Innoc   Deception

Shabibi Shah Nala

Cover photo by Ernesto Hernandez Fonte used under Creative
Commons licence.

For Shafi and Nisar.

For all the displaced children of Afghanistan.

With much love.

ACKNOWLEDGMENTS

Dear Reader,

When I was young and ambitious one of my childhood dreams was to be a writer in my mother tongue Dari. It never happened due to my difficult circumstances. But throughout my life this dream slept with me, woke up with me, lived with me and travelled with me all these long years until I reached the age where it was impossible to concentrate on it any more. But this dream never went away so I decided to follow it for better or worse.

To be a writer or a novelist it helps to be fluent in that language, have talent and skill with an array of vast vocabulary in mind. Something which I feel I lack. How could I do that? Why I am writing? Why do I have the urge to write?

Because I believe every human being has a story to tell and needs someone to listen to it, we need to empty it from inside us or we explode.

Because I have been witness to so many tragedies throughout my life. Because the world is unjust, the cruelty in many parts of the world is high and the sufferings continue. So I thought I don't have to be a writer to see. I can see the tragedies of ordinary people. I don't have to be a writer to feel. I can feel deep down in my soul the power of corruption which affected millions of lives.

Some of the stories in this book are loosely based on true stories. To my knowledge the nature of the political situation in Afghanistan presented here, where the last thirty years turned that beautiful land to ashes, is true but the characters and names in the book are fiction.

I would like to thank my friend Mary Simpson who gave her precious time and patiently read and re-read every page, and Veronica Doubleday who read the first draft and encouraged me to continue writing.

I would like to thank Dr Elaheh Rostamy Povey for

her many suggestions and her friendship.

My thanks go to Lucy Popescu for editing the book, and to Tom Green at Counterpoints Arts, a hub of creative projects by and about refugees and migrants, who kindly offered his help with the publishing.

Shabibi Shah Nala

CHAPTER 1

The staff at the Bukhara Banquet Hall in West London were waiting for their guests to arrive. It was *Nawroz*, the Afghan New Year's Eve, the first month of Hamal in the Afghan Calendar which falls on the 21st of March, the beginning of spring. The hall was one of the best venues for religious *Eids* , *Nawroz* , weddings, parties, birthdays and funerals. The owners of the venue were a young Afghan couple, who knew how to satisfy their customers' needs and decorated the hall in keeping with their colourful taste.

Entering the L-shaped marble corridor, a massive chandelier hung from the ceiling capturing everyone's attention. The white painted walls made the corridor unbearably bright and wide. Portraits of Afghan landscapes and the national sport of *Buzkashi* (played on horseback with the headless carcass of a calf or a goat) were fixed to the wall. At the end of the corridor stood two huge coat rails and a mirror, taking up the entire wall and doubling the room's size. Two attractive, young women welcomed guests and took their coats with a job-supplied smile plastered on their faces. Tonight the atmosphere was cheerful.

Entering the massive hall, the red carpet and cream curtains all around the room immediately attracted one's gaze. There were white tablecloths and fake red, white and yellow flowers on each table, which were occasionally changed depending on customers' tastes. Sometimes there were fresh flowers, if budgets allowed. In the middle of the hall was a laminated wooden dance floor with two huge chandeliers hanging down from the ceiling, blinding the guests with their brightness. There was also a decorated stage for performance and a special stage for the bride and groom, if the occasion was a wedding party.

In Afghanistan, *Nawroz* has been celebrated in every household for centuries. The celebration was banned during the *Taliban's* reign of power as they believed it to be sinful and non- Islamic. This festival was celebrated long before Islam was introduced in Afghanistan and is one of the most ancient festivals, dating back to 555-330 BCE, and is deeply connected with Afghan culture. After Islam became established in Afghanistan, *Nawroz* was given its religious aspect. The first day of *Nawroz* was dedicated to Imam Ali, the prophet Muhammad's cousin and son in-law, who became the fourth leader of Islam in the Sunni tradition and the first leader in the Shi'a tradition.

During *Nawroz* thousands of people travel from all over Afghanistan to Mazar-e-Sharif, a northern city, to visit the famous mosque and Ali's shrine and they pray together on this special day. There is a strong belief that even a blind person who goes to this sacred place will be able to see, a cripple will be able to walk, and a sick person will be cured if they pray hard. This special day is for families to spoil each other. This is the day for forgiveness amongst enemies and friendship amongst foes.

In London the festival, though small, was celebrated with style and extravagance and was heavily publicized by the manager of the banquet weeks in advance. At 7.30 the guests began to arrive. Men in their best suits stood behind their women and waited for the staff to take their coats. Ladies with vibrant red, dark green, orange and yellow dresses created a colourful atmosphere. They were generously made up and wore gold jewellery in their ears, around their necks and their fingers. This had become an essential ritual for some Afghan refugee women in London as the more gold they wore, the wealthier they appeared. Older children were dressed in expensive new clothes, and some young boys wore suits. They looked the spitting image of their fathers with their blue or red ties.

Some women loosely covered their heads with scarves and others wore Western style clothes, dressed as if they were on the Hollywood red carpet at the Oscars. In contrast, one or two women wore long black robes copying the style of wealthy Arab women living in London.[i] (see endnotes after page 205)

The staff members were a mixed bunch: Afghan and Eastern European men and women wearing white shirts and black trousers. They stood shoulder to shoulder, ready to welcome their guests and escort them to their tables. As the first guests entered the hall, the musicians began to play loud Afghan pop. The young musicians had developed their careers in the diaspora and created their own style of music aimed at keeping both the old and young guests happy. Some of the musicians, too young to appreciate traditional Afghan music, created their own mix of music, losing much of the true artistry of the original.

As the sound of music became louder and faster, one or two men left their chairs and headed onto the dance floor. Heads down, they started dancing; copying the Indian Bollywood film stars. Then slowly other men followed and within a few minutes the dancing floor was full of young men dancing with each other or in groups. They didn't dare to ask any women to dance and they stayed put in their chairs, knowing their place in public.

Akbar parked his blue Fort Fiesta outside the hall, turned off the satnav and opened the car door for his wife and two daughters, seventeen-year-old Sittara and eight-year-old Jamila. They all adjusted their outfits and slowly walked toward the building. Akbar, a tall, handsome man in a black suit and a red spotted tie, led his family towards the hall. He was all smiles. His wife Simeen was dressed in an elegant, dark green, sleeveless dress with a black shawl around her shoulders.

She wore black high-heeled shoes that matched her handbag and her head was uncovered. Her make-up was relatively light. She had no gold around her wrists and wore a simple cream pearl necklace. She was a beauty. She had an oval face, rosy cheeks and long black hair reaching to her waist.

Entering the hall the family looked around for other people they knew, hoping to be able to join their table but saw no one. Akbar and Simeen knew one or two Afghan families in London but it was the first time that they had attended such a big gathering. They sat at a round table near the entrance hoping that the empty chairs on their table would soon be occupied. After a while three chairs were taken by another family, new to Akbar and Simeen. They all stood up to welcome them.

'I am Jaweed Karimi and this is my wife and my son Abdullah,' the new guest said. He was evidently from a family used to giving orders. But he was clever enough to act humbly and politely in public. He wore a black suit which could not hide his big stomach.

'Nice to meet you,' Akbar extended his hand. 'I am Akbar Ali, this is my wife and my daughters Sittara and Jamila.'

They all sat down. Simeen's hands had started to shake under the table and her face drained of colour. Her body had turned to stone, and she was overcome with dread. Suddenly her past, which she had tried hard for years to forget, had become present in a second, right before her eyes.

'Oh Allah please help me, oh Allah please help me,' she murmured under her breath. She recognised Jaweed, his wife Hosna and their son Abdullah. She knew they also had a daughter, Fahtama, who was older than Abdullah but she was not with them that night. 'She must be married by now,' Simeen thought.

Although nearly two decades had passed, apart from Jaweed's bulk the couple had changed very little. Despite all the chandeliers in the hall Simeen's evening had turned to darkness. She felt dizzy, her heart moving up into her throat. Pieces of her past had returned for her to re-live right then and there. She recalled the big imposing house, the long marble corridor, the room that she sometimes shared with Begum, the nightmares she had suffered. After a few minutes she couldn't stand it anymore and excused herself from the table, walking away with as much dignity as she could muster toward the toilets, her black Kashmir shawl draped over her elegant body. Her face was crimson, her brain was on fire and her heart pounded. She was sure everyone could hear it. Her stomach was churning. She opened the bathroom door with such force that the other ladies refreshing their make up in front of the mirror jumped, but Simeen did not notice. She went to the toilet and locked herself in.

For a while she stayed in the tiny cubicle, her emotions running high. She did not know how to handle this unusual situation or what to do. Fifteen minutes later, having forced herself to calm down, she opened the door and came out. 'Should I go back to the hall? Should I stay here? What will Akbar think?' She faced a big dilemma.

At the table the conversation between Jaweed and Akbar had built up about their children, where they lived and what they did. Then they found something else in common to talk about –

Afghanistan. The conversation turned to politics as in every Afghan men's gathering, large and small. Jaweed's self-confident manner impressed Akbar who was much younger and did not know much about the current political situation and history of Afghanistan. Akbar had been a child when he left his country and had not had the opportunity or the time to know Afghanistan as he wished to. All he knew was that Afghanistan's problems started with the Russian invasion in 1979. He felt a little insecure talking to a man who seemed so knowledgeable. Jaweed, in his late fifties, had recently arrived with his family as refugees while Akbar and Simeen had already become British citizens and had an established life.

'How long have you lived here?' Jaweed asked Akbar.

'Nearly fourteen years.'

'Oh good! You must be British by now,' Jaweed said

enviously.

'Yes we are, thanks to this country,' replied Akbar.

'How about you sir, how long have you been here?' Akbar asked.

'Not very long, nearly four years but we are still waiting for the Home Office decision.'

'I am sure you will be accepted as refugees,' Akbar said.

Then the conversation turned again to politics. Jaweed never failed to engage on the subject although his knowledge was limited. He charmed people into believing that he knew more than he did. Jaweed's wife, Hosna, and Akbar's youngest daughter, Jamila, were bored, but listened politely to the men's conversation. Politics was not usually a woman's favourite subject but Sittara listened with interest. In Afghanistan, Hosna had not even finished school when she married. All she had been interested in was fashionable clothes, make-up and jewellery.

Coming from Afghanistan and Pakistan where the *Taliban* forbade even the smallest of pleasures like playing football or flying kites, Abdullah watched the dancing with hungry eyes. He would have liked to ask Sittara to dance. But it was just a stupid wish. He knew he couldn't ask her. He was just a newcomer from a closed society. On the dance floor young men were dancing in a group. One or two brave young women started dancing on their own at the corner of the dance floor, trying not to mingle with the men. They knew that the older generation would not approve but they couldn't resist it.

Abdullah gazed at Sittara with shy eyes and wondered how he could open a simple conversation with her. Growing up in an open society Sittara had no difficulty talking to young men. But dancing was out of the question as far as her mother was concerned. The music stopped for a short break and people's conversations filled the hall.

Another family joined their table. A middle-aged couple and a young man. They all stood up again to welcome them. The newcomers introduced themselves as the Tarakhel family. It was obvious to everyone around the table that the new comers were of Pashtun origin. They could guess from their surname and their accents. The woman was dressed modestly and covered her head with a dark-green scarf. Her husband was a tall, slim, dignified man with silver hair. They took the three remaining chairs. Mrs Tarakhel found herself next to Hosna. The conversation on politics continued among the men. It was pure accident that the families came from three different ethnic groups and backgrounds, Pashtun, Tajik and Hazara. This would not have happened in Afghanistan, during the decades of invasion, violent conflicts and war when the different ethnicities were always fighting each other.

Sittara grew bored and disengaged from men's conversation. She picked up a small plate of sugar-coated almonds and offered them first to Jaweed, his wife and the Tarakhel family, as they were the eldest in the group, then to her father and finally she extended her hand to Abdullah and tried to start a conversation with him.

'What do you do for a living?' Abdullah's heart began to beat fast. He had not expected Sittara to start the conversation. He knew that in Afghanistan girls never voluntarily talk to boys. But he loved the attention from Sittara.

'I am at the School of Oriental and African Studies, SOAS.'

'What are you studying?'

'At the moment I am trying to improve my English but I plan to study law. How about you? What do you do?'

'It is my last year at college. I want to study media,' she said.

'So you want to be a journalist or study film?'

'I love journalism.'

'Good for you,' said Abdullah.

'Hopefully one day I will be able to go to Afghanistan and make reports,' she said. They both laughed.

'Being a journalist requires much knowledge. You must already know a lot about Afghanistan,' Abdullah said.

'Oh no! I don't know much. I was a child when we

came here. I don't remember anything.'

'But why do you have an interest in a country you don't remember?'

'I don't know, perhaps because my parents are from there and speak Dari at home or perhaps because sometimes people ask me about my origins and as I don't look English it makes me feel that I don't belong here. Therefore, I feel that I should know a little about where I come from.'

'Yes I agree with you.'

'You must know a lot about the *Taliban* then,' Sittara said.

'No, not much,' he said. 'When the conflict reached its highest point between the Soviet-backed government and the *Mujahideen*, we escaped to Pakistan and lived there for a few years. I was too young at the time to understand the political situation but I witnessed various tragedies.'

'It must have been hard for the people who lived under their control.' Sittara said.

'Yes, of course, but luckily we lived in Islamabad which was not *Taliban* territory. The *Taliban* mostly live in Peshawar, on the border of Afghanistan. We were not there when the *Taliban* took control of Kabul. Just before they arrived my father spent a lot of money bribing people to get us out.'

Listening to their conversation Akbar said, 'I saw a photo of Dr Najibullah, the last communist leader of Afghanistan, in The Guardian. The *Taliban* had hung his body from a lamp-post and stuffed cigarettes and money between his lifeless fingers in a crowded area for civilians to see. What savages they must be.'

'Yes they are,' Jaweed agreed.

'I wonder why they stuffed cigarettes and money between his fingers,' Sittara asked, unaware that she was intruding in the men's conversation.

'To symbolise that he had sold the country to the Soviet Union for money and cigarettes,' Mr Tarakhel volunteered.

'How did they manage to capture him? Didn't he have any bodyguards?'

'He was a fallen leader by then and he took refuge in the UN headquarters for his own safety thinking that he would be protected but the *Taliban* attacked, captured him, tortured and killed him. Yes, it is true the *Taliban* are savage but people do not easily forget what Najibullah did to Afgahnistan,' Mr Tarakhel said

'What did he do?' asked Akbar.

'He was the head of KHAD, the secret police, he was a brutal man and filled up the notorious Pul-i Charkhi prison.' Jaweed, a strong supporter of the Communist regime at one time, kept quiet and tried not to give away too much.

'Who exactly are these *Taliban* and what do they want?' Sittara asked.

'Well it is a long complicated story. Perhaps you need to have some lessons from my father, he knows a lot,' Abdullah said. He laughed and looked to his father for further explanation. Jaweed was trapped. He knew it was a sensitive issue but turned to face Sittara.

'Yes, young lady. What is your question? You seem very interested in Afghan affairs.' He sounded surprised that a young woman was interested in politics. Sittara suddenly felt shy and couldn't look Jaweed in the eye.

'I read somewhere that the *Taliban* are children of the wars. They escaped Afghanistan and lived in refugee camps. How did they manage to overthrow the Communist regime?'

'The *Taliban* did not overthrow the Communist government, the *Mujahideen* did. They were one step ahead of the *Taliban*,' Jaweed said.

'Oh I'm so ignorant about my own country. Who were the *Mujahideen* ? They must have been powerful people if they managed to overthrow the Communists,' said Sittara.

Jaweed rubbed his black and white goatee beard. He looked around the table with his usual self-importance and said, 'The yellow dog is the jackal's brother.' Sittara couldn't get the Afghan proverb and waited for Jaweed to continue, but his attention turned to a group of newcomers and he forgot about Sittara's question.

'To my understanding they are all same,' Mr Tarakhel

said. 'To my eyes they are all the same,' he repeated. 'The *Mujahideen* called themselves freedom fighters and were against the Communist regime. They defeated the invaders and changed the regime, but unfortunately they started fighting each other for power for many years. They disgraced themselves. People were sick and tired of war. When the *Taliban* came to power in 1996, the people actually welcomed them with open arms but they turned out to be the most vicious group that Afghanistan had ever experienced in its bloody history. They turned the beautiful land of Afghanistan into a wasteland.' Mr Tarakhel explained.

'Who are the *Taliban*?' Sittara asked again.

'They grew up in refugee camps in Pakistan. Most of them lost their family in the war. They lived in orphanages and from early childhood were indoctrinated by the conservative *mullahs* to recite the Quran without knowing its true meaning. Those who provided them with food and shelter also taught them about their own conservative interpretation of Islam and brainwashed them,' he said. As Sittara became engaged in her conversation with Mr Tarakhel, Jaweed grew annoyed.

'I never saw an Afghan girl so much of a chatterbox,' he thought. 'She doesn't know her place.'

The music started up and the dance floor became crowded with young men once more. When the music stopped again Sittara resumed her conversation with Abdullah.

'I wish I knew more about my country.'

'It's not too late. You can read about it,' Abdullah replied.

'I don't think there are many books written in English about Afghanistan politics.'

'Why in English? Can't you read in your own language?' Abdullah asked.

Sittara blushed. 'I can't read or write.'

'But you speak very good Dari.'

'Because my parents speak Dari at home,' Sittara said.

'When you finish college, which university would you like to go to?'

'I don't know yet, if I have my own choice I would like to study journalism but my parents think I should study medicine. They think it has a more secure future,' said Sittara. 'I'm interested in politics and would love to know about the history of Afghanistan and the present situation. It is always in the media nowadays.'

'Yes I agree with you. If you love politics go for it. Maybe it's a good idea to study journalism.'

Sittara lowered her voice. 'My parents think politics make people's lives difficult and that most politicians are corrupt, especially in Afghanistan. They always find fault with people who disagree with them and drag the country into war. It's such a shame I do not know more about my country.'

'I have a few books in English. If you're interested you can borrow one. It's not too late. You can start now; I can help if you'd like.'

'Thank you, I'll think about it.'

Sittara knew she couldn't take up Abdullah's offer as she was already busy with her studies at college and it would create problems with her mother who insisted that she avoid young men.

'If you are interested just give me your address and I will post one or two books. Abdullah didn't wait for Sittara's reply. 'Can I have your number?' he blurted out.

'Yes, sure,' Sittara said without thinking. She was about to give Abdullah her mobile number, but stopped herself just in time. This was an Afghan gathering and she should follow cultural rules. But it was too late to make an excuse because she had already said yes. So she gave him their home number instead. Akbar was relieved to see that Sittara did not give Abdullah her mobile number.

'Thank God Simeen is not here,' he thought. Abdullah saved the number in his mobile and thanked her. He perfectly understood why she had not given him her mobile number.

'Go and see if your mum is OK,' Akbar told Sittara.

Reluctantly Sittara stood up and excused herself. She picked up her phone from the table, put it in her pocket and walked towards the toilet, feeling rather annoyed with Akbar. 'Why must he always ask me to do things while Jamila is just sitting there and is not involved in the conversation. He could have asked her,' she thought. Perhaps her father did not want her to continue to talk with Abdullah. She had noticed recently that her mother had become stricter with her.

Sittara opened the toilet door and saw her mother's reflection in the mirror with both hands on her face. She rushed towards her.

'Are you all right Mum?' she asked, holding her hand.

'No, I am not,' Simeen replied.

Sittara found a chair and Simeen sat down in the corridor to get some fresh air, her face colourless. Sittara fetched her a glass of water.

'I am not feeling well at all. Go and tell your dad he needs to take us home.' Sittara was disappointed. She had just started to enjoy the evening and was not keen to leave early. She walked back into the hall, leaned towards Akbar.

'Mum is not well,' she whispered. Akbar excused himself and rushed to the corridor.

'What's the matter?' he asked his wife.

'I think my blood pressure has gone up again, I have a splitting headache. This music is so loud my head is bursting. Can we please go home?'

'Yes of course but dinner has just been announced. Please let the children finish their meal and then we'll go,' Akbar said 'Can I bring you some food?'

'No thank you. I don't feel like eating. You go and help the children. Give me a few minutes and I will join you,' she replied. Slowly and painfully Simeen followed Akbar to the table, trying hard to look normal and avoiding eye contact with Jaweed's family.

In one corner of the hall a long narrow table was set up with a variety of dishes and after the announcement the guests walked over to get their food. The music had stopped playing. The food - an assortment of traditional Afghan dishes - was excellent. A variety of chicken and lamb kebabs were served with pilau rice. Spinach with rice, *manto*, *oshaak* and various other dishes. Akbar took some food for Simeen but she pushed it around her plate, patiently waiting for her husband and children to finish their food. Every minute seemed like an hour to her. Once they had eaten, they excused themselves, said goodbye to the other families and left the hall.

All the way home, Simeen was in such a state that her husband thought she was going to faint.

'Can I pull over and get you some tea or water from somewhere?' Akbar asked.

'No, I think if I get home, take my medication and get some sleep I will hopefully be all right. This has happened before.' she said.

'I've not seen you this bad. I've never seen your face so pale,' Akbar said. Arriving home, Jamila was boiling with rage. Their evening had been spoiled completely. She had just started to enjoy herself. 'This kind of Afghan gathering didn't happen very often,' she thought. Simeen did not notice her children. Her mind was fully occupied. 'What if Jaweed and Hosna recognized me?' she thought. 'What if Akbar senses something? What if they create problems for my family? My life will have to end.'

Simeen had never forgotten the details of her life in Afghanistan. She had never forgotten that large house in Kabul and that tiny curtain-less room. Over the years, she was unable to forget all the terrible things that had happened to her. Now, seeing Jaweed and his family, she was terrified that the secrets of her life would unfold. She was terrified that if Akbar found out about her secrets nothing would ever be the same again.

For many years, Simeen had tried to bury her past and to deal with her headaches and high blood pressure. But the psychological scars that had been left on her soul ran deep. The best thing that had happened to Simeen was marrying Akbar, who was a loving husband and a good father. He was clever and fun to be with. She had tried to tell herself that with him at her side she would be fine for the rest of her life, and that her wounds would heal. She thought she would succeed. Now, seeing Jaweed and his family, she could not sleep, she could not stop thinking, as her past paraded before her eyes. She desperately needed someone to tell her that everything would be OK, to put an arm around her and calm her down. She could see the whole scene clearly like a field of mushrooms after the rain.

Simeen and Akbar had been living on the third floor of a rented three-bedroom council flat in a slum area of South London since their marriage. Being on the top floor, they shared the stairs and corridor with many other families. All nationalities were represented here. English, Asian, African and people from all over Europe. Sometimes when Akbar was in a good mood he would joke to Simeen, 'You could hold a United Nations meeting in the hallways. It feels as though we have invaded this country, look around, there are more foreigners than English.' The smells that filled the corridors ranged from the delectable and inviting (mainly around dinner time) to the mostly unpleasant and, at times, downright foul. Most of the time the stench of cigarettes, stale alcohol, dogs' urine, empty milk bottles and other rubbish was over-powering. The state of the corridors was something to behold, always cluttered with people's junk.

When Simeen lived in her native village of Bamyan she had never heard of Britain and did not know that such a country existed. Her world was small and simple but when she moved to Kabul and later to Pakistan, she had met large wealthy families who went to Britain and she heard a lot about the country they described as paradise. Now, living in London herself, the reality was a more sobering experience. She found the place frightening and over-populated. A bunch of strangers keeping themselves to themselves. No 'hellos' as you passed people in the streets. No smiles. The residents passed each other with their heads down and avoided each other's eyes. Just blank faces with eyes fixed on the ground in front of them. 'What is there on the ground that these people seem to find so fascinating?' Simeen asked herself. Occasionally the sound of a neighbour's music was deafening and there was loud banging on the wall that would end up in arguments and sometimes police intervention.

The following morning, Simeen woke up at half past eight with a severe headache and turned her tired face towards an empty space. Akbar was not there. She slowly went to the kitchen to take her tablets and realized that her daughter was late for school.

'Jamila, wake up you're late, get ready quick!' she shouted. Then she found a note from Akbar on the table. 'Don't worry I'll drop Jamila at school, you get some rest.' She was so relieved. 'I don't deserve you,' she mumbled to herself, as she returned to her bedroom and tried to sleep to no avail as there was a commotion below.

A young Indian family lived below them. The father was an alcoholic, and the mother was a shy woman who rarely left their flat alone. They had a nine-year old boy who suffered from anxiety every time he went to play outside. He was ashamed of his father's addiction, and his mother's lack of English. The children around the block tormented the poor boy every time he went out to play. Sometimes they knocked on their door and ran away for fun. That day Simeen heard the children go one step further. They knocked on the door, and shouted, 'Go home Paki!' The father had had enough. He opened the door and ran after them. He had on just a pair of underpants. He started shouting and cursing. 'You bloody potato eaters. You lived in my country, you looted my country for two hundred years. It is payback time, my darlings. Go and tell your stupid parents.'

Simeen remembered that Kabulis insulted the Hazara people by calling them 'mouse eaters' as Hazaras were the poorest in the country. She was fascinated as to why eating potatoes was so shameful. She couldn't understand it. The children stopped knocking at their door, but the little boy remained indoors.

CHAPTER 2

Akbar had escaped the war after his family were killed in a clash between the *Mujahideen* and the Soviet-backed government in 1982 in Kabul. His family, who were Hazara were not involved in politics. His father Hussain Ali had a corner shop attached to their family house in Tiemany, a poor, crowded area situated on the outskirts of the Shar-e-Now, which was where the rich and middle class lived. In his small shop Hussain sold all sorts of goods from clothes and household items, to fruit and vegetables. As the eldest son, Akbar helped his father every day after school. Life was a constant struggle but they were a relatively happy family.

Akbar had one older sister and two younger brothers. They lived in a small house made of mud that his grandfather had built with his own hands without any help from builders or surveyors. In Tiemany all houses were made more or less in the same way. Their house had just two bedrooms and a toilet at the end of their dusty yard. The open cooking area was covered by a big plastic tent. During the winter or on rainy days they had to cook in one of their rooms. They had no running water and Akbar and his siblings were responsible for carrying water from their neighbour's well. Despite being very poor, the wife was a part-time cleaner and the husband a shopkeeper, they had a very happy life. Akbar's day was shaped by his father going to work and arriving home in the evening with some shopping for a simple dinner together. They didn't expect much from life.

It was a Friday morning when their house was bombed. The only survivor was Akbar who, by chance, had been sent to town to buy some goods for the shop. On Fridays, the schools were closed and Akbar would help his father in the shop all day. When he returned home after a two-hour journey he found his entire family and their neighbours under the rubble. Their small mud house did not exist anymore. Life for this young boy was shattered.

After the funeral, Akbar had no choice but to move in with his uncle Najaaf who already had a large family to support. Losing the family and moving in with his uncle was not easy for a young orphan. His uncle was a cobbler and rented a small shop in a poor area down town. He was barely able to sustain his own family and now had another mouth to feed.

When the war reached its height in Kabul, thousands of Soviet soldiers and tens of thousands of Afghan fighters were killed. The effect of war on ordinary citizens in towns and villages alike, especially in Kabul, was enormous. There were always food shortages and plenty of tragedies. Many tried to escape from this unbearable situation. Civilians disappeared every day without having had a chance to say goodbye to their extended families or neighbours. Millions of Afghans became refugees. The rich, wealthy and educated managed to bribe the officials and get passports to go to America, Germany, Britain, France and other countries, but the poor had to choose the harsh way and walk over the mountains to Pakistan or Iran. Their journeys were extremely difficult, often taking them through deserts or thick forests, in hazardous weather conditions.

One day, Najaaf woke as usual to the sound of *Azan* calling people to morningprayer from the nearby mosque. His family was fast asleep. He sat on his bed for a few seconds, half asleep, and then reluctantly got up. He walked out to the yard, filled a small bucket with water and headed towards the toilet in the corner of their dusty yard. After washing his face, hands and feet he was ready for prayer. He returned to the room and placed the prayer mat facing toward *Kaaba*. Najaaf was a very religious man and never missed his morning prayer. But he was not strict with his wife and children.

After having a piece of bread without tea, he left home for his shop. He was thinking about the previous night when he had come home with just three pieces of flat bread, no tea, no sugar and no potatoes. Recently Najaaf hadn't had any customers. They usually ate potato stew, but yesterday dinner was only hot water with pieces of bread. He hurried to his shop hoping that he might have some customers today.

He opened his tiny shop and tidied a few things on the table. No one came. He got up from his chair and went to sit a few steps away on the pavement, his hands in his head. It was midday and all of a sudden there was the sound of a rocket exploding somewhere close by, followed by the high pitched whine of an engine and people's screams. The noise filled the whole town. Shopkeepers closed their shops and people began rushing to get home. Within a few hours the area was empty except for a few bodies lying on the deserted streets.

Najaaf quickly closed his shop and rushed home empty-handed again but happy to find his family alive. His young children were playing in the back yard and his worried wife met him with a hug. She was so relieved to see him alive.

'You have to do something, we cannot live in this madness,' his wife said. 'Everyone has left. The whole area is empty now.'

'I don't know what to do,' said Najaaf, his hands under his arms, his colourless face suddenly weary, his eyes moist. The recent wave of violence had been close to their home and he was frightened. He had already lost his brother and now, if he didn't do something, he would lose his own family too.

'Everyday people escape to Pakistan,' his wife said.

'We can't go empty-handed. We don't have any documents, no ID to get through the borders and I know the government is reluctant to provide any facilities, knowing that once people get out, they will never come back,' Najaaf said.

After a week of hard thinking, he realised that the only option was to leave town. They had to go but how, without money and direction? Going to Iran was ideal, as the majority of Iranians were Shi'a Muslim, but Najaaf needed money and the journey was long. He began desperately looking for someone to buy his shop.

After two weeks he pawned his shop for very little. The family picked up their few belongings and quietly left early in the morning when the curfew had finished. They had decided to travel to Pakistan through the mountains. The journey was particularly hazardous with four children walking all the way. After fifteen days, struggling on foot over the high mountains, hiding from the police, sleeping rough in deserted areas and begging for food, they reached the safety of Pakistan. Najaaf was overwhelmed with relief. It was his first proper journey abroad.

They reached Peshawar, an ancient Islamic city. Najaaf did not know anything about the city's past and its volatile present, although it was notorious for bombing, murdering, kidnapping and assassinations. Najaaf was illiterate and did not know much about history. He did not know that a large part of Peshawar had once belonged to Afghanistan. He did not know that between 1881 and 1901 Abdur Rahman Khan, the monarch of Afghanistan, with the help of the British, ruthlessly crushed ethnic dissent and attempted to create a strong centralised state. The present borders were established according to the strategic needs of the British and Russian Empires rather than the socio- political needs of Afghanistan's diverse ethnic groups. Najaaf did not know that the subsequent ethnic conflicts and the backlash against modernisation could be traced back to this period. In 1893 an agreement was signed between king Abdur Rahman Khan and Mortimer Durand, the foreign secretary of the colonial government of India. As part of this agreement, the Durand Line was drawn to mark the boundary between Afghanistan and the British

Indian Empire. In 1947, following the partition of India, it became the border between Pakistan and Afghanistan. To this day, the dividing line has never been recognised by the Pashtuns in these two countries.

Najaaf had no money, no place to stay and knew no one in this strange land, where people spoke languages that he did not understand. He spoke Dari with a slang dialect of Hazaragi. Eventually, Najaaf and his family found their way into a refugee camp. Najaaf knew that Afghan refugees received support from the Pakistan government, but had no idea that refugees received help from other Muslim countries and the United Nations. He felt so grateful for Pakistan's hospitality. What good Muslims they are, he thought. After a long interview, Najaaf came out of the UN office with a tent, a small parcel of food and a few blankets. He managed to erect the tent on a patch of dry, packed earth. Although Najaaf's pride and dignity were crushed, he was relieved that his family were out of danger.

The camps were full of people from different walks of life: university lecturers, doctors, lawyers, teachers, builders, farmers and nomads alike. They all lived in similar tents and experienced the same trauma of displacement and loss. It was a new home. A tent but still a home. They were safe and tried to make sense of all that had happened to them. In the first few days after their arrival, the family felt completely cut off but slowly they came to accept their new situation. Najaaf stayed inside the tent while his wife found her way around, befriending other women in the neighbouring camps and sharing their miseries.

Najaaf discovered that well-off refugees rented houses and flats in the cities and sent their children to special schools. Some even set up businesses, while the poorer refugees relied on the camps for food and shelter. After a few months Najaaf learned that the refugee camps were funded by the *Wahabis* in Saudi Arabia, the UN and other Muslim countries.

'What is *Wahabi*?' Najaaf asked Hamidullah, the only friend he had made in the camp. Hamidullah, a disabled man who lived on his own, had been a history teacher in

Kabul before the war. Hamidullah looked up at the sky and thought of a simple way to explain Wahabi to his friend. He fingered his goatee beard before replying.

'*Wahabi* is a sect of Islam founded in the eighteenth century by a man called Abdul Wahab who thought he was going to purify Islam. Since then his strict form of Islam has been practised in Saudi Arabia and has slowly found its way to other Muslim countries. These neo-Wahabists did not just help refugees in the camps but also provided the *Mujahideen* with arms and ammunition against the Soviet Union. They established guerrilla training camps in Pakistan and sent fighters from other Islamic countries to help the different resistance groups.'

Najaaf was fascinated by this information.

The camps were situated in a large, bone-dry, tree-less, water-less, filthy area in Peshawar. The food rations were limited and there were no power facilities. Thousands of young children would walk bare feet for hours to the nearest town to beg for food. Those unwashed, naked young orphans, who were too young to walk, played with dirt in the hot sun. Their faces were dirty and their hair full of lice.

They were like small adults robbed of their childhood. If some fathers were lucky enough to find a job, their children worked alongside them. After months of hunger they forgot to complain about wanting more food. They silently swallowed the hard pieces of naan bread and dreamed of eating a plate of potato stew.

Then the idea of *madrassas*, religious schools for children, began to be promoted and funded by conservative Muslim countries. Thousands of traumatized, hungry, displaced boys rushed to these schools. These young men had never seen their country at peace and had no knowledge of its complex ethnic identities. Many were orphans who had grown up without families in the confines of segregated male refugee camps, and these *madrassas* promoting puritanical conservative Islam gave meaning to their lives.[ii]

Cobbler Najaaf had been happy back home in Afghanistan. He worked hard in his tiny shop in downtown Kabul and knew all the local people by name, where they lived, how many children they had and which tribe they belonged to. He was gentle with his customers. He had a bubbly personality, and made friends easily. He never earned enough but he didn't complain. 'God created us and it is His responsibility to feed us,' he believed. Since moving to Pakistan, he found it hard to find his usual work, as he did not have his tools with him. Buying tools required money. He looked around for other labouring work, but it was impossible to find any. After a long search he began to lose hope.

One day, while Najaaf was sitting in front of his small tattered tent deep in thought, his friend Hamidullah approached him. He was the only person to occasionally come and talk to Najaaf. He was older than Najaaf, and lived a few yards away from him in another small tent. He was ill, not just because of his amputated leg but because he suffered from shell shock and depression. In Kabul, he had been forced to join the army by the Soviet-backed government to fight the *Mujahideen* or *Ashrar*, the terrorists as the Afghan government called them. He lost one leg in a bloody war in Kondoz province and was hospitalised for many months. Eventually he returned to Kabul to discover that his entire family had been killed by a bomb set off by the government. Hamidullah had found his way to Pakistan's refugee camps. Despite losing his leg, he had a friendly attitude toward everyone. He walked towards Najaaf, bent over his crutches, and sat next to him on the ground. Najaaf looked disconsolate with his hand under his chin.

'It seems that all your camels are drowned. What is the matter?' Hamidullah joked.

'Life is the matter,' Najaaf said.'I am fed up with my life, I have no job, no money, not even a country anymore. Now my children are burning like dry leaves under the tent, and my wife is pregnant.'

'Oh my dear brother,' said Hamidullah after a few seconds. 'Look around yourself; you can see that you are not the only one. There are thousands of people in the same situation as you are. Be grateful to God. At least you have two legs and a good family. You can walk. Look at me. I studied hard to make a good life and look what the war has done to me. I lost my home, my family and my leg.' He paused.

'What did you do in Kabul?' He asked Najaaf.

'I was a cobbler.'

'You can resume your old job here. Can't you?' Najaaf laughed sarcastically.

'How many pairs of shoes do you see around here for me to repair?' he asked. 'Look, men, women, children are all walking barefoot.'

'Yes it's true, but you can go to the town. There are rich people there. I wish I had my leg and your skills,' said Hamidullah.

'What did you do in Afghanistan?' Najaaf asked.

Hamidullah raised his left hand, touched his snow-white beard and massaged it, his eyes fixed on one spot for a long time as though he was hoping to find his former happy life there again.

'I was a *moallem* at Istiqlal School,' he said. 'I was a history teacher, bloody history.'

'Why 'bloody', were you not happy? I don't know much about our history but people say we have to be proud of it,' Najaaf said.

Hamidullah paused for a few seconds and then replied, 'If you want to know my honest opinion, as long as I remember our history has been full of conflict, killing, savagery, oppression, injustice, ruthlessness between powerful people. I reached the point when I realised that human nature never really changes and people won't learn from their history. People always find something to fight for: religion, ethnicity, politics, clans, any disagreements, you name it. Who suffers the most? Of course, the poor and the innocent. Oh my dear friend, sometimes ignorance is a blessing. I wish I was a cobbler, like you, with good skills. Go to town. I am sure you can find some work.'

'I don't have my tools. I left them back home. How can I work without tools?'

'You can buy some here.'

Najaaf hesitated. 'I do not have any money,' he said

Hamidullah stroked his white beard again. 'Why don't

you send your boys to the *madrassa*?' he replied. 'They feed them and your life may be a little easier.'

'I believe they do not take children who have parents. The *madrassas* are for orphans, and also they are Sunni and I am Shi'a' Najaaf said.

'No. That's not true, they take other children too. You can say that you are looking after your brother's son, Akbar, and he is an orphan.'

After a long pause Najaaf said, 'Although I would feel really bad about it, I have no choice, he has to go to the *madrassa*.'

'I am sure God will help you,' Hamidullah murmured to himself. 'Tomorrow is another day, don't lose hope, God will help you in mysterious ways.' Saying that, he got up, adjusted his crutches under his arms and slowly walked back to his tent.

Najaaf appreciated Hamidullah's friendship and company, and he was surprised when he did not return the next day, nor any after. Two days later his neighbours found his body in his tiny tent. He had left a small note on his pillow which read:

'Oh God please forgive me for my sin. There is nothing left for me to live for. What I am going to do now I should have done a long time ago, when I lost my family, but I was a coward. I have left a small amount of money in my pocket to go towards my burial and I'd like the rest to go to my friend Najaaf for his tools. I don't have much to say to my people but just a few words in the last moments of my tragic life. We have been betrayed by our leaders, Communists or conservative Islamists, both have acted in a similar way. They fight for greed, for power, not for the country and not for us. The fact is that I have realised too late to change anything now. I do not have any desire to live anymore. I am just praying in the last moments of my life, hoping that God may forgive me.'

The neighbours in the camp buried Hamidullah on a hot summer's day. A bearded man read a few words from the Quran and they all said goodbye and left. No one grieved for him except Najaaf who missed his only friend, and felt grateful for the help he had received from him.

Three weeks later, Najaaf bought a few basic tools and went to the nearest town to find work. He did not have a permanent place to work, so after a long search he asked a Pakistani man who owned a vegetable shop if he could use an empty space nearby and the shopkeeper agreed.

'How much will you pay me?' asked the shopkeeper.

'I thought as it is an empty space on the pavement, it might be free.'

'Wake up brother, nothing is free these days, even speaking,' the shopkeeper replied, laughing.

'I have a large family and do not have anything right now but if I earn money I will pay you,' said Najaaf.

'Good, I will not charge you a lot,' said the shopkeeper.

'Thank you. God bless you.'

Najaaf stationed himself near the shop's entrance, placed his tools behind him and waited for customers to come. For a few weeks he worked hard and gave a small amount to the shopkeeper. He was happy. As the place was crowded, passers-by often sat on his chair, extended their feet and Najaaf happily cleaned and polished their shoes. 'Life is good, thanks to Hamidullah,' he thought. He always prayed for his friend, hoping that God would forgive his sin. A few weeks passed without any problem. Then a policeman approached Najaaf. He knew that the Pakistan police were not nice to Afghan refugees but he was confident he hadn't done anything wrong. The policeman sat on the stool and Najaaf thought he would ask him to clean his shoes.

'My friend, you are not allowed to work here,' the policeman said.

'Why not, sir?' said Najaaf, sheepishly. 'I pay my rent to the shopkeeper.'

'Still, you are not allowed. Move on, move on.' He shook his stick in the air and stood up.

Najaaf knew there was no point pleading, he picked up his belongings quickly and put them in a plastic bag ready to go.

The shopkeeper, watching the incident and seeing the tension between them, came outside. He spoke to the policeman in a low voice as they walked together down the road. After a while the shopkeeper came back and told Najaaf that the policeman wanted some money.

'This is your shop. You agreed with me I could stay here. Why should I pay him?'

'I know it's extortion but you can't argue with the police in Pakistan. This is not your country and they will create problems for both of us. Pay him a little and I'll reduce my weekly rent,' the shopkeeper said.

From that day on, Najaaf could barely afford to buy food for his family. Whatever he earned went to the pockets of the corrupt policeman and the shopkeeper. After a few weeks he decided to move to a less crowded area in order to escape having to pay the policeman.

Life went on without change. After a long sleepless night Najaaf decided to send Akbar to the *madrassa*. It may be good for him, he thought.

The next day, Najaaf asked his nephew casually, 'Would you like to join the *madrassa*?'

Akbar panicked and looked up at his uncle questioningly.

'It would be good for you to learn the Quran.'

'I heard from other boys that the *mullah* beat the children,' Akbar said.

'If you are a good student and follow the rules I am sure the *mullah* wouldn't beat you,' Najaaf replied.

So Akbar joined the *madrassa* but found it hard to keep up with the lessons which involved memorising and reciting the Quran in Arabic. The only thing that Akbar was happy about was that he had enough food to fill his stomach. After one year, when he had finished learning to recite from the holy book, it was time for his Islamic duty, preparing for *jihad*, the holy war. At this point, Najaaf realised his mistake and started to worry about his nephew. But it was too late. Akbar and Najaaf were trapped and Najaaf knew that within one or two years Akbar would be sent to the war zone, back to Afghanistan.

One hot summer morning, as Najaaf set up his station for work, a tall, well-dressed Afghan man approached him.

He was bull-necked, about forty with dark skin and watchful eyes. He was wearing a white *shalwar khamiz*, a black jacket and a shawl on his right shoulder, his black hair was shiny with oil, and he was smoking an expensive cigarette. From the way he walked, Najaaf guessed he was a businessman. The man sat on Najaaf's stool and asked him to polish his shoes. He did not bother to take off his shoes, but just extended his legs toward Najaaf.

'Clean my shoes.'

'*Baly agha sahib*. Sure, sir,' said Najaaf, happy to find a rich customer.

They started a conversation about family issues, how many children they had, where they lived and which family and tribe they belonged to. It was obvious that Najaaf belonged to the Hazara tribe because of his round face, white skin and small nose, but it was difficult for Najaaf to work out which part of Afghanistan this arrogant man came from. He spoke very soft Dari. Najaaf thought he might be a warlord but which tribe did he belong to? Najaaf could not figure it out.

'This is not a good place for your work. Why don't you find a crowded area to make more money?' the man said to Najaaf.

'I couldn't make enough money after paying off the Pakistani police. If I don't give them what they want, they will not let me work there. I had to keep changing my place every day.'

'The policemen are worse than criminals. They are nasty,' agreed Najaaf's customer.

Curiosity caused Najaaf to ask him, 'What do you do for a living sir?'

'I run a business, a good one,' he said.

'I thought you might. What sort of a business?'

'Helping people.'

Najaaf laughed, but the rich man's face was serious and Najaaf reddened.

'How come you make money by helping people?'

The man put on a business-like voice. 'I take children to Europe. Have you got a boy or two? I can take them.' Najaaf knew that rich people went to live in Europe but he had never heard that poor children could go too.

'What do you mean, sir?'

'I mean I take boys to Europe who can send money home to their families.'

Najaaf thought he was joking. 'How? Does money grow on trees in Europe?'

'No. It's a long story,' he said and then fell silent. Najaaf polished his shoes and tried not to mark his white clothes with black shoe polish. At the same time he was thinking about what the man had said.

'Tell me a bit more about it,' he said. The rich man knew he was targeting the right person.

'I will tell you if you have someone for me to take, otherwise there is no point.' The more the man resisted revealing the full details, the more curious Najaaf became.

'I have a nephew but he is too young, he is just fourteen-years-old.'

'Fourteen is a good age, the younger the better.'

Najaaf did not know why a younger child was better or where the child could get money from to send home, and the man did not explain any more. All he said was that children could easily find jobs in Europe and that there was lots of work available. Najaaf could understand this as in Afghanistan young children often had to work for a living.

'Akbar is a very strong lad. He is ready to do all sorts of work.' Najaaf tried to advertise his nephew's ability for work in the best possible way and laughed nervously. The man saw his yellow tobacco-stained teeth. He knew he had found the right person.

'Yes, he can work and go to school. He has a chance to make something of himself'.

'I do not want him to go to school,' Najaaf said.

'That is the silliest thing I have ever heard. Why not? School is good.'

'School is for rich people,' Najaaf said.

'It is a good opportunity for him to become literate and work in an office, wear a nice suit and have a good comfortable life. You never know, he may become a big man, a politician, one day when he gets older and then he can come back home and work for the government. You do not want him to be a shoe polisher like you, do you?'

Najaaf did not like his tone of voice but kept quiet. He did not want to lose his customer but deep down he was annoyed.

'I do not want him to be a politician,' he said.

'Why not?' said the man, surprised.

'Look, what did the politicians do to Afghanistan, apart from making everyone's life miserable? Look what has happened in the last couple of years. If it was not for them I could have had a peaceful life in my own country and my brother and his family would have been alive today. He raised his voice. 'I hate politicians.' He paused and suddenly thought, 'What if this man has some connection with politicians or is a politician himself?' He softened slightly. 'Well, I suppose you are right. Education could be good for the boy but I need money. A little money would be handy,' Najaaf said, trying to stay calm.

'Yes, if he works hard, believe me, you will be rich and will not have to sit here anymore,' the businessman said.

'What sort of jobs are available for him if I let him go?'

'Any sort of job.'

'What if he can't find a job? Will he be on the streets'?

'Do not worry. Before they find him a job the government will give him some money and a place to live. He can send some of his credit to you. When he reaches eighteen he can work hard and send a lot of money to you.'

Najaaf put his brush on the ground in bewilderment.

Najaaf was not yet forty yet but seemed much older. He looked at the ground for a few seconds to give himself more time to think. Then he straightened his back, lifted his chin and looked at the rich man in disbelief. He had never heard of such a thing in his entire life; a government giving away money to children for no reason.

'I know that British people are *kaffir*. How come they give away their money to Muslim children?'

'They are Christian, they believe in God but their

religion is different. *Kaffirs* are people who do not believe in God,' said the smuggler.

'If they don't follow the Prophet Muhammed they are *kaffirs* to me. What if they try to convert Muslim children to become *kaffirs*?'

The rich man laughed loudly, stood up and lit a cigarette. 'The government don't care about the children's beliefs. They help children from all countries who need help.'

'What good people,' Najaaf said, not fully believing what the man said.

'And how do you make your money? Does the government give you money for taking them there?' He was even more confused. The rich man laughed again, raised his right hand and slapped his knee.

'No, I take my money from you, from the children. Look! Let me explain. Normally when I take the children to Europe their fathers or relatives pay me half of the money that we agree in advance and the rest of it when their child reaches his destination. But don't worry. In your case, I know you don't have money so I will not charge you now but when the boy starts sending money home, then you can pay me back bit by bit. You do not have to pay me in one go. Think about it. I have a large group of children in Europe and now they have all started sending money home.'

'How much do you want?'

'For each child, I receive ten or twelve thousand dollars or sometimes more.'

'Wow!' Najaaf was shocked. 'It's a lot of money. Where do the parents get that much money?'

'Well, they sell their land or house to save their children's lives and it's a good investment in the long term.'

'If I had one thousand, I wouldn't send him away,' Najaaf said.

'In your case, as I said, I will not take the money right now. I'll only take it when I know he is making money.'

'What if he doesn't?'

'Then the government will give him a bit, not much, but enough for him to give me some and send some to you.'

When the man's shoes were clean and shiny, he paid and left. Najaaf faced a real dilemma.

CHAPTER 3

After two years of living in a refugee camp in Pakistan, Akbar arrived in the UK aged fourteen. Akbar always remembered that cloudy, late afternoon in Pakistan when he said goodbye to his uncle's family. Tears rolled down his small cheeks and he felt like a wingless butterfly caught in a storm. He felt powerless, confused, and sad that he had no control over his uncle's decision. It was the second displacement in his young life and he was devastated. His uncle looked into Akbar's eyes.

'Don't be so worried, you're fourteen-years-old and a man now. I am sure you will be OK,' he said. 'Please look after him,' he begged the smuggler. The man chain-smoked as he reassured Najaaf.

Najaaf bent down, hugged Akbar and kissed him on both cheeks. Then, without looking back, he entered his small tent, his face wet with tears, consoling himself with the thought that he had at least saved Akbar from *jihad*. Left alone with a complete stranger, Akbar's sense of rejection was like a door slamming in his face. He looked at the strange man with pleading eyes.

The trafficker picked up Akbar's small bag and indicated with his head that it was time to go. Akbar walked behind him. On the way, the smuggler collected three other teenage boys from different areas. Then the long journey started from Pakistan to Iran, at night, through deserted, dark and unknown surroundings. Occasionally they would see a tiny glimmer of light in the far distance. At four o'clock in the morning, when they were tired and couldn't walk any further, the trafficker let them rest in a forest.

For days on end they did not see a single soul around. They walked for miles and miles in the hot desert until, at last, in the middle of a pitch-black night they reached Mashad, a town in north east Iran. The smuggler took them to a dilapidated house hidden among tall trees, where they met another man who was waiting for them. He had a long face with a scar on his right cheek, a dark bushy beard and moustache and a belly that bulged through his worn-out shirt. He spoke Dari with an unusual accent. He was not Afghan but the boys could not figure out where he came from. Perhaps Iran or Kurdistan? He had a strange way of laughing and made a sound like a bird. Every time he laughed it was as if he had a pain in his stomach.

The children were all given a piece of bread, a large tomato and a glass of water and then were sent to sleep in the same dark room which smelt of unwashed bodies and sour metallic objects. The two men took a *chalam* out of the room to smoke their hashish as they discussed how much this trip had cost them. The next morning when the boys got up, a different man came into the room.

'Get up, get up you lazy boys. Breakfast is ready,' the new man said.

Breakfast consisted of a thin piece of flat bread and a cup of black tea with lots of sugar. The new man told them that he was in charge of them from then on. The previous one had disappeared.

'Why, where is Easanullah?' the eldest boy in the group dared to ask.

'He has gone back to Pakistan to bring more boys.'

There was nothing in their faces but panic, fear, and anxiety. 'How long will it take him to come back?'

The smuggler was surprised the boy had a tongue. Normally children didn't ask questions.

'He won't return for a long time. Don't worry, from

now on I am in charge,' he repeated. 'We have to start our journey in a couple of days and in the meantime you are not allowed to leave this compound, you understand. I'll bring you your food.'

'I am sorry but I don't know you. My father gave money to Easanullah and arranged for him to take me to Europe, not to you. Now you are saying he is not coming. How did this happen?' the eldest boy said.

This time the man raised his voice loud and clear. He moved towards the boy and looked him straight in the eyes.

'I'll tell you one more time. Don't ask any more questions, OK? We are a team working together. My job is to get you out of Iran. When you are out, there is another man waiting to take over. You will probably see a few of us before you reach your destination.

'This means you will give us to another man?'

'Yes, any more questions?"

The boys had no choice, they nodded their heads in agreement and did not dare ask anything further. They remained in the dark room, sharing their bed with lice and mice. There were no facilities for them to wash themselves. Occasionally they were allowed out into the dusty compound, surrounded by high mud walls, to stretch their legs. They were in a remote area and did not hear any cars, people or animals. The smuggler gave them very little food; just plain flat bread, black tea and boiled potatoes. Sometimes he gave them a flat naan bread with water.

Two weeks passed. Then one night, when the boys were fast asleep, the man came into the room and banged on the door loudly.

'Wake up boys, get ready. We're going now.'

The teenagers did not move. He shouted harder this time. When the boys still did not move he got angry and pulled off the dirty blanket covering them. 'Come on! Get up! We have to go now. We don't have time.'

'Where to?' the eldest boy asked sleepily.

'You have a big mouth. Why do you ask so many questions? I told you not to ask any questions.'

They hurriedly put on their dirty coats and   followed

the man out of the room, not knowing where he was taking them. The man gave each of them a piece of flat bread and a few dry apricots and told them to keep them in their pockets for their breakfast.

The journey was horrendous. They walked all night through pitch-black forests, over hills and on empty roads. They were not allowed to talk for fear of animals and possibly policemen finding them. At dawn they arrived in another forest. They stopped walking, exhausted and hungry. There was a wooden shelter and the trafficker pushed them towards it, told them to have their breakfast and to rest.

'I am going to buy some food from a nearby shop. Don't go anywhere from this spot. If you hear a noise or footsteps just hide under those bushes.' He was away for hours and the boys started panicking. He returned that afternoon bringing some naan bread and two bottles of water. 'Now we have to wait until it gets dark again and then we start the next part of our journey.'

As night fell they started walking again for hours until they reached another deserted area. At the end of an empty road a giant petrol tank awaited them. It was cleverly divided into two sections, the bigger part was for petrol, while the second part was a tiny box. This was where the boys would hide. On the surface it looked like a normal petrol tanker so that the police would not get suspicious. The smuggler handed over the children to a new man and said goodbye. The new man pointed towards the tank. 'Get in quickly,' he ordered, looking around to make sure no one could see them. The boys jumped in, the engine started and they continued their journey.

The children could hardly move. The smell of petrol was overpowering and they felt dizzy. Akbar vomited all the way and eventually passed out, leaning against another boy's shoulders as there was not enough room to lie down. They lost count of the hours. It seemed to take forever to reach their next destination.

Arriving in Turkey, the driver took the boys to another dark, dilapidated room and shoved them inside. The boys were astonished to find that there were six more children waiting for them. Two of them were Kurdish and two Pakistanis but they had been told to pretend to be Afghan. The rest were all Afghans. The Kurdish boys spoke a little Dari and the two Pakistanis spoke Pashtu fluently. Akbar wondered why they had to pretend to be Afghans but was too shy to ask.

The boys lived in the small room for a month waiting for the right time to continue their journey. They began to lose hope and stopped asking when they would move onto the next stage of their journey. Again the food consisted of just naan bread and sometimes yoghurt, boiled potatoes or dried apricots.

Eventually, the promised day came. Another man took over the responsibility for the next stage of the journey. He was slightly built with squinting eyes and dark skin. At each stage of the journey the group became bigger and bigger. One evening they found themselves beside a vast ocean. Where was this place? They did not know. Perhaps somewhere in Turkey or Greece?

They all stood around anxiously, not knowing how they were going to travel across the water in such a small boat. Some of them had never swum in deep water before. What if something happened? They would all be dead, Akbar thought. All the boys were scared but Akbar, the youngest in the group, started sobbing, tears and snot running down his face.

The smuggler tried to comfort him at first but then Akbar refused to get into the boat. It was obvious that the smuggler did not want to create a scene in case the police heard them so he quickly grabbed Akbar by his neck and threw him into the middle of the boat before telling the others to get in. The scared teenagers did not have any life jackets and pushed each other to get to the middle of the overcrowded boat. The boat slipped off into the night like a giant animal in the dark water.

In the early morning, before the sun rose, they reached the shore of Greece. No one was around except another smuggler waiting to take over the job. The boys were exhausted. Their heads down, they silently followed this new smuggler to a small family house. A woman gave them some cooked food which tasted better than anything they'd had the entire journey. The room they were given was windowless and dark, and the light was on day and night. They had to sleep on the floor. They were not allowed to go out for any reason.

In Greece the boys were separated from each other and no one explained why. The next stage of Akbar's journey was from Greece to France and then on to Dover. Seeing the massive chalky cliffs of England, surrounded by fog, Akbar suddenly missed the snow-topped mountains of Afghanistan and the clean, fresh, sunny air. He felt a sharp pain in his small chest.

CHAPTER 4

In Dover, Akbar was surprised to see the first smuggler who had made the deal with his uncle in Pakistan. He seemed different. He wore Western clothes and looked smart. His hairstyle was smarter and he looked much cleaner. Akbar was pleased to see him and felt safe. The trafficker seemed satisfied that so far his long-term investment was secure.

The train journey from Dover to London Euston was the smoothest that Akbar had ever experienced. Looking out of the window at the vast green fields of England was like a dream. Akbar knew nothing about Britain or what was expected of him. He thought he would have to work the moment he arrived in London, as the smuggler had promised his uncle. He felt excited. He would be good at physical work, he thought. He did not know that under-age children are not allowed to work in Britain and were protected by the law. He did not know that it was compulsory for children to finish school. He did not know that in Britain most children enjoy their childhood before they become adults.

The smuggler knew all about child and human rights, but he also knew that desperate, unaccompanied minors could work unofficially in the UK for long hours in take-away shops, butchers or as car-washers in order to pay their debts t traffickers. Some walked long distances every day, delivering leaflets for hours for petty cash. Smuggling children was a profitable investment for many different nationalities and there was a network of international criminal gangs.[iii]

After a journey of four months, Akbar arrived in London in the summer of 1985. The next day, Akbar and the trafficker left the tiny flat where they had stayed the night in order to go to the Home Office in Croydon. Akbar left the flat with the smuggler walking behind him. He was like a lost sheep, not knowing where he was being taken. The smuggler hailed a taxi. London felt huge. A few yards from an imposing building the taxi stopped and they got out.

'You are to go inside by yourself,' the smuggler told Akbar, pointing at the building.

'Why?' Akbar asked, his heart beating fast, a sinking feeling in the pit of his stomach.

'Because my job is finished here and those people are going to take care of you. I cannot go with you.'

'I thought you were coming with me. How can they give me a job if you are not going to introduce me to them?'

'They don't give you a job, they give you a place to live.'

'On my own?' Akbar panicked.

'No, probably with some family. But don't worry, I'm around all the time,' the smuggler replied. Akbar had not moved.

'If they knew I had brought you here they would put me in prison,' the trafficker said.

Akbar was confused. 'What if they put me in prison?'

'No, they will not put you in prison because you're a child, but you must not tell them anything about me. You understand?' Akbar blanched. 'They may take you to another building. Just don't panic. I'm around and watching you closely. OK?'

'I don't know how to explain myself. What should I say to them?' Akbar said.

'Don't worry, when they realise that you can't speak English they will provide an interpreter. In the meantime just keep quiet and don't panic. Remember not to mention me or your uncle will be in trouble. And remember if they ask you how old are you, tell them you're twelve.'

'But I'm fourteen,' Akbar said. The man lost patience and started to push him towards the Home Office entrance.

'Just say it, OK? You will understand later on,' he said.

'Will you wait for me outside?' Akbar pleaded.

'Yes, I'll wait. But when you come out of the building don't look around for me. If you see me, pretend that you don't know me. Don't panic, I know where they will take you anyway.'

Akbar was anxious and could not stand still. His hands were shaking like dry leaves in the autumn, his heart was an empty cell, and his brain was on fire. He moved around in circles like a fly trapped in a spider's web. The man pushed him again toward the building, before walking away and disappearing from the scene.

Reluctantly Akbar entered through the glass doors, his mind empty of words. His tongue, as dry as sandpaper, stuck to his lips.

Inside he was confronted by a large, bald security guard who had a ring in his ear and tattooed arms. He asked Akbar what he wanted. Akbar was tongue-tied. He stood there speechless and looked at the floor.

The guard knew why he was there. Recently a large group of unaccompanied children had arrived in the UK. He asked the boy to empty his pockets and put all his belongings into a tray. Akbar stood there still like a statue. The guard then realised that the boy didn't understand English. He made the boy take off his coat and put it on the tray. Then he searched the boy and told him to pass through the security gate. Akbar retrieved his jacket from the tray and the guard pushed the lift button. The guard motioned towards the open door and said 'third floor.' Akbar did not move. An Asian family arrived and the guard searched them. They approached the lift and the guard pushed Akbar into it along with them.

Inside, Akbar felt even more confused as the lift

moved up and stopped. The door opened and they all got out. This was like a magic. This was the first time that he had used a lift. The Asian family walked away from him and Akbar did not know where to go. A well-dressed Indian woman with a dark suit approached him.

'Can I help you?' she asked. No answer. 'What is your name, where do you come from?' she tried again. Akbar felt dizzy. He had lost his tongue and looked down at the grey carpet. 'Come with me,' she said and Akbar followed her.

They reached a door and entered a large, empty room with a big table in the middle and two chairs. She indicated to Akbar to sit.

The woman was nice, and she tried to help him by naming various countries: Iraq, Pakistan Syria, Afghanistan. When Akbar heard the name of his country, he looked up for a second and then returned his gaze to the floor. She said something in English that Akbar did not understand and left the room. Akbar sat on his chair and looked around the huge reception room full of files, books, papers, and a tape recorder. It was daunting. He was amazed when she came back with an Afghan interpreter who shook his hand and introduced himself. Akbar began to feel human again and slightly relaxed. Apart from the smugglers, it was the first time that he had heard the familiar language.

The assessment took place in a small room with another man who introduced himself to Akbar and tried his best to comfort him.

'Would you like to have a glass of water?' he said. Piles of paper and a tape recorder were in front of him. This was another new experience for Akbar. The questions about his family and why he had come to Britain lasted a full hour. The interpreter translated them for Akbar.

'What is your name?'

'Akbar Ali'

'How old are you?'

Akbar was just about to say fourteen and then he remembered what the trafficker had told him. He hesitated for a few seconds and then said 'twelve'.

'Exact date please?'

'1st January.'

'Which year?'

Akbar started to panic. He did not know which year. He was not familiar with the Western calendar although the trafficker had repeatedly told him the year he should say that he was born.

'What is your father's name?'

'Hussain Ali.'

'What is your surname?'

Akbar looked at the interpreter, perplexed and no words came out.

The officer repeated the question.

Akbar had no idea what he was talking about. He looked up at the interpreter, his eyes begging for help. 'What is a surname?' he asked.

The interpreter held up his hand. 'Can I explain something?' he asked. The officer stopped the tape. 'In rural parts of Afghanistan people do not have a surname as such. If necessary they use their village name or their ethnicity.'

'You have a surname,' the interview officer said to the interpreter.

'Yes because I grew up in a big city where the lifestyle was different. I went to school, college and university. There was peace at that time. But most of these children come from villages, they are illiterate and modernity never reached the rural areas.'

'But some children that I interviewed before had surnames.'

'I'm sure the traffickers chose surnames for them. Perhaps he forgot to give this boy a surname. Most of these children have two first names, for example Abdul Mohamed or Mohamed Bashir so they invent a surname for themselves. Abdul becomes his first name and Mohamed his surname.' They both laughed.

'They're very clever,' said the interviewer.

'No they're not, but the smugglers are expert at their jobs,' said the interpreter. He turned to Akbar. 'Are you happy to have Ali as your surname?'

'Yes,' Akbar said, indifferent.

The officer turned the tape back on. 'What part of Afghanistan do you come from?'

'I was born in Kabul but my parents were from Bamyan.'

'What is your mother tongue?'

'Dari.'

Then he was asked some general knowledge questions to make sure that he was from Afghanistan. The Home Office had recently noticed that the smugglers were bringing young boys from Afghanistan's neighbouring countries, Iran and Pakistan, into the UK. They spoke Dari and Pashtu and pretended to be Afghan. It was therefore hard for the immigration officer to differentiate between true Afghan asylum seekers and those who pretended to be Afghans.

'Who are Afghanistan's neighbours?'

No answer.

'What is Afghanistan's capital?'

No answer.

'Where did you live before going to Pakistan?'

'In Kabul.'

'Can you name a few provinces in your country?'

No answer.

Akbar had started school at the age of seven and attended on and off before the war disrupted his education. Schools were closed down and the teachers disappeared. He could not remember anything from that time. The officer wanted to make sure that Akbar had a correct record, but it was hard for him to answer all the questions. He had been just twelve-years-old when he became a refugee in Pakistan.

The interview terminated and the officer turned off the tape recorder as there was not enough evidence to prove Akbar's country of origin. They needed an expert from Afghanistan to confirm the boy's nationality. According to child protection law, Akbar was entitled to be protected until he was eighteen-years-old, then the Home Office would reopen his case. If the case was strong enough they might grant him refugee status, but if not they would send him back to his country of origin as an adult.

'I will have to conduct another interview as your file is not complete yet,' the officer told him. 'The council will provide you with somewhere to stay for the time being, OK?' The officer stood up, and shook hands with him. Akbar felt grown up and respected. No one had ever shaken hands with him before. He was then accompanied to the local authority.

Entering another large office was nerve-wracking but he had no choice. Much to Akbar's surprise he found a small group of Afghan boys in there. It was a relief. He sat among them, too scared to talk for fear of giving something away. The smuggler had told him not to talk to anybody, but they all were in the same boat. They had dark frightened eyes and did not know what fate had in store for them. Some of them were well informed about the UK from their smugglers or relatives, while others had no clue what to expect. All Akbar knew was that they would send him to live with a family.

Akbar was wondering whose house he would go to, what sort of people he would live with and what he would eat. He felt listless, his clothes were dirty and hung off his skinny body. His eyes were dark red with tiredness, his hair messed up and unwashed for God knows how long.

In the local authority office a social worker, a tall, gentle, black woman with Afro hair, introduced herself to Akbar through an interpreter. After filling in a few forms she gave Akbar the address of a nearby Bed and Breakfast to stay in until she could find a foster home for him. Akbar did not know how to get to the new address and what she meant by foster care. He was disconcerted by his surroundings. He did not ask how to get there, but stood head down, looking at the floor without moving.

The interpreter noticed Akbar's confusion and offered help. 'Come with me. I'll take you there.'

Akbar walked behind the interpreter. His brain raced ahead. 'Who are these people? Why are they taking me to different places? Are they going to put me in a prison or give me a job? What if I do not see the smuggler?' At the time, all Akbar wished for was to see the smuggler. He was the only one he knew in this strange country. But he had vanished as if he had never existed at all.

The interpreter tried to comfort Akbar. 'I came to this country as an asylum seeker myself. Don't worry. You're safe here. This is a good country,' he said. Akbar had many questions in his mind but was too shy to ask. When they reached the Bed and Breakfast the interpreter rang the bell. An overweight, middle aged Indian man opened the door. He wore bifocal glasses, flowery shorts and a red T-shirt which, for Akbar, seemed unusual.

'Hello,' he said to Akbar and the interpreter. 'Is this Akbar?'

'Yes it is,' said the interpreter and extended his hand toward the man.

He asked Akbar to come in and showed him the bathroom, kitchen and his bedroom, which was on the second floor, and then left him there. Akbar liked the Indian man, but wondered why he was wearing women's clothing.

The room seemed empty, soulless, and cold. Akbar had never slept alone in a room before. He'd always been with his parents and his siblings in the same room back home. When he was in Pakistan he slept with his uncle's family in a tiny tent. Here, the ceiling seemed too high. The flowery-carpeted floor was huge. Suddenly, he felt like crying. All this was happening so fast, it did not seem real to him. Was he dreaming? Where were his family? Why had he ended up in a strange land? What had happened to that happy, peaceful life they had shared under that bright clear blue sky, so beautiful that it felt like it was smiling at them all day? Where were those tall trees surrounded by the mountains?

He looked around the room, stood up, went to the window, and looked out at the quiet and empty street. A few people were walking with their heads down and a group of children were fighting, a young lady walked by with a child in a pushchair. He came back and sat on the bed, deep in thought.

Yes, this is reality, he convinced himself. His mind travelled back to Afghanistan. He remembered his family. They were poor, but happy. Then the war, the hateful war, had changed everything. It all started like a tsunami from the east, the west, the north and the south and had drowned the whole country, including his family. The politicians and the warlords attacked each other like savage animals, and the war had spread to every part of that beautiful land like an epidemic, overwhelming every family, rich or poor. He felt like a small leaf that the strong wind had blown far away to a strange land. The pain of dislocation was too much to bear.

He lay awake that night thinking of his home, his parents and his siblings and started crying. He could not sleep until two in the morning. At seven he was woken up by a big bang, jumped out of bed and rushed toward the window, his heart in his mouth. Then he heard an indignant conversation between two people but did not understand a word of. He thought that maybe they were arguing over him because he was occupying someone else's room. He was too scared to leave the room. But no one bothered him.

Akbar stayed in that small hotel for three days. He hardly came out of his room and ate very little of the food that the kind Indian man offered him. On the fourth day, an English woman came to pick him up. It was another surprise. The doorbell rang and the manager put his tea on the kitchen table. 'I'm coming I'm coming,' he shouted and rushed toward the door.

'Good morning, I am Mrs Smith the foster carer,' she said.

'Come in please. I was expecting you,' said the manager. 'I'll fetch the boy.'

Akbar came downstairs, Mrs Smith extended her hand and shook Akbar's hand. 'I'm Mrs Smith, your foster carer.'

Akbar didn't understand what she meant and looked at the floor again. 'What is foster care and where is she taking me?' he wondered.

Mrs Smith smiled at him but Akbar did not respond. They both fell silent and then she said, 'Let's go!'

Akbar grabbed his few belongings and his coat, which was far too big for him. The trafficker had given it to him on the way.

He followed Mrs Smith to her car. She opened the

door and indicated for Akbar to get in. Akbar's heart started pounding in his chest again. He did not know where she was taking him. Why had he ended up in this strange and mysterious country, so different that he could feel it with all his body and soul? All he could see around him were high buildings, shops, houses, endless cars, buses, roads and of course new faces. This was in sharp contrast to the slum area where his uncle had lived in Peshawar, a town where smoke was in the air and filth on the streets, where carts, horses, animals, beggars, children used the same road. Now everywhere he looked was cleaner and fresher and not dusty at all.

To Akbar, the biggest surprise was the way women dressed. London seemed so wealthy but women's clothes were tight and revealing, as though they were short of material.

The foster carer drove Akbar to the shopping centre to buy him some clothes. She bought him shoes, T-shirts, trousers, socks and underwear from a cheap shop, and then they returned to the car.

He walked behind her, with a dreamlike uncertainty, thinking to himself, 'Why has she bought me so many things? Who is she?' Her blond hair was tied in a ponytail and she wore light red lipstick and a grey sleeveless top that revealed most of her ample breasts.

She took him home to her three-bedroom flat on the third floor of a council block. Before entering the flat, Akbar heard the sound of dogs inside and started to panic. When she opened the door two big dogs leaped excitedly on Akbar. He backed away terrified and started screaming. The lady cursed the dogs, rushed toward them, held their collars, dragged them into the kitchen and closed the door, apologising.

Leaning against the corridor wall, his heart beating fast, his face white, Akbar did not know how to handle this unusual situation. He was embarrassed and ashamed. 'Come in,' she said and Akbar entered the room and looked around fearfully while the dogs barked loudly behind the kitchen door.

In most Muslim countries, people do not keep dogs

indoors as pets, as they consider them dirty. They use dogs for hunting and keep them outside. Once in the flat Akbar felt nervous at being completely alone with a strange woman, who could not speak his language, and the idea of living with dogs under the same roof was a nightmare.

The lady ran a bath for him with bubble bath. She handed him a pink towel and pointed towards the bathroom. Akbar knew rich people in Afghanistan owned luxury bathrooms but he had never experienced a bubble bath before. His family had always used the public baths in Kabul. Akbar felt he was going to faint with shame. 'How could he wash in a strange house with no man around?' Even the soapy water seemed dirty to him. He stood there frozen. The lady closed the door and left him alone.

Reluctantly, Akbar undressed himself and got into the warm, sweet-smelling water. For a short time he felt relaxed but his mind was full of unanswerable questions. 'Who is this woman? Where is her husband?' He was shocked to see a woman living on her own. 'Why am I in this house? Why did the smuggler disappear?' Suddenly he missed the familiarity of the camps in Pakistan. He missed that piece of bone-dry land, the dusty and dirty slum that had become home for thousands of refugees. He missed his uncle and his cousins.

He rinsed his body, dried himself with a soft, clean towel and put on his new clothes. He liked the new trousers, they were blue jeans, the sort that he had always coveted back in Kabul. He put on the white T-shirt but discarded the underpants, they seemed too girly to him, and left the bathroom. He kept his head down because he did not want to face the woman.

'Did you have a good bath?' she asked. He did not answer as he did not understand the question. He just nodded his head.

The lady was kind but did not know how to communicate with Akbar without a common language. When he was in Pakistan he had heard a few simple English words from other children in the camps: 'Yes' and 'No'. Since arriving in England, Akbar had managed to understand some words and gestures but one of the main problems for his host, which frustrated them both, was that when she was talked to Akbar, he avoided eye contact, out of respect, which she found extremely rude. 'Look at me when I am talking to you,' she said. Immediately Akbar heard his father's voice. 'Don't look at me when I am talking to you.'

That first evening, Akbar felt completely lost although he had washed himself in a luxurious bathroom, had new clothes and his own private and comfortable room for the first time in his life. Sleeping alone made him feel grown up, but uneasy. The food was so different that he found it hard to swallow. That first day he ate fish and chips with boiled vegetables. It seemed such strange food. In Afghanistan no one would ever eat tasteless boiled vegetables and certainly not with fish. He missed the familiar hot, oily and spicy food. In the morning she gave him a bowl of corn flakes with cold milk and he did not touch it. 'How could he drink milk that was not boiled?' he thought.

For weeks he did not hear any news from his trafficker. Every time he went out with his foster carer he was hoping to see the trafficker. He felt like a fish out of the water. After four weeks in the tiny flat, spent mainly in his room for fear of the dogs, his carer knocked on his door.

'I've found a school for you,' she said, happily, knowing that he was bored at home. Akbar smiled vaguely, wondering if there would be more surprises for him. He had expected to hear 'I've found a job for you.' as his trafficker had promised his uncle.

The first day at school took shape in Akbar's memory and remained there like a clear picture in his mind throughout his life.

How fragile he was on that grey morning when he entered school for the first time. The teachers were so nice. He liked his uniform which was black trousers, blue jacket and a white shirt. It was so different from his school in Kabul. He joined year nine without any knowledge of the English language. He sat there like a zombie. He felt so out of place, but was happy to be away from the dogs. He found it hard to make friends. Sometime he was bullied but couldn't express his feelings. For many months he was not able to communicate with anyone. He kept his distance from others. The only friend he made was a boy from Africa who had recently arrived in England and spoke no English. Although their communication was through facial expressions and body language, they enjoyed each other's company and, slowly, their bond strengthened.

Akbar began to accept his situation and appreciated the kindness of his teachers. He started to enjoy school. He had extra English lessons, worked hard and proved to be a good learner. He even received a reward from his school for good attendance which was a huge achievement. The foster carer noticed his good work and held her thumbs up. 'Well done Akbar,' she said. By now he knew that 'thumbs up' was not considered rude in the UK, but he would never repeat this gesture to a fellow Afghan as it was the equivalent of two fingers in Britain.

His biggest discomfort was sharing the flat with the dogs. The hardest thing for Akbar to bear was that the food was cooked in the kitchen while the dogs roamed freely around. He tried not to eat. After six months he had lost weight and couldn't sleep at night. He started having nightmares. His foster carer used to wake him up when he was crying out loud. 'Wake up Akbar. You are having a nightmare again,' she would say. As he awoke, he would move his head slightly and cover his face with the blanket to hide his tears.

CHAPTER 5

After a while, the local council placed Akbar with an African family. Again it was a change of food, and a different way of life. In four years Akbar had lived with three different families. The nightmares continued for a long time. Gradually, with the help of his third foster family and his social worker Akbar overcame them.

Akbar had had no contact with any Afghan families in the UK but when he finished school and joined a college he discovered a group of Afghan young men who lived semi-independently. He was happy to meet them and began socialising with them. However, he realised that too much freedom could harm you and decided to stay with the foster family who were kind and supportive and treated him as part of their family.

Every year they organised a birthday party for him. Akbar had never celebrated his birthday before and he had already forgotten the fake date of birth that the smuggler had tried hard to inject into his brain. There was always cake on the table with candles, presents and cards. This act of kindness touched his heart and he was always grateful.

Gradually, Akbar's English improved and he proved to be a gifted student. He grew into a confident young man. He made a lot of good friends at college and enjoyed

English culture, although it was not always an easy process. He was still wary of cameras and policemen every time he went out. Three months travelling from country to country and hiding from cameras and police had made him nervous. He would jump at every loud noise.

Akbar had a hunger for education but this was disrupted with the sudden reappearance of the trafficker who started demanding money. Because of this, Akbar could not concentrate on his studies. The trafficker followed him like a shadow wherever he went.

When Akbar left college with his friends he noticed that the trafficker was following him but he knew he would not approach him when he was with a group of people. It was only a matter of time until he found Akbar alone.

'I want you to start paying me money,' he said.

'I do not have any money.'

'Why aren't you working?'

'How can I work when I go to college?'

'Do you think I was born yesterday?' said the trafficker. Akbar did not answer. 'Do not make excuses. Other boys work and go to college too.'

'I don't know where to work.'

'I can find you a job, after college.'

'How?' Akbar shrugged his shoulders, helplessly.

'Leave it to me. In the meantime you get enough money from the government to give some to me. You have to finish your debt. I brought you to this country to have a comfortable life.'

Akbar did not know how to handle this nasty man. He was too scared to reveal his secret to the foster family. He also became anxious about going out, in case he was approached by the smuggler again. A few weeks later the smuggler reappeared. 'I have found you an after-college job.'

'What is it?' Akbar asked, nervously.

'Working in a pizza kitchen.'

'I have never worked in a kitchen before. Plus I have to go home after college.' Akbar said.

'I know you are allowed to be out for a few hours

after college. No one will question you.' The man was adamant.

A week later he approached Akbar again. 'Let's go to the pizzeria,' he said and Akbar had no choice but to follow him. The restaurant was in a crowded area full of Indians, Afghans, Africans, Chinese, Pakistanis and Colombians. They entered the tiny kitchen which smelt of food and spices, human sweat and rats. Six Afghan boys, all unaccompanied minors, already worked there and none of them had a work permit. The trafficker introduced Akbar to the manager and negotiated his wages.

'I want you to come every day after college and work for four hours,' the manager said. 'Do not worry about food. There are plenty of pizzas and you can eat as much as you like.' Akbar smiled at the Afghan manager making Italian pizza. In Afghanistan men never cooked and had never heard of Italian pizza.

'I don't have any experience I'm afraid,' said Akbar.

'That is not a problem. You will learn quickly but remember to stay in the basement kitchen.'

'OK,' Akbar said, resigned to his fate. The money he earned would go directly into the smuggler's pocket.

The manager took Akbar on a small tour around the kitchen and showed him everything. Akbar noticed that at the end of the shelves there was a dirty grey curtain and behind it was another small room with a few blankets and thin mattresses tied up in a roll. He realised that these were for some of the young men who slept there overnight. The smell of rats was so strong that he felt suffocated.

He was under the supervision of another Afghan, Najibullah, who also had to work out of desperation. He had a large family back home to feed. After a few days they became good friends.

'We have a gathering tonight after work. Would you like to come?' Najibullah asked Akbar.

Akbar was tempted. He missed his own people, language and culture, he missed the few friends he had made in the refugee camps in Pakistan. He felt isolated as he did not have any other activities after school.

'I have to be home by a certain time. Let me call my foster carer and ask if I am allowed to be late.'

That night the young men left the pizzeria and they cautiously walked down the High Street with their heads down. They did not have work permits and they did not want to be confronted by the police who would sometimes stop them for no reason.

'What is your name? Where are you going? What is your address? Show me your ID?' Whenever there was vandalism and crime in the area, some people blamed the foreigners for it. The young men were not familiar with the system and were scared of any sort of interrogation by the police. Their cases with the Home Office were not yet approved. They had to be careful and keep a low profile.

They arrived at a flat above a bakery where some of the young Afghan men lived. The flat was far from the pizzeria, but they did not mind the long walk. They felt safe together. The small council flat was allocated to three young men, but most nights four or five of them stayed there. Entering the room Najibullah turned on a bare bulb covered with a spider's web. A small rat moved into the shadows and ran under the bed. 'Hello my friend don't run away from us we are all friends here,' Najibullah said and everyone laughed.

Akbar felt grown up among them, although he was the youngest in the group. Normally the men were too tired to cook for themselves, and they got free pizza from the shop. But occasionally they cooked kidney beans with lots of oil and spices and had it on pitta bread or chicken qurma with potatoes.

Cooking was fun. When the food was ready, they covered the flowery carpet with a piece of plastic and started eating from one big plate with their hands. They drank lots of green tea and coke, listened to Afghan music and talked about their families. This was the only time when they could enjoy being with one another. Sometimes they also met at a shelter, where a group of church volunteers provided them with food. They liked the shelter because it provided them with the opportunity to get together with a larger group. They played Afghan pop music and danced together.

Their conversations were all about their cases with the Home Office.

'I have been refused,' one said.

'What does that mean?' asked a newcomer who was not familiar with the system.

'It means they can kick me out, but I saw my solicitor and he is going to appeal.'

'What are you going to do if they refuse you again? asked another teenager.

'I have something in mind.'

'Like what?'

'I'll go undercover, work hard and save some money. If they catch me and send me back at least I'll have some money with me.'

'Find a girlfriend, get married and you will be OK,' suggested someone else.

'No, God forbid. Those girls are good fun but not for sharing your life with. I don't want to give my parents a heart attack.'

'Some of them are very good girls.'

'No, not for me. If you marry, they make you wash, clean and cook for them.' They all laughed.

After a few weeks of working in the tiny basement Akbar realised that the real reason why the shop manager asked them not to leave the kitchen was because they did not have National Insurance numbers, health and safety insurance and were not officially allowed to work. They worked for very little money, which suited the manager. The teenagers were like slaves with no rights. They were desperate to help their family and pay off the traffickers.

Five weeks passed and Akbar was just getting settled in when the police found out about the illegal workers. They fined the owner and closed down the pizzeria. Akbar was relieved to leave.

During that short time, working in the tiny kitchen with other Afghans, Akbar learned not only how to make pizza but also about his friends' lifestyle. He felt lucky to have a kind foster family.

One morning when he was on his way to college the

smuggler approached him again.

'I've found you another job,' he said.

'The family I live with are very strict. I cannot come home late after college every night,' Akbar replied.

'Look boy! As far as the Home Office is concerned you are 16 years old. I know you are older. You can live independently now, like other boys,' said the man.

'How can I do that?'

'Tell your social worker that you are not happy there.'

'But I like the family. I am happy there.'

The trafficker frowned.

'Listen to me you have more freedom when you live independently. You can work hard and save money to send home and pay off your debt to me. You know that I won't leave you alone until I get my money back. The sooner you pay me, the better for both of us,' he shouted.

'I do not have the money,' Akbar said.

'I know how much you get.'

'My foster carer puts most of my pocket money into the bank. She doesn't give me any more.'

'Do not lie to me. I can make problems for your uncle.'

By this time, Akbar had had enough. He had been in England for nearly four years and knew that young asylum seekers were not allowed to work. He knew the traffickers were acting against the law, and if the police caught them, they would go to prison as criminals.

'I don't care. Go ahead. If you approach me again I will give your name to the police.'

The man's eyes widened, he laughed nervously and then his face reddened. It was the first time that he had been confronted by a rebellious, young man.

'You do not know my name,' the smuggler shouted,

'Yes I do, you're Easan.'

'Stupid donkey! Do you really think I would give my real name to you or your uncle?' he said.

'Look, I told you I am not leaving my studies. I will pay you one day when I get a proper job. However, if you make trouble for me, I can easily make trouble for you,' Akbar said, confidently.

After that the smuggler did not bother him again,

knowing that he could make money elsewhere and that it was not worth the risk of Akbar reporting him. He had other teenagers to harass.

Akbar never missed college. He proved to be an excellent student, had a good record and won awards. He had not had opportunities like this in Afghanistan where his education had been disrupted many times due to war or his uncle's poverty.

In the diaspora, Akbar achieved something that he had never dreamed possible. He was grateful for the support of his social workers and the foster carers. However, he felt sad that he had lost contact with his uncle. He did not have his address and he did not want to confront the smuggler.

When Akbar was in the last year of college, he received a refusal letter from the Home Office. They were not convinced by his case on the grounds of his first interview in Britain. They refused to accept him as a refugee and as an adult and he would have to go back to Afghanistan. Akbar was thrown into uncertainty. How could he go to a country where he had no family, friends or relatives? He was just twelve years old when he left. He did not even know if he could survive there. 'What should I do?' he asked his solicitor on the phone.

'We will appeal again. And we will defend your case in court.' A few weeks later Akbar received a letter from his solicitor confirming the court date.

Akbar arrived at the central London court at 9.30am. He waited for hours. His faded confidence was concealed by the cheap suit that he borrowed from one of his friends for this fateful day. He asked two of his English friends and his foster mother to accompany him to court for support. It seemed such a strange system to him. His solicitor, an attractive, middle-aged woman, with fair hair, wore a dark blue suit. She sat next to Akbar and advised him how to present himself in the courtroom. He grew more and more nervous. His suit began to crease as he sat hunched up over himself.

Finally, at 2pm, the court was ready to see Akbar. He entered a hot and musty room where the judge, an old gentleman with grey hair, was sitting between the   two solicitors. Akbar's heart was beating faster and faster and he was not able to look at the judge. The Home Office representative, a small woman, looked Akbar straight in the eye as if to say, 'Hmm...I don't believe this young man.' Akbar tried to avoid her intimidating look. He was flanked by an interpreter, a rather chubby and clumsy man.

'How old were you when you left Bamoun?'

'It is Bamyan,' Akbar wanted to correct the judge but of course he just answered the question.

'I came from Kabul.' he said

'Was your father involved in politics? This was a question the judge might think a twelve-year-old Afghan child would know but, in reality, children would get a slap round the head if they spoke to their fathers about their political involvement. 'It was not a child's place to know such things' Akbar thought to himself.

The court finished after three hours of investigation, questions and answers. Akbar felt under a lot of pressure. He remembered the pain of losing his entire family that early morning in Kabul. He revisited that scene in that big courtroom.

'You will hear about the decision in three weeks time,' the judge said. Akbar and his supporters left the courtroom, uncertain of his fate.

Two weeks later, Akbar received his 'Leave to Remain' papers from the Home Office. He was a free man and had big ambitions for his future. He also planned to find his uncle and his family through the Red Cross. After graduating from college he applied for a university degree course to study law in London.

Three years later, Akbar graduated with a good degree, completed his training as a solicitor and began working for a law firm that dealt with immigration cases and unaccompanied minors. It was a rewarding job. But it involved a lot of emotional struggle and reminded him of the time when he was seeking asylum himself. He always supported the teenagers and felt their pain, sorrow and their plight.

Akbar bore a deep, psychological scar from his

family's death. It was a wound which he tried hard to heal, to forget that period of madness in Afghanistan which he had lived through. Sometimes working with those young children disturbed him deeply and a sense of rage erupted in his heart.

'Who is responsible for these children's displacement?' He asked himself. 'The Soviet Union, war lords, smugglers, businessmen, or international weapons manufacturers? Or perhaps all of them have their hands in this crime against humanity? Why do the bigger countries invade the poor, powerless countries? It was like the law of the jungle. The bigger animals eat the small ones.' Those children had lost everything: parents, relatives, friends, and they had to start from scratch in a foreign country.

Akbar worked on many heart-breaking cases where victims of war and conflict had been forced into exile. He also experienced a few isolated cases where Afghans and other refugees had abused the system and this gave ammunition to the politicians and the media to attack asylum seekers generally.

He had genuine child clients that the Home Office refused and tried to send back when they reached eighteen years of age. Some of them, desperate not to be returned, were advised by the smugglers to lie.

'Tell your foster carer that you are suffering from headaches, insomnia and depression. You'll get help on compassionate or medical grounds,' the smugglers would tell them.

Akbar knew that those teenagers were the product of a failed system throughout the world. They learned to lie from an early age.

There was a large group of Afghan children as young as eleven or twelve-years-old in London with no basic education, no hopes or ambitions, no family, no love or real purpose. They were dragged into drugs and alcohol. Some had girlfriends that they thought of as 'cheap tarts' ready to be used and to be thrown away whenever they wished. They had never known such freedom. The sudden changes to their lifestyle confused them.

Akbar knew that their experience in the UK was in

sharp contrast to what they had learned in Afghanistan. Even if a young man was engaged to a young woman, he was never allowed to go out with his fiancée alone. In Afghanistan, children lived with their parents, grandparents until they married. Even then, the newly-weds often continued to live with the groom's family. Akbar's own wedding and marriage was also to follow a different path.

CHAPTER 6

Simeen had developed severe headaches from a very early age. For the last couple of years she also suffered from high blood pressure and was regularly on medication. A week after the *Nawroz* at the Bukhara Banquet Hall, Simeen felt a little bit better. She tried hard to forget the horrible evening as she had tried, unsuccessfully, to forget her past by putting it in a locked, wooden box. A few weeks later the nightmares returned, triggered by one phone call that changed her life.

Simeen was in the kitchen washing the plates when the phone rang.

'My hands are wet. Pick up the phone please!' Simeen shouted. She knew that Akbar didn't like talking on the phone, especially in the morning, as he was always rushing to get ready for work. Akbar reluctantly picked up the phone.

'*Salaam*-hello, can I speak to Sittara please?' said a young male voice.

'I am afraid she's just left home. Can I take a message?' Akbar said.

'I hope you remember me. I am Abdullah Karimi. We met at the Bukhara Hall on New Year's Eve. Sittara wanted to borrow a book about the history of Afghanistan but I don't have your address. Could I please have it? I would like to post it to her.'

'Yes of course. Have you got a pen?' After giving their address to the man, out of curiosity Akbar asked 'What's the name of the book?'

'It's called *Afghanistan In The Course Of History*, written by Ghobar, the famous historian.'

Akbar had no idea who this historian was. He did not know much about his country's long history, but was proud that Sittara had expressed an interest. Simeen came into the room, dried her hands on her apron and stood near her husband to listen to the conversation. Akbar said goodbye and put the phone down.

'Who was it?' Simeen asked.

'Oh, someone wanted to send a book to Sittara. I gave them our address.'

'What was her name?'

'Why do you think it was a girl?'

'Oh was it a boy then?' Simeen was alarmed.

'Yes it was. Why did you think it was a girl?' he repeated.

The question irritated Simeen. 'OK, does he have a name?' she asked.

'I think he said Abdullah. Do you remember we met him and his family at the Bukhara Hall?'

The name did not register in Simeen's mind at first but after a few seconds she felt a sharp pain in her chest. 'Oh my God, how can I get away from this nightmare?' she thought. All the agony she had experienced in the past returned like an avalanche into her mind. Her mental anguish became a sharp, physical pain and she felt as though her legs had been wrenched from beneath her.

'You shouldn't give our address to young Afghan men,' she said. 'It's not good for Sittara's reputation'.

'He just wanted to send a book to her, that's all. What's wrong with that? You know how Sittara is interested in Afghan history.' Simeen's mood had changed and it made Akbar argumentative. 'This is Britain and we have to accept some of the culture. Here young men and women talk all the time, at school, college, university, shops, parks, offices, everywhere. You have to trust her.'

'I do trust Sittara but I don't like people talking behind our daughter's back,' Simeen said.

'No one talks behind her back. This is not Afghanistan and we are not the *Taliban*, are we?

Sittara is living in this open society. I am sure she can look after herself. She's a sensible girl,' Akbar said.

'But it's not our culture. You know that, we are not British. She should behave like an Afghan girl.'

' I think she is a very level-headed young woman and knows her limits.' Akbar said.

When Simeen didn't reply, Akbar grew angry 'What is an Afghan girl? Do you know how many Afghan families are living in Britain?' He moved closer to her and sat down at the dining table, trying to keep his voice down so as not to upset his wife. He answered himself. 'Around 60 or 80,000 families, and each family has at least two or three girls and boys. They go to school from an early age, they socialise with British children, learn from them, eat with them, talk to them. How can you expect our children to keep our culture hundred percent pure in the way you want it? It is like telling them to swim but not to get wet. Does it make sense to you? They will find their own way if you trust them and direct them on the right path, talk to them, be their friend. If you press them hard, they'll choose the wrong way. Do you want her to be like that Afghan girl?'

'Which Afghan girl are you talking about?' Simeen asked. 'There are a lot of Afghan girls.'

'The Afghan girl who lived near us with her family when we were in Acton.'

'So many Afghan families live in Acton. Which do you mean?' Simeen was impatient.

'Perhaps I didn't tell you about it. A very respectable Afghan family lived just two roads away from us. One late afternoon I saw their daughter walking along the road wearing a black *chador*, covering herself from head to toe. She was in a hurry and did not notice me. When she was out of sight of her home, she took off her robe, folded it and put it in her handbag. Then she put her make up on. When she turned into the next road she got into her boyfriend's car, kissed him on the mouth and they drove off. I felt sorry for the family and for the young girl too. Surely you do not want this sort of double life to happen to our children. You have to trust them, direct them on the right path and leave them in God's hands. The best way is to be friends with them and listen to their problems. Too much pressure on children forces them to create a double life. At home they may follow our culture, but when they are out they will behave very differently.'

But Simeen did not hear the rest of Akbar's lecture. Her mind was occupied with the phone call from Jaweed's son.

After Akbar left for work, Simeen went to her bedroom which was her refuge. 'What does he want from Sittara?' She knew the answer already. 'What will happen if Jaweed remembers me?' So many other questions stopped Simeen from concentrating on anything else. She stood by her bedroom window biting her lip, looking outside but seeing nothing. That simple call had taken her back to Kabul and a horrible memory began to replay like a scene on a TV screen. She could not find the right button in her mind to switch it off. 'Why had she fought poverty, shame, losing her family and now this? When Simeen and Akbar had married she thought her nightmares were over, but now this simple telephone call had cast a shadow over her life again.'

Simeen, like Akbar and many others of her generation, was the child of war and the victim of horrific circumstances. Each had had their share of misery throughout their young lives. But they were also different in other ways, Akbar had a stronger personality. He was open and passionate about his rights and beliefs. Simeen's attitude was more conservative and she hated confrontation. Her childhood had been spent in Bamyan province, a closed, mountainous environment, while her teenage years, supposed to be the best of one's life, had been painful. She had lived in poverty, worked in Kabul, and then became a refugee in Pakistan and later in London. She had spent most of her adult life with unhealed wounds.

That day, the phone call took Simeen back to Afghanistan and her past returned to her like a sad song ringing in her ears. She remembered that small, dark room on the corner of the roof where she had to sleep alone every night. The horrible smell of that filled the room that night replayed itself again and again in her head.

Her childhood in Bamyan had been a happy, carefree time that she thought would never change. Although people were poor, they were rich in love. They dressed in rough, dust-covered clothes but had good hearts. She did not know where their simple food came from or who provided it. The whole family, mother, father, grandfather, grandmother, brother, sister, aunties and uncles lived together in a large mud house in a small village. Living with three generations under one roof was a sign of unity and pride and breaking up the extended family was considered a source of shame.

She thought their village must be located in one of the most beautiful parts of the world, a hot, dry and spicy land. The grass lay like green velvet, the sky was clear and bright blue and in the spring the trees were covered in blossom. Simeen loved the sound of water running in the nearby river and it made her sleepy when she closed her eyes.

They led a simple, rural life, far from the turmoil of the big city and without education. The technological age had never arrived there and they knew nothing of television or telephones, cars or buses. Men and women followed their set roles and the desire for equality was not an issue for them. The people demanded no more than to live in peace and contentment with their donkeys, hens and sheep. Their faces were honest, and straightforward. Their lifestyle had not changed for centuries.

Simeen missed her mother terribly. She also missed the farm, the animals and the clear skies. She remembered playing barefoot in the dusty, open space in front of the house all day long with other village children. It did not bother her that she had no shoes. Nobody   had shoes.

Sometimes, Simeen and her cousins were responsible for looking after the goats and the sheep in the fields or for carrying water in large pots on their heads from the river, where the villagers washed their clothes and the young boys swam. In their free time they played with small stones and straws, climbed trees or played hide and seek. They never saw a toy in their life, never knew that children in Kabul played with toys.

Simeen's grandfather was the head of the family, an honest man who never raised his voice and was always able to forgive the wrongs of the children or the adults. He was always out in the field and working hard. He loved his large family and was proud that they all lived under one roof. He felt blessed. He was illiterate but it never bothered him as most of his fellow villagers were uneducated. Simeen called him Baba and she was his favourite grandchild. When she was young she used to sit on his lap and he told her stories whenever he had the time. He would tickle her small hands and she would giggle.

Every night when Baba came home from working the land Simeen jumped on him and asked for stories. 'Baba it's story time,' she would say and Baba could never resist her. He took her small hand and kissed it and repeated the same story again and again. Her favourite one was the story of the demon and a fairy. When she was older, her grandfather told her different stories, especially about the bravery of Imam Ali, the great hero of the Shi'as, who fought with his enemies and was never defeated. Ali was another favourite story of hers as her grandfather had explained to her 'God gave him such power that no one could beat him.'

When Simeen reached the age of eleven, the rules changed. She had to stop playing outside with the boys. Instead she started helping her mother and grandmother. Simeen did not mind staying at home.

Her grandmother would also tell her stories. She had many tales about boys and warned Simeen to be suspicious of them all the time. 'We must obey the rules of our clan,' she said. 'If a girl's reputation is spoiled, not

66

only does she ruin her honour so that no one will marry her but she also damages the honour of her father, brothers, uncles and her clan,' her grandmother would say. 'You cannot mix fire and cotton together,' she concluded, meaning that boys and girls should not play together after a certain age.

Simeen knew that her parents treated the boys differently. They were spoilt, and had the freedom to go out, but she did not mind as it was part of their culture. But in Kabul, things were different. The girls had more freedom. They went to school, college, even university and socialised with boys.

Simeen remembered when her cousin was born. He was the first son in the family after four girls. The family gathered in front of their house to celebrate the arrival of the little boy by firing a gun in the air to inform the other villagers of the good news. But if it had been a baby girl there would have been no gunfire or party. Six days later, the grandfather slaughtered two lambs and invited the whole village to share the feast and celebrate the naming ceremony. He asked an elderly relative to read a page from the Quran and then they named the child Darwesh Ali. Most Hazara families, whatever name they gave to their male children, they added Ali or Hussain at the end. Ali was the Prophet Muhammad's cousin and Hussain was the prophet's grandchild and it was a sign of respect to Imam Ali and Prophet Mohammed.

After naming the child, the men gathered in a separate room to play music and sing songs. The instrument they used, a *danbora*, was very basic; it was made of wood and had two strings. When the sound of singing and music reached the women, they clapped, danced and sang in the warm *tandoor khana* room where they baked bread.

You went and I was watching you, oh my flower

I was saying prayers for you, oh my flower

I did not realise on that day of separation

That I'd sacrificed my soul for you, oh my flower.

It was such a happy occasion. The words of the songs sounded so sweet and gentle that Simeen always remembered them and sometimes she would sing the lyrics when she was alone in their flat in south London.

It was the job of the grandmother to distribute *noqul*, sugar-coated almonds, to the whole village. Then it was the villagers' duty to bring small presents to the happy family. The mother of the new-born baby rested for forty days. She was released from all cooking and cleaning. Everyone in the house had to serve her. When the forty days was over, she had a bath and was ready to start working again.

Visitors were not allowed to see the baby's face for a set time to protect him from the evil eye. For forty days, every morning, Simeen's grandmother burnt some seeds of *espand*, the plant rue, in every part of the house, believing that it kept the evil eye away from the new-born. Simeen loved the freshly aromatic smoke.

Simeen always remembered the poetry evenings her grandfather organised with his male friends when, as a young child, she was allowed to sit on his knee. Only a few people in the village could read and write but every month the male villagers got together and the few who could read poems from Shah Nama, the book of Ferdousy, a famous 12th century poet who wrote about historical stories and imaginary heroes. People were fascinated and encouraged by these heroes. Simeen loved those special nights resting in her grandfather's arms. Their names, King Jamsheed, Rustam and Sohrob, became engraved in her memory for ever.

During the summer nights, when the weather was very hot, the family took their beds outside into the wide field or onto their roof where they slept, side by side. Looking up at the sky, watching the bright moon and the stars, they talked, joked and laughed together.

Simeen's favourite occasions were wedding parties. She always remembered her cousin's wedding to a girl from a nearby village. As the head of the family, her grandfather thought it was time to marry his grandson

Qurban Ali when he turned seventeen-years-old. It was up to the grandfather to choose the bride for his grandchild. No one could argue with him. Marriage was a contract rather than just an act of love. When everything was agreed between the parents and grandparents, and the wedding was arranged, they informed the couple. Grandfathers decided the age of marriage. They went to the chosen family and asked for their daughter's hand in marriage for their grandsons.

It was customary that the young woman's family refuse the request of marriage a few times. It was believed that the more the process was prolonged, the more respect their daughter would gain. At last, when they reached an agreement, sugar-coated almonds were brought with the news of the engagement to every family in the village. Then the negotiation for the price of the bride started. If they did not have money, they gave animals instead. It depended on the wealth of the groom's family.

The negotiations would go on and on with discussion of how many sets of clothes and what type of jewellery was to be included. The groom's family also provided presents for the bride's family. In some cases, if the bride's family did not want to accept the marriage proposal, animosity started between the two families and in some rare cases this ended in murder. At other times, if the man was determined to marry a particular young woman, then in desperation the young man's family took the holy Quran to the young woman's family. The minute the holy book reached the home of the young woman's family, the arguments finished. They could not say or do anything against the power of the Quran.

Marriage between cousins was a common practice. Sometimes this was agreed when the boys and girls were small children and sometimes before the babies were even born. Simeen's grandfather promised Simeen to her cousin when she was three years old and the boy was five.

Simeen's father, Share Ali, a slight, wiry man, grew up in Bamyan. He had a large family; three brothers and six sisters. They all lived in the same brick house as their parents. They had a small piece of land as well as working for other landlords. There were no schools, but sometimes the villagers organised Quranic lessons for the boys.

Throughout the spring of 1977 there was no rain in Bamyan and in the summer the weather was burning hot, the rivers dried out, the grass became yellow, and the trees lost their leaves. The drought affected Bamyan severely. Thousands of people and animals died of starvation and cholera spread throughout the whole village. Share Ali lost his mother, father, two brothers and two sisters and his large family was reduced by half. Many children from the village lost their lives too. People were reduced to eating grass and grasshoppers. There was no help from the government that year. When Share Ali's eldest son died, he decided to move to Kabul to save the rest of his family. There would be more opportunity to find food there and a job, if he was lucky.

Simeen remembered the end of that sweltering, harsh summer when the remaining family gathered outside their house to see them off. They were tearful and heartbroken. It was an extraordinarily sad day for Share Ali as he had never travelled more than forty miles from his birthplace. Most villagers were born in Bamyan, lived and died there.

CHAPTER 7

Hazar means 'one thousand' and the Hazara are a large population who live in central Afghanistan. Historically there are two narratives about the Hazaras. Some historians believe that when Genghis Khan invaded Afghanistan in 200BCE, on his way back to his own country, he left behind a thousand (hazar) of his soldiers in Afghanistan. In more recent times, there is another narrative, told by Afghan and non-Afghan historians who believe that the Hazaras are the original people of Afghanistan who have lived there throughout its long history.

In Afghan history, two important events had a great impact on the Hazaras' fate. The first was in the nineteenth century when the Pashtun King Amir Abdur Rahman Khan extended his power over the whole country by force. The Hazaras were the first ethnic group to revolt against him to maintain their independence from the rule of the capital. As a result thousands of Hazaras were killed and their women and children were taken as slaves and concubines by the wealthy Pashtuns. Having lost most of their fertile land to the Pashtuns, the Hazaras migrated to Kabul and other cities in Afghanistan. In Kabul, the Hazara men took work as porters and labourers and the women worked as servants in the houses of wealthy Pashtuns and Kabulis. In 1919

King Amanullah abolished slavery but it did not change the Hazaras' status as the lower class.

The second event was in 1933 when King Nadir Shah was assassinated by Abdul Khaliq, a Hazara student. Abdul Khaliq's mother worked as a servant for a wealthy Charkhi family, who was one of the King's greatest political rivals. The King killed the head of the Charkhi family and put his family members in prison including his young children. Abdul Khaliq, who was just seventeen years old, boiled with rage as he looked to the head of the Charkhi family as a father figure. The day the King presented students with their certificates, Abdul Khaliq shot and killed him in front of pupils at the school. In consequence, a large group of Hazaras were killed in retaliation and Hazara children were forbidden to go to school. This attack on the Hazaras made a deep mark on the ethnic group, and they became even more of an underclass. Ironically, since the 1980s, the war and violent conflicts have played an important role in improving the status of the Hazaras, who fought alongside other Afghan ethnic groups to defeat the Soviet Union.

Simeen's family was Hazara, and her father Share Ali had never been to Kabul before. To move to Kabul was a painful decision that he made for the sake of his family. In Bamyan, Share Ali had never faced any prejudice as the villagers were from the same race. He knew that Hazaras were not treated fairly in Kabul but desperation left him little choice. When they reached Kabul, Share Ali rented just one room in the old part of the town called Chin da Wool, where Shi'a, Hazara and other minority ethnic groups lived in appalling conditions. He was willing to take any job available but could not find anything. His wife, Gulchaira, tried to find work as a domestic servant in the neighbouring area for several months, but had no luck. Out of desperation, she travelled a long distance to a wealthier area. She knocked on every door for days. Finally, a young woman opened the door for her.

'I am looking for a cleaning job. Do you need a cleaner?' Gulchaira said.

'What good timing.' The woman smiled at her. 'Yes I
do, but I cannot offer you a room for you or your family.
Do you have any family?'

'Yes I have a family, but I don't need a room. I could
come in the morning and go home in the evening if that's
OK with you?'

'Yes it suits me perfectly,' said the woman. She
paused and then added, 'I hope you're not one of those
Agha Khan followers.'

Gulchaira's face reddened with embarrassment. 'No
I am not.' She was aware of most Kabulis' racism towards
her religion and ethnicity, the Ismaili Shi'as. The Ismailis
are a branch of Shi'a Islam and their leader is Prince
Karim Agha Khan. He is the 49th Ismaili *imam* or leader
in line to Imam Ali, the cousin and son in-law of Prophet
Muhammad, and lives in Europe. Agha Khan is the
hereditary title of the *imam*. The Ismailis live in thirty-
three countries across the world. Those who lived in
Afghanistan were the poorest of the poor. They had been
neglected for decades by their own leaders and had been
oppressed not just by Sunni Muslims but also by the
other Shi'a minorities.

'If you are telling the truth you must insult the Agha
Khan,' the woman said.

'What do you want me to say?'

'Say Agha Khan is a *kaffir*.'

'OK he is a *kaffir*.' Gulchaira repeated.

'All right, you can work for me. I'll give you 200
Afghani per month plus breakfast and lunch and you can
take your dinner home if you wish with three naan bread
every night.'

'Thank you and God bless you, 'I can start today if
you like,' Gulchaira said.

Gulchaira was delighted to find a job. She was not
comfortable about denying her faith and insulting her
religious leader, Agha Khan, but she had no choice. At
the end of the day, she received her food as promised.
She had mixed feelings. She was happy that she could
feed her family, but felt guilty for being disloyal to her
faith. All the way home she was praying to God for her sin.

It was not an easy job, and every day Gulchaira woke

up at four o'clock in the morning. After praying and providing some simple food for her children and husband, she left home and walked for one and half hours to get to Shar-e-Now. She could not afford to get the bus. She could barely manage to feed her family, but this job was better than nothing. After five months of hard work, the lady of the house summoned Gulchaira.

'Do not wash the dishes today. Come to the garden. I want to talk to you,' she said.

Gulchaira dried her hands on her scarf and rushed to the garden wondering what the lady might want.

'Why did you lie to me?'

'What lie?' she said.

'You are a follower of the Agha Khan.'

Gulchaira felt the blood rush to her face and looked down at the ground without answering, her mouth empty of words.

After a long pause the woman said. 'I do not want you in my house. You must not touch anything, as your hands are not clean and pure. Go, pick up your things and leave.'

'Can I have my ten days' wages?' Gulchaira asked.

'No you can't. I have to hire someone else and will need to pay extra for them to clean the house and everything in it,' the woman said. 'My whole house needs to be purified.'

Gulchaira picked up her things and quietly left. She reached home in the middle of the day which was not her usual time. Her eyes were red, and her face was swollen with anger and humiliation. Share Ali immediately guessed what had happened. He did not ask any questions, just sat there, with his arms crossed and a sad face. After a long silence Gulchaira turned to her husband.

'Don't you want to know what happened?'

'I guess you lost your job. Why?' He asked.

'She found out that I am Ismaili,' Gulchaira said.

'How?'

'I don't know. I assume, someone told her.'

'You could have denied it.'

'I couldn't.'

After a few weeks, Gulchaira found another cleaning job for an Indian family. Hindus had migrated into Afghanistan at the time of the civil war between Hindus and Muslims in India, which resulted in the segregation of Muslims and Hindus and the creation of Pakistan in 1947. As a result a large group of Indian civilians reached Afghanistan as refugees. Although they were allowed to stay, the Afghan people never socialised with them as their religion and beliefs divided them. The Hindus existed peacefully and socialised among themselves. They started their own businesses importing Indian goods, especially material for clothing. They built shops on both sides of the road in Sar-e-Chawk, the old part of Kabul, and soon became wealthy.

Finding the job was good for Gulchaira but there was a problem. Not even the poorest in Afghanistan had any social contact with Hindus, even as servants. The Afghans considered them dirty because they were not Muslim. So Gulchaira's job had to remain a secret. No one knew she was employed by a Hindu, not even her children. When the Indian family gave Gulchaira some food, she politely took it home but never touched it and threw it in the bin because Indian food was not *halal* and it was a sin to eat their food. She worked for the family for a couple of months until Share Ali found a job as a porter for a short period in the Kabul Custom House. Gulchaira was then able to give up her job.

CHAPTER 8

Simeen thought about the time that she had worked as a maid in Kabul in Bibijan's house. She clearly remembered sitting on the step of a wooden ladder in the backyard with a piece of naan bread in her hand, looking up to the sky. It was early in the morning. One of her dreams since she had arrived in Kabul was to go to school, make friends, read books, and have fun like other city girls. But it was just a daydream, nothing else.

The mansion looked like a palace. It was built on a beautiful hill from where one could see the whole town. Every room was furnished with pure silk Afghan carpets. The huge dining room had a large cabinet, full of silver cutlery and fine china. A modern kitchen was attached to the dining room. This massive room was cleaned by different servants every morning. The huge garden with trees full of apples, pears and apricots gave a majestic aspect to the house. Amongst the lush green grass was a variety of flowers. There was a vegetable garden at the back of the building with a special gardener to look after it.

That morning the whole household was asleep. Simeen swallowed each bite of bread, too lazy to get a glass of water from the kitchen or make herself a cup of tea. She adjusted her black cashmere shawl to protect herself from the early morning cold. Her feet were bare, her long, plaited hair was uncombed but it did   not matter. No one could see her this early in the morning, her beautiful young face tired from working at last night's party. But she had had a good time, she thought. It was Jaweed Agha's 35th birthday party. Jaweed's wife had prepared for two days and asked everyone not to mention the surprise party to him. She asked the servants to clean and dust the whole house and tidy the garden. All their close friends and relatives were invited in advance. Simeen had never heard of a birthday party before and did not know what people did to celebrate.

The sun rose and warmed Simeen's body and her daydreams abruptly ended with the sound of Hanifa's voice. Hanifa had a kind nature and gentle manner towards everyone. She never got angry with her servants. The servants addressed her as Bibijan as   a mark of respect. 'Make yourself useful,' she said to Simeen. 'Go and prepare for breakfast.'

Simeen stood up, dropped her shawl on the garden chair, secured her scarf on her head and went to the shed to pick up the brush and the dust pan. She cleaned the long corridor and tried not to make too much noise. After she finished she went to the kitchen to put the breakfast on the table and boil the water for tea. She enjoyed her leisure time in the early morning, before the household woke up and the children went to college or work.

The day before, when everyone was   busy cleaning and tidying the house and garden, Simeen was working alongside the cook in the kitchen preparing a variety of dishes.

She asked, *'Khala Jaan*, dear auntie, what is   a birthday party? Normally women servants are called 'Begum' or 'Opha' but Simeen called her 'dear auntie' out of respect.

Begum made a gesture with her left hand, waving it in the air. 'To be honest I don't know. Rich people know how to invent things to enjoy themselves and spend their money,' she said, and then she added, 'It means that Jaweed Agha was born thirty-five years ago today.'

'Are they going to read the Quran to him then?'

'No, you silly girl! They are going to dance and   sing

and the men will lift up their glasses of *sharbat*, juice, and say *basalamaty*, cheers, good health. But I know it's not pure sharbat. They mix alcohol with it to mislead poor Bibijan,' she laughed. 'Why do you think they would read the Quran?' Begum asked.

'I don't know'. Simeen was confused. 'Because in Bamyan when someone is born a *mullah* reads the Quran to the child. I thought if he was thirty-five the *mullah* would read the Quran again to him.'

'I suppose people learn all sort of things from those *kaffirs*.'

'Who are *kaffirs*?' asked Simeen.

'Those infidel, foreigners, non-believers,' Begum said. The word *kaffir* was embedded deeply in people's minds as Godless. Many uneducated people believed that anyone who didn't follow the Muslim faith was Godless and a *kaffir*. To them *kaffir* was an insult. Begum did not know that there were many people in the world who follow different religions and still believe in God. In her eyes anyone who was not Muslim would go to hell.

Simeen wanted to know more, but she had asked too many questions already and Begum did not have time to answer them all. She had to cook the dinner. How different the Kabulis' lives seemed to Simeen, how different it was to Bamyan where she had never heard of a birthday party. Birthday celebrations were not a traditional custom amongst Afghan people, especially in rural areas, although under foreign influence some members of the upper class and the monarchy had begun to celebrate the event.

That night's party seemed perfect to Simeen. A table was set up in the corner of the marble corridor for the presents. A big cake, decorated with candles, sat on another table. Colourful balloons hung from the walls. When Jaweed arrived home everyone sang *salgera et mubarak*, happy birthday to you, happy birthday to you. Everyone clapped. 'Such a happy atmosphere,' Simeen thought. Jaweed was a tall, handsome, dark-skinned man.

After dinner it was time for Jaweed to cut the cake. Everyone had a piece and clapped and sang again. Jaweed opened all his presents and thanked everyone.

Then it was time for music and dance. The sound of *tabla* filled the big room. They danced in pairs, men and women together, and the beat of the loud music made a vibrant atmosphere. When the dancing finished there was a ripple of applause. Simeen thought it was wonderful, and wished her family could do the same for her. It was such fun.

Jaweed was the fourth son of the late Karim Khan, who had left behind a large family when he died at the age of seventy. In the 1920s, Karim, a young, light-skinned Arab from Yemen, arrived in Kabul on a dilapidated bus. He hoped to find some sort of labouring job in Afghanistan where the winds of destiny had brought him for the first time. He was tall and thin with a long curly moustache, wore a white turban and a long Arab gown that was now grey, worn out and far too big for his skinny body. He carried a small bag on his back and a note in his hand. He had never been to Afghanistan before, but he believed that someone would help him.

Karim was just twenty-five years old. He walked alongside the Kabul River. Throughout the summer, the big river had less water and children were swimming in dirty water, while adults washed their clothes. He walked along the river until he reached the nearest mosque. It was a Friday afternoon and people were hurrying there for the afternoon prayer. Karim walked slowly toward the mosque's minaret.

When he reached the gate he put his bag near the door, took off his shoes and entered the mosque repeating to himself, *Bismilahi rahmani rahim* . In the name of God. He prayed with the rest and when the prayers finished he gently moved towards the *imam* and gave him a slip of paper with an address in the hope that he could help him with the directions. He could not speak fluent Dari but managed a little mixed with Arabic.

'Where are you from?' the *imam* asked.

He pointed toward the paper and in broken Dari said, 'I am looking for this address if you could please help me.'

The *imam* took the paper but couldn't read it as he was not literate. He asked his disciple, who could read a little but the handwriting was strange and he also failed to read it. It was getting dark and the *imam* realised that Karim had no place to go so he let him stay in the mosque. They gave him some simple food and a blanket so that he could sleep on the bare floor.

Just a few years later from this inauspicious beginning, the ambitious Karim Khan had established himself in Kabul. He married a beautiful young Afghan woman from a rich family, and took a position in his father-in-law's business using his name and contacts. He moved up the ladder fast until he eventually took over his father-in-law's position.

Soon he had produced a large family. He learned the language, to dress differently, to socialise with the upper class and the rich, where to send his children to school. He never returned to Yemen. He started his own business and, within a few years, became one of the most powerful and richest men in Afghanistan. His social status improved much more than he had expected and so did his appearance. He began to wear a dark, three-piece suit, ironed perfectly, and a handkerchief matching his tie in his upper pocket. He managed to establish close ties with the wealthy and famous. He was generous with money and was able to buy himself a good reputation. No one knew about his past, so Karim Khan invented a family and background that had never existed.

Karim Khan moved to Karta e Chaar at the foot of the mountains, where the air was cooler and fresher, and began to build up his kingdom. He started buying properties in every part of Afghanistan as holiday houses for the summer and winter. Karim employed watchmen, drivers, gardeners, cooks, sweepers and many female helpers. He loved his dynasty-like lifestyle and his snobbery spread among his children like a contagious disease.

Karim's wife, Hanifa was much younger than him. Karim had a huge sexual appetite outside his marriage, not just with the maids but with other women too. His money protected his reputation. Hanifa was just sixteen when she married Karim. She had had a very basic education and never knew about her husband's activities outside the house. She produced children one   after another without any break. She had a kind heart but was weak-natured, a sad lady with many anxieties but no one to share them with.

When Karim died, he did not leave a clear legacy for his spouse and his many children, eight sons and two daughters. His children grew up and married and each one of them produced a large family of their own. Some moved out while others lived in the same mansion. They swam in the pool of their father's wealth for a short time. The girls married with lavish wedding ceremonies and the boys went crazy spending, pawning and selling their father's properties one by one and when there was little left they started fighting with each other, which created a lot of unresolved problems and hatred in the family. Within a few years Karim's wealth began to collapse like a house of cards. His children had few ambitions.

Jaweed, in particular, attracted many young women around the town. He had everything in life; charm, money and social status. But he was a dreamer who spent the majority of his time following girls after school. He had no interest in education at all, driving his mother crazy, and was distrusted by friends and family alike. By the age of seventeen he was following in his father's footsteps.

After breaking many hearts, Jaweed claimed that he had fallen in love with a girl younger than himself. For days he looked for the right moment to talk to his mother about his new love. One evening after dinner when everyone had left the dining table, he stayed put which was unusual. He put his hands on his mother's shoulders and hugged her.

'What do you want? You don't hug me for no reason,' she said, suspiciously.

'It's amazing you read my face so well, Mum,' he said, and hugged her again.

'Because I am your mother. Tell me, what do you want?'

'I've seen a beautiful girl I want to marry,' he said.

'Good, who is the unfortunate girl this time,' his mother replied, sarcastically.

'No, Mum. I am serious.'

'How do you know her?'

'She is my friend's sister. I glimpsed her when I went to their house,' he lied. In fact he had met the girl many times behind her brother's back.

'You are just seventeen and have to finish your education first, then get married.'

'I cannot wait because her family have already found another suitor for her. If we don't move quickly they are going to marry her to someone else,' he said.

'How do you know that?'

'My friend said so.'

'Don't lie to me. Afghan men never talk about their sisters even with their friends. It is shameful.' Hanifa read her son's face like an open book. Hanifa loved her children but found it hard to reason with them, especially Jaweed, who always got round his mother.

When Hanifa's brother came to visit her she told him, 'Jaweed wants to get married.'

'What is the rush? I thought you had learned your mistake when you married your other son too young. He is not responsible. Let him finish his schooling. He has to learn some responsibility first,' her brother advised.

'Jaweed is very much in love. If we don't move quickly they will marry the young woman to someone else.'

'Who said that?'

'Jaweed.'

'Do you believe him?'

'Yes I believe him,' Hanifa lied.

'Well he's your son. If he was mine I wouldn't let him.'

A few days later, Hanifa, her two brothers and eldest son, went to see the young woman's family. They put on their best clothes to impress them. They knocked at their door and the lady of the house opened it.

'*Salaam alaikom*,' Hanifa said with a smile.

'*Salaam*, said the lady, surprised to see unexpected guests.

'I am Jaweed's mother, your son's classmate. We are here,' she pointed at her brothers, 'to talk to you if you have time please.'

The lady welcomed them into the sitting room, knowing immediately their purpose for visiting but she did not offer them tea. After a brief conversation Hanifa said suddenly, 'We are here to ask you to accept my son Jaweed as your son-in-law. We want to be part of your family.'

'Isn't Jaweed a bit too young to get married?' the mother said. 'How is he going to support a family when he's still a student?'

'Oh you shouldn't worry about that. His father left him enough to support a family,' she said.

'Hosna is too young to get married.'

'Oh she is not the first to get married at fifteen. I was fifteen when I married. Haven't you heard what the wise man said, 'If you hit a girl with a feather and she does not fall down it is time for her to be married.' The sooner the better,' Jaweed's mother said and they all laughed.

'Yes I know that, but she has to finish her education,' insisted Hosna's mother.

'If that's the only reason, she can finish her education after the marriage.'

'How? By law, as you know, a married woman is not allowed to go to school and mix with other girls.'

'She can go to *Masisa e Niswan*, the Women's Institute, and finish her education. It's a proper college for married women,' Jaweed's mother persisted.

Hosna's mother was pleased that her daughter was being asked to marry a man from a rich family. But she pretended not to be convinced in order to gain more respect for her daughter.

'I will talk to my husband and let you know.'

'Thank you so much. When is a good time for us to come again? We would like to talk to your husband if it's possible?'

'Of course, but I would like to talk to him first,' she said.

After that first visit, Hanifa continued visiting Hosna's family and begged the parents for their agreement. It was not unusual for a sixteen-year-old to marry a seventeen-year-old man. But it was unusual to agree to a marriage with the groom's family at the first or second time.

The family finally agreed and Jaweed and Hosna became engaged. The engagement party was organised by Hosna's mother in a big hotel in the best part of Kabul, and hundreds of people were invited. When the time came for the wedding, there were negotiations between the parents over the wedding ceremony, the jewellery and the marriage venue which went smoothly.

'I want the wedding to be in the Continental Hotel,' said Hosna's father.

'Yes it was in my mind anyway,' agreed Hanifa.

Jaweed's mother and older brother organised a lavish wedding party and invited two hundred people to join them and share their happiness. Deep down Hanifa was worried about Jaweed's lack of responsibility but she thought if he married the girl he loved perhaps he would improve, finish his education and leave other girls alone. Hanifa bought a full set of diamonds and rubies for the bride as an essential part of the marriage agreement. The girl's parents argued over how many sets of clothes the groom's family would provide for the bride, and even about the gifts for the bride's close relatives, and how much money the groom's family would put aside if they divorced at any time in the future. Jaweed did not know where the money would come from and did not bother to ask his mother or his older brother who were responsible for the wedding. His mother and brother pawned another property in the hope that they would manage to get it back when Jaweed finished his education and got a good job.

The married couple continued to live in the same house as the rest of the extended family.

Within three years Jaweed's wife had produced two children. It was Hanifa's responsibility to feed and to provide for his wife and children. In Afghanistan, when the head of the family dies the sons are responsible for the rest of the family. But Karim Khan's family was not an average Afghan family. The children had grown up with a lifestyle like Bollywood film stars when Karim was alive and continued their lavish lifestyle after he died. They did not know where their father's money came from, nor who was responsible for paying taxes, collecting rent and dealing with the expenses.

Over the years Jaweed had built up two different personalities. He could be friendly and charming, but also angry, forceful and extremely selfish. In the first year of their marriage, Hosna interpreted his aggressiveness as the sign of a strong character. However she soon realised that his behaviour was the result of an inferiority complex. As her love gradually diminished, she began to pity him. But marriage was a big commitment. As her mother had said: 'Remember you go to your husband's home in your white wedding dress and you will come out in a white coffin.'

Jaweed dropped out of school and started drinking alcohol at any occasion, big or small. After two years of marriage he went back to his old habits and had secret affairs. Hosna had no choice other than to accept her fate.

Simeen had just turned thirteen when she found a cleaning job in the late Karim Khan's household through Begum, an elderly Hazara woman, who was their cook. Simeen was bright, beautiful, slim with soft white skin, a small nose and almond-shaped blue eyes, which was unusual for a Hazara. Working as a maid in a rich family was an opportunity for Simeen. She had to grab it with both hands.

The first day, as they walked toward Karim's mansion, Begum turned to Simeen. 'Bibijan is a very good woman, kind and considerate, and as long as you work hard you will eat enough food.'

'I promise I will,' Simeen said.

They got off the bus and walked through an empty park. It was early morning and freezing cold, but Simeen did not mind. She was looking forward to seeing the household and was prepared to work hard. To Simeen's eyes everything in this part of town was clean. The streets were smooth, the shops were big, the houses were painted white and the people wore different clothes from those living in the slum area where she lived with her parents. When they reached the house Begum introduced Simeen to Bibijan.

'Oh she is very young. Are you sure she can do the job?' Bibijan smiled at the girl.

'Wait and see how good she is.' Begum replied, wanting to convince her boss.

'OK she is your assistant. If you are happy I am happy,' Bibijan said and left them to get on with their work.

For every job there was an allocated servant. Simeen's job was mostly in the kitchen area, and cleaning the big corridor. She quickly settled into her new environment and learned how to wash the dishes how to clean the kitchen, how to make tea and tidy the dining room. Simeen loved working there and got on very well with Begum. She thought the lady of the house was a bit crazy and spent too much time changing her outfit in the morning and changing again when she went to bed. No one changed their clothes twice a day in Bamyan.

Working-class Hazara families used to send their male children to learn practical skills in carpentry, building work or other non-skilled jobs. But sending Hazara girls to school was not the parents' priority. Usually girls had to stay at home or work as child-servants alongside their parents. Education was not compulsory.

Since the assassination of King Nadir Shah in 1933, the Hazara minority were not allowed to have jobs in the army or hold any high positions that would give them security or status in society. When King Zahir Shah came to the throne, the Hazaras slowly and cautiously started to go to school in Kabul but in Bamyan nothing improved. As a result, most Hazara students went into the field of medicine. In the 1950s and the 1960s Afghanistan had a large group of well-trained Hazara doctors.

The sense of superiority and arrogance of other ethnicities, especially those who lived in Kabul, over the Hazaras was undeniable. No Kabulis sat at the same table, socialised with or married a Hazara. The servants cleaned toilets and bathrooms but were not allowed to use them. The men worked as *jwali*, porters, and carried heavy household goods on their backs for miles for very little income. Hazara women worked in Kabul households, cooking, cleaning and washing.

Simeen dreamt of being like other children and of being able to go to school, make friends with Kabuli girls, read books, and wear a school uniform with a black blouse, black skirt, black socks and a white scarf. But her dream was far from reality. She had no choice other than to work. This was her first paid job, and she had to take it seriously. Simeen liked the grand house and the people around her. She did not mind working hard. The pay was good and there were fewer mouths for her father's large family to feed.

Simeen secured her scarf on her head, put on her slippers and rushed to the kitchen. She started tidying the kitchen for breakfast. After everything was ready she sat on a chair in the adjoining dining room and put both hands on the table. She knew she was not supposed to do this but she was young and wanted to treat herself. There was no one in the dining room anyway. Suddenly Bibijan's teenage grandchild entered the room and started laughing. 'Grandma, grandma come quick and see who is sitting on your chair,' she called out. Simeen quickly stood up knowing she had crossed a boundary, but Bibijan ignored her grandchild. Simeen was embarrassed and rushed back to the kitchen. She washed a plate and waited for a lecture or a telling off from Bibijan, but she said nothing. After this Simeen would never sit on another chair as long as she worked in that house. Similarly, she was never tempted to use the household's toilets. The servant's toilet was in a corner of the backyard.

'Tomorrow is my day off. I would like to finish all my work today because my mother is not well. I would like to stay one or two days. Is that OK with you?' Simeen asked Bibijan politely.

'What is wrong with your mother?'

'I don't know but she is in bed all the time.' said Simeen.

'Has she been to a doctor?' asked Bibijan.

'I don't think so,' said Simeen.

OK you can stay with your mother if you wish' said Bibijan and left the kitchen.

When breakfast was finished and every one had left the room, Simeen started cleaning the table and taking the plates to the kitchen to wash them. She jumped at the sound of the kitchen door slamming, a plate dropped from her hand onto the floor and shattered into pieces. It was from the best set of china, which Bibijan used when they had guests. Jaweed Agha came over and started to help Simeen pick up the pieces. Simeen's face was flushed with embarrassment. Her upper lip trembled and her eyes welled up with tears.

'I am so sorry, *Agha*, sir,' she said.

'Do not worry,' Jaweed said as he stood up. Bibijan who had heard the sound of a broken plate rushed into the kitchen.

'Sorry mother, I broke the plate,' Jaweed said immediately. He was holding a piece of broken crockery in his hand. Simeen's face was now a crimson red. Bibijan looked suspiciously at her son and then at the plate and realised that it was from her best set of china.

'The kitchen is not a man's place. What are you doing here anyway?' Bibijan demanded.

Jaweed mumbled something, looked at the floor and left the kitchen without responding. Simeen was grateful, but felt uneasy. Although Bibijan was kind, Simeen did not know her well. She had only started working there a few months ago. 'How would Bibijan have reacted if she knew it was her fault?' Simeen wondered.

Simeen washed the rest of the plates, tidied the table and went to her room, which was on the third floor far away from the rest of the family. The cook did not live in but occasionally stayed overnight when she was needed and shared the room with Simeen. She changed her clothes, and packed her bag with some nuts and sugar coated almonds which she had kept for her siblings and left the house.

Simeen walked for twenty minutes to the nearest bus stop. When the bus arrived, she couldn't get on as the women's section, which consisted of four seats and a small area for standing, was occupied. The   men's section, was empty, but women were not allowed to cross the boundary. So she decided to walk. At least she would save some money. Public transport in Kabul was not regular and the buses did not keep to a proper timetable. Sometimes, especially in the mornings, there was lots of pushing and arguments which often ended up in physical fights.

As she walked, Simeen thought how different Karta e Chaar was from where her parents lived, a forty-five-minute drive away in the old part of Kabul. Karta e Chaar had wide, clean streets, a park, cinema and shopping centre. This was in stark contrast to the ramshackle irregularity of the old part of the city where mud-brick buildings with windows made of plastic nestled into one another at the foot of the mountain. In winter, when the snow melted, it turned the whole area into a mud river. Animals, humans, cars, and beggars used the same long road, and the smell of animals' waste was strong, especially on summer days. It was one of the most crowded and poverty stricken areas in Kabul but ironically also one of the most cheerful and lively. There were all sorts of small businesses from carpenters, builders and bakeries to goldsmiths, fish markets, butchers and even second-hand shops. Their world was simple, friendly and carefree.

Simeen thought about the broken plate, and the way Jaweed Agha covered up for her. 'Why he was so nice to me?' she wondered. During the past few months that she had worked in their house he had barely noticed her.

Simeen reached home. Her parents lived in Chin-da-Wool, south of the Kabul river, part of old Kabul. There was no running water. Children walked around half naked or wore rags. They had no shoes but that did not bother them. It was normal not to own shoes in that part of the town. Some earned their food by begging or by burning seeds of *espand* in a small can to get rid of the evil eye and to purify the passers-by. In return they received a little change.

Educational opportunities for children did not exist in that part of the city. It was the very heart of the working-class community. On either side of the narrow street there were arcades of small shops and stalls where one could find whatever one needed. From dawn to dusk there were crowds of shoppers, porters, beggars, donkeys and mules.

At the end of the narrow street there was a dilapidated mosque. Sometimes mostly on Fridays, a *Sadu*, a bearded man in a long robe, stood in the middle of the tiny road and sang songs about the leaders of Islam or invented religious stories. At the end of his sermon, people donated money. At the back of the long street there were houses, built with mud and bricks centuries ago without any architectural plan. They looked like match boxes stuck together divided by tiny muddy paths full of sewage and germ infected flies buzzing around.

Simeen hated living there. Sometimes she wished they had stayed in their own village in Bamyan where the lifestyle was completely different. She missed the open land of her father's farm, the fresh air, and the silvery water cascading down from the nearby mountain. She missed socialising with her own people. In Shar-e-Now and Karta e Chaar nearly every family had their own car. Simeen loved those areas and hated going back to Chin-da-Wool to see her parents. Even in Bibijan's house she had her own room. It was small, but clean and tidy, while her whole family lived in one room.

Simeen's parents lived in one dark, claustrophobic room with bare mud walls. In the summer time, when the weather became very hot, the air was filled with the smell of rats, and the room became as hot as an oven. Scorpions crawled freely around as though their territory had been invaded by the family. The room had a tiny window covered with clear, cheap plastic. The family ate and slept in their one room. Although it was cleaned every day they could never eliminate the smell of tobacco, sawdust and rats. A black and white striped kilim carpet covered the floor and two dirty mattresses and a few pillows were piled in the corner of the room. They were the only possessions they had.

One part of the room was used as the kitchen area when it rained but on sunny days they used the corner of the dusty yard and cooked on an open coal oven. The families living there shared one toilet in the back yard. It consisted of three mud brick walls and one big hole in the middle of the dusty ground for the waste. A dirty curtain was hung on the door to give some privacy. Every other week, a man came with a donkey to take the waste away. They did not have a bathroom but occasionally went to the public baths, which cost money.

In Bamyan, when Simeen reached the age of ten, her parents had started to teach her how to pray which involved washing herself beforehand. Her grandfather accompanied her every morning and sometimes there was warm water available. But in Chin-da-Wool Simeen was reluctant to wash, especially in the cold winter. Early in the morning she had to wake up and find her way to the yard with a jug of freezing water, wash her feet, arms and face, then lay down the prayer mat facing *Kaaba*. In Bibijan's house she had plenty of warm water and praying was a pleasure.

Share Ali and Gulchaira were both heavy smokers. Whatever Share Ali earned, the first priority was food for the family and then tobacco. They could not afford to indulge themselves with luxury cigarettes as they were expensive, so they bought leaf tobacco. They used a *chilam*, water pipe, and usually smoked before dinner. This was the only pleasure they had. The room filled with smoke to the extent that they could hardly see each other's faces. Then it was time for dinner, which consisted of tea with lots of sugar and naan bread. Occasionally Share Ali brought home some potatoes for his wife to cook. Everyone washed their hands, sat around a cloth spread on the floor and ate. When it was their bedtime they pulled their thin mattresses out from the corner into the middle of the room, made their beds and slept side by side with their children. Gulchaira had developed an illness which started with flu but went on and on for a couple of months.

'I brought you some medicine from the Indian shop,' Share Ali said. 'It is good for your chest.'

Gulchaira knew they could not afford to see a doctor. He boiled the herbs and asked his wife to drink the mixture. But it didn't help. When Gulchaira's health worsened Share Ali became really worried. He often went to the nearby mosque to pray. One evening, after prayer, he approached the bearded *mullah*.

'*Mullah Saheb* I need your help.'

The *mullah* stroked his bushy beard and asked 'How can I help you?'

'My wife is very sick. Would you be kind enough to come to my home and pray for her or perhaps give her some *taweez*?'

'Yes of course. Give me a few minutes and I will be with you.' The *mullah* adjusted his white turban, took his long sleeved *chapan* from a hook on the wall, threw it over his shoulders, picked up his small prayer book, his fountain pen, a small bottle of black ink and a piece of paper and accompanied Share Ali.

The *mullah* sat near Gulchaira's bed and read a few lines from his notebook.

'I'll give you a *taweez*. Hopefully you will be OK in a few days,' he said, sure of himself. Then he tore out a piece of paper from his notebook and drew grids. 'What is your mother's name?' he asked the sick woman.

'Sanowber,' Gulchaira answered in a weak voice.

He asked a few more questions and wrote strange Arabic words in the grids. Then he folded the piece of paper many times until it looked like a tiny matchbox.

'Cover this *taweez* with clean material and put it under your pillow,' he said.

Then he prayed again and left. Share Ali offered him a small amount of money, which the *mullah* happily took. Share Ali waited for an improvement. But weeks passed and his wife lost her appetite and became weaker and weaker, lying in bed, almost invisible under the heavy quilt. Share Ali again asked the *mullah* for help. He suggested taking her to the shrine of Abulfazil, the grandchild of Ali, the Prophet Muhammed's cousin, to pray for her.

In desperation Share Ali took his wife to the shrine of this holy man. It was a small room, decorated with colourful materials and shiny scarves. A blind man was sitting near the shrine reciting the Quran loudly, moving his head from side to side. Share Ali and Gulchaira took off their shoes and entered the room. They lit a candle and started praying. When they had finished Share Ali gave some small change to the blind man and left.

When Simeen got home that Friday her mother was in bed, hardly able to move, and her father was out, sitting somewhere under the hot sun waiting for work. Simeen put her bag down and started tidying the room. She looked around for some food to give to her mother but could not find any, so she offered her the nuts which she had brought from Bibijan's house. Her brothers were out, collecting papers and sticks for cooking and her sister was playing outside, too young to realise that their mother was seriously ill. When their father came home that evening he had managed to buy just three loaves of flat bread, sugar and tea. Simeen boiled the water and made black tea with enough sugar for her brothers and sister to have with their bread. Her father refused to have tea, pretending he had had some earlier. Their mother was too sick to have tea. After two nights Simeen had to return to her job.

A few weeks later, on a hot summer's day, Gulchaira died without having seen a doctor throughout her illness. Simeen was informed of her mother's death by a distant relative working in the kitchen. She rushed home to find her mother laid out on the floor, lifeless and silent, a piece of white cotton material tied around her chin and head to keep her mouth shut. Gulchaira was in peace but had left a large family behind for her husband to cope with. Share Ali mourned soundlessly and the children joined him.

Gulchaira's funeral was very simple. A female neighbour washed her body and covered her with white cotton material, and four men put the body on an old wooden *charpiee*. Share Ali and his two boys followed them to the cemetery at Karta-e-Sakhi on the slopes of the famous mountain with the shrine of Imam Ali. A bearded man read a few Arabic words and finished with '*Innaa Lillaahi wa innaa illaahi raaji'uun*', 'We came from Allah and we return to Allah.' He gave a short talk about heaven and hell and how people who say their prayers go to paradise and those who do not, go to hell. As simple as that. He spoke with certainty as if he was talking from his own experience. The family said their goodbyes to Gulchaira and left. The four men who had carried the body came back to Share Ali's house, read a chapter from the Quran, had a cup of tea and left the family to deal with their grief.

Simeen did not know where her mother was buried as women and girls were not supposed to go with men to the graveyard. But she heard that it was on the slopes of the famous mountain, where Shi'a people celebrate New Year's Day and bury their loved ones near the shrine.

Bibijan heard the sad news through Begum. She sent a donation of cash and a big bag of rice, a bottle of oil, a bag of sugar and some black and green tea to Simeen's family. She also promised to raise Simeen's monthly salary which was good news for them. Simeen had hoped Bibijan would come and comfort her but there was too big a gap in the lifestyle between the rich and poor in Kabul. In Bamyan, when someone died, the whole village, no matter how rich or poor, went to pay their respects to the mourners. Close family and friends brought food for three days and stayed with them.

A few days later two of Simeen's brothers started working in a butcher's shop and a bakery. The money helped but life had become unbearable for Share Ali without his wife. He could not manage to look after his daughter Ferosa who was six years old. He needed Simeen at home.

'At the end of the month when you get your pay tell Bibijan that you can't come anymore.' He said to Simeen.

Simeen's jaw dropped. 'Why? I love my job.'

'Your mother is not with us and now your two brothers are working and I am out all the time. Your sister needs you and I can't manage without you. I need you at home to look after Ferosa.'

The next day when Simeen returned to Karta e Chaar she told Bibijan that she would not be able to continue.

'Why?' said Bibijan 'I will raise your wages if you stay.'

'Thank you. I am happy to work for you, but my

father said he needs me at home.'

Simeen's job was not that important and finding a replacement would not be difficult, but Bibijan liked her and wanted to keep her.

'When are you going to leave?' Bibijan said.

'My father said at the end of the month.'

'OK, so you have another fifteen days to go.'

At dinner Bibijan asked the cook if she could find a girl or a boy to help in the kitchen.

'We have Simeen already and don't need another one, do we?' said Begum.

'I thought you knew. Simeen is leaving soon,' Bibijan said.

'Oh no, she didn't tell me,' said Begum.

The announcement did not bother anyone around the table, apart from Begum who felt sorry for the girl. Apart from Bibijan no one asked Simeen why she was leaving. Simeen was not very important and the others in the house hardly noticed her existence.

After dinner, everyone went to the sitting room to have tea. Preparing the tea was Simeen's job. When they finished, she cleared the table, washed the dishes, tidied up the kitchen, turned off the light and closed the door behind her. She had enough time to sit in the garden, which she loved. It was the only free time she had. The house was quiet. It was a summer's evening, the stars were out and the moon shone so brightly that she could see everything around her. 'I was so comfortable here,' she thought. It was such a shame that she was leaving.

After a while she moved inside and entered the bathroom to wash herself for evening prayer. Since her mother had died she found praying comforting. It was a practice that her mother had taught her from an early age and it had become a big part of Simeen's life. She wished she could read the Quran to give her comfort. She remembered the time when her father asked a bearded *mullah* to teach his sons the holy book. Once or twice his wife mentioned teaching the girls too but Share Ali refused saying that the girls just needed to know how to pray. She left the bathroom, went to her small bedroom on the third floor, unfolded the prayer mat, positioned it toward the *Kaaba*, and started to pray.

She heard a noise on the stairs but did not move as she was not supposed to be distracted from praying. 'If during praying you move your head from the *Kaaba*, you break your prayer and you have to start all over again,' her mother used to say. So she ignored it and continued her praying.

When she had finished she folded the mat, turned off the light and went to bed. Simeen had a nightmare. She dreamt that she was standing next to a mud wall in Bamyan, her homeland. Suddenly there was an earthquake, the land moved under her feet the wall collapsed and she got stuck under it. She gasped and woke up. She opened her eyes, but could not see anything at first. There was a strong smell and a something on top of her. No, it was not a bad dream. It was a dreadful reality. Jaweed Agha inhaled a lungful of air, as he towered over her with his hand on her mouth. Simeen had already lost her strength and her voice.

Jaweed left Simeen's tiny room and disappeared down the stairs like a dirty dog satisfied with his meaty bone. Simeen did not move for a long time. She thought that if she did not move everything would be normal again but the reality was that she was wet with sweat and blood. She leaned against the wall. Her half-naked body was covered with scratches. She shivered not because of cold but with shame and horror. She wished that the ground would open its mouth and swallow her in one go. She imagined her dirty body lying a long way from her. Her tongue was stuck to her mouth, her head was dizzy and her mind was on fire. She started hitting her head against the concrete wall, and then buried her face in her pillow which smelled of alcohol. She badly needed her mother. She needed someone to reassure her that things would be all right. She needed someone she could trust and lean upon. But she knew that nothing would ever be all right again, as long as she lived.

She cried all night and did not rest until four in the morning, when she fell into a deep sleep for a short time. She dreamt that she was stuck in a barn, the door was locked and she could not get out. She shouted for help but no voice came out. She tried to walk but her legs were buried in deep mud. A wooden beam resembled an eagle that was about to swoop in and attack her at any second. The smell was like rotten meat or dead bodies in a battlefield. Cobwebs had formed on every corner of the barn. She felt like a fly trapped inside a grey net curtain, moving her arms and legs, trying in vain to escape but without success. And then the dark walls of the barn moved closer and closer to sandwich her. She screamed loudly and woke up. Sweat was running down her forehead, neck and back. She found herself in an unfamiliar place. Where was she? Her mouth was dry like an arid desert. She tried to lick her lips to moisten them but felt a fresh taste of copper. And then she remembered everything and the reality hit her hard. Her body was full of pain and her soul felt like a crushed leaf in the autumn. She did not want to go downstairs, did not want to face the reality of her tragedy. How could she face her father after this? She put her head on her pillow again and drifted off to sleep.

At 8 o'clock in the morning Bibijan entered the dining room but tea was not ready. She was surprised and angry. She raised her voice calling Simeen's name, thinking that she might be around. There was no trace of her. She came out of the dining room, down the long marble corridor and slowly climbed the stairs to Simeen's room. The girl was sitting on her mattress hugging her knees, her eyes were red and swollen. Bibijan opened the door gently and entered the room. Simeen looked up, her face awash with tears.

'What happened? Are you not well?' Bibijan asked. Simeen closed her eyes and felt a sob rising in her chest. Her helplessness frustrated her but she couldn't express her anger to Bibijan.

Simeen bent her head and wept, her throat tightened and she could not manage to answer. She pulled the blanket over her face. Bibijan asked again but, deep down, she guessed what had happened. She stood there motionless hating herself for not being more careful. 'Why do I never learn that I shouldn't have young female servants?' she kept repeating to herself. She could have protected Simeen knowing her sons. But it was too late. Bibijan moved closer to Simeen, put her hand on Simeen's shoulder and asked, 'Which one?'

'Jaweed Agha,' Simeen answered immediately.

Bibijan slowly got up and sat on the window sill, her hands on her face, boiling with rage and sorrow murmuring something under her tongue which Simeen could not understand. 'You dirty man, you left your mark on your sons.' She remembered her own miserable life with her husband who had been obsessed with sensual pleasure outside marriage. She remembered every time she caught her husband, he had bought her a diamond necklace or a gold bracelet as compensation for hurting her, which she had never worn because she did not want to remind herself of what had happened. She knew her husband had at least one illegitimate child from a female servant.

Bibijan sat in that deadly silent room for a long time inhaling the sorrowful atmosphere that polluted the air and that her son had created. She did not know what to do. She did not have the guts to confront her son just as she had never stood up to her adulterous husband. She did not want her daughter-in-law to know. She did not want another scandal in the family. What if her relatives found out? A woman from a good family keeps secrets and lives her life pretending, she thought. It did not cross her mind to worry about what would happen to motherless Simeen, nor how she would cope for the rest of her life, knowing no one could marry her.

Bibijan stood up and gently touched Simeen's shoulder again but could not find the right words to express her feelings. She went downstairs and fetched a small electric stove that she brought back to the room and turned on. When the surface was hot she sprinkled a few seeds of *espand* over the stove. The noise of the seeds burning and the smoke filled the room like a huge dark cloud ready to rain. Simeen did not know or care what she was trying to do. Bibijan hoped the *espand* would clear the sinful atmosphere where her son had committed the crime. The *espand* would work its magic, the evil eye would be blinded and no one would know about Jaweed's crime.

Although Bibijan was upset about Simeen, she did not know what action she could take to heal her wounds apart from burning the *espand*. She was cursing herself for not having learned from the past. Jaweed had always abused the servants. But Simeen was too young. In the end Bibijan decided to remain quiet for the sake of her family. She had not been brave enough to fight with her husband and now she was not brave enough to confront her son. All she could do was to allow Simeen to stay in that small room. She brought some tea to comfort her. Simeen did not touch it.

Simeen remained in that claustrophobic room for the day. The following morning, Bibijan gave her a full month's salary and discharged her like a pair of old shoes as if nothing had happened. Throughout her own married life she had been a victim herself, and made sacrifices for the sake of her family honour. She did not know what else to do.

CHAPTER 9

Simeen's life changed for ever. From then on her brain was on fire, her thoughts moving round and round in circles, like a non-stop train never reaching its destination. She was broken and powerless. She knew that once you are molested or raped in Afghanistan you are disgraced. You are no longer a normal member of your family and society. She gathered some of her belongings in a plastic bag and, hardly able to walk, left the house in the early afternoon. Her feet were unsteady, her eyes red and her face swollen. Her thin legs were barely able to carry her body.

It was raining. She felt that the sky was crying for her tragedy. She did not know what to do. Surely she could not tell her father or anyone else. She was dirty, untouchable, unworthy, reduced to nothing. Simeen reached home later that day, and handed her salary to her dad. Share Ali did not even look at his daughter's face. He did not notice any difference in her. He took the money and counted it. It was more than usual.

'It is not the end of the month. She gave you more, kind lady. I wish I did not need you at home. You could have worked longer there,' he said.

'Bibijan doesn't need me anymore,' she said. 'I am not going back.'

'Oh! It's good of her to give you the full amount for

this month,' he said, counting the money again and putting it in his pocket, very satisfied with himself.

With a broken heart, Simeen walked out of the room to the dusty yard and the toilet. It was the only place that she could have some privacy to cry. After a while she came out, and decided to act as a mother to her brothers and sister as if nothing had happened. Her pride was shattered, her body was dirty and her carefree dreams had turned to nightmares. Over the next few weeks her father did not notice that Simeen was unusually quiet and just did what was required of her.

One morning Simeen got up early to make tea for her family. As usual she laid papers and sticks over the coal in the fire and then lit it and put the kettle on to boil. The smoke from the paper hit her face and she suddenly felt dizzy and sick. She rushed to the toilet.

The smell in the toilet was so overpowering that she fainted. Share Ali got up to go to work and when he saw that the tea was not ready, he rushed into the yard.

'Simeen, Simeen where are you?'

Simeen dragged herself slowly from the toilet. Her face had lost its colour and she was shaking. Share Ali noticed something was wrong. He rushed toward her, his feet bare and his head turbanless. He held Simeen's hand and helped her back inside the room.

'What is the matter?' he asked. 'You don't have a fever, do you?' He put his hand on her forehead. 'I'll go and make the tea.'

Simeen dragged herself toward her bed. Share Ali went to the yard and made her some tea. Then Share Ali left for work with his two sons. Slowly Simeen got up and did the usual house work, washing the cups and tidying the room. During the day she felt better. But the morning vomiting continued for a couple of weeks. Finally, to Simeen's relief, the sickness stopped. Simeen did not know what was happening and why she got better. Even if her father had noticed that his daughter was not well he could not afford to take her to a doctor.

Deep down Simeen's mental state was on fire. She was restless, sleepless and scared. During the day she kept herself busy with cleaning the only room they had many times over, or washing their clothes or just playing with little Ferosa, whose company she thought was a blessing. During the night a wall of anger pushed her to the point where she simply wanted to die. Over the months, Simeen lost a lot of weight but her stomach got bigger and bigger and she felt something moving inside her. It was frightening. There was no one around to tell her what to do. She went to bed every night praying that the next morning she would be dead. She desperately missed her mother. Sometimes she went to bed with her mother's clothes and buried her face in them for comfort. At last, Share Ali noticed that Simeen was extremely unhappy, didn't have any appetite for food and had lost weight although her tummy had become bigger. He thought Simeen had developed some sort of illness related to malnutrition. He was unable to grasp what had happened to his daughter.

'My daughter is very sick,' he said to his only close friend. 'I am worried about her.'

'What's wrong?'

'I don't know but she does not eat.'

'It is understandable. She misses her mother,' his friend said.

'No it is not just that. I think she has got a serious stomach problem.'

'Why don't you take her to the doctor?'

'You know I don't have the money,' Share Ali said.

Finally they both went to the doctor and then Share Ali realised what had happened. The shock hit him badly. When they returned home, he was burning with rage. The minute they entered their room, he stood above her, his eyes on fire, lifted his right leg and kicked her with all his might. The second blow split her lip and loosened her front teeth. She tasted the salt of blood and, after the third blow, warm blood spurted from her nostrils. Then Simeen lost consciousness. Her sister Ferosa and her brothers Rostam and Moraad stood there shaking from head to toe. They did not know what had happened to their father, who had always been gentle with his children.

Share Ali left home like a complete madman, running

down the street without knowing where to go or how to face this shameful tragedy, nor how to face his own people. Why had he come to Kabul? Why had he let his daughter work far away from home? He did not know who had done it, but it had definitely happened in Bibijan's house. He was running aimlessly round and round like a blindfolded horse not knowing what to do. Someone had destroyed his honour.

Who did it? When? Where? Why was he so stupid to let her work far away.

Simeen regained consciousness. She had a three to four second period of grace before she remembered who she was and where she was. Slowly she opened her eyes but could not focus properly. She tried to move, but felt a burning pain in her back and left arm, and a pounding headache followed by a wave of nausea. Gradually she remembered what had happened and the tragedy of her situation hit her again. She looked around and closed her eyes again.

Share Ali came back to the room exhausted and frustrated. He did not look at Simeen. She was a piece of rotten meat. He told the boys to get ready for work. The boys left with their father. Simeen was left alone with Ferosa. Her six-year-old sister looked at her motionless state, then she moved toward Simeen and touched her arm. Simeen hugged her and cried loudly for a long time. Tears mingled with the dry blood running down her injured face. The room was cold and dark. She held her sister's hand and moved towards the door. She wanted to wash her swollen face. She grasped the door handle. It was locked. They were locked in. It was the first time that their father had ever shut them in the room. She had no idea what her father would do to her.

Simeen moaned, 'Oh God, please help me.' She went and lay on her mattress.

Share Ali came home late with his sons. That evening the atmosphere in the room was tense. Share Ali was normally good-natured and kind to his children. He wrestled with the boys and little Ferosa. But that evening the children knew that their father was upset and angry.

Simeen stayed in her bed, unable to move. Her left shoulder was dislocated, her father didn't even look at her. To him she was like a dirty animal. Everyone was scared and quiet in the tiny room. Two nights passed and Simeen was in agony but she did not even groan for the fear of being beaten up again.

Simeen woke up in the middle of the night. She had excruciating pain in her shoulder but before she could change her position, she heard a whispered conversation between her father and another man. The room was dark. She thought she was dreaming. But it was real and someone was in the room talking in a low voice to her father. She did not move and pretended to be fast asleep. She tried to recognize the voice of the other man, but failed. She hunched up in bed and tried to keep her body away from her sister. Since their mother had died her sister, Ferosa, stuck to her day and night.

'I know I have no other choice, but how and where?' Simeen heard. 'I am not going to do it in this room in front of my other children,' Share Ali said.

'This is the only safe place,' said the other man.

'No I am not doing it here,' he repeated.

'The best time is when the children are asleep. They won't notice anything,' said the man.

Simeen's father did not reply. 'Just provide a bag and shovel. We have to dig the ground at least one day before. It must be in the dark,' whispered the other man.

'Where?'

'Let me think.'

'What should I say to the children, if they ask where she is?'

'You can tell them you sent her back to Bamyan to your village,' the stranger's voice said.

Simeen did not hear any more but her body had turned to stone, and sweat had accumulated around her neck and down her body. She wanted to know what exactly the plan was but couldn't hear anything else, just the repeated words of her father, 'I have no choice. I have no choice. I have no choice.' The man left the room and Share Ali sat on his bed. The pain of humiliation and disappointment was unbearable. He started weeping aloud at his powerlessness. How was he going to face the world and his people?

If Share Ali had had the power to fight the dirty animal who had violated his daughter he would have done, but he knew he couldn't. He knew that rich men were above the law. He knew his position in Afghan society. He had no money, no power, he was just a porter. Who was going to listen to him even if he wanted to complain? Who should he complain to? How could he prove what had happened?

Simeen couldn't sleep all night. She listened to the sound of her own breath, harsh on the air. She felt empty, devoid of hopes that had been filling her mind. The room was dimmer by the minute. At five o'clock in the morning, everyone in the room was fast asleep and she could hear her father's snoring. Simeen quietly got up, trying not to wake her sister. She looked at her innocent face for a few minutes so she could remember her for the rest of her life, bent down and kissed her small carefree forehead.

Then she dragged herself out of bed and looked at the wall where the only family photo was hanging on a single nail. It was black and white, taken long ago by some distant relatives when they came to Kabul and Simeen loved it. In the photo her father wore his big white turban, and he sat on a chair, both hands on his knees looking formal and stiff. Next to him were her two brothers and her mother, with the two girls standing behind them. Her mother had covered half of her face with her scarf, so you could only see her shy eyes. Simeen took the photo, and tiptoed barefoot out of the room downstairs into the dusty yard. She unlocked the wooden gate, went outside and closed the gate behind her.

CHAPTER 10

In 1978 the political situation in Afghanistan was unstable. The Soviet-backed Communist regime came to power in a bloody coup that shook the entire country. It affected every single person and changed everything. In the early 1960s, the Communist Party had been secretly created in Kabul under the name People's Democratic Party of Afghanistan (PDPA). At that time, ordinary people were uninterested in their gatherings. Later, the party had some influence over a small number of university students in Kabul, and gradually attracted others in other provinces. In 1965, the PDPA won a few seats in the parliamentary election. In 1969 it split into two branches, called *Khalq*, 'people' and *Parcham* 'flag'. Noor Muhammad Taraki was the leader of *Khalq*, and the majority of their members were Pushto speakers. Babrak Karmal was the leader of *Parcham* whose supporters were mainly Dari speakers. Over the next few years the two branches of the party became increasingly hostile towards each other. But in 1977, under the influence of the Soviet Union, they reunited as a coalition government, in preparation for the 1978 coup.

Afghanistan's real tragedy started with the murder of Mir Akbar Khaibar, one of the leading members of the Communist Party, on 17th April 1978. The Communist party blamed Daoud's government, and gained support.

Rumours quickly spread throughout the city that Khaibar was killed by one of his own party's rivals in order to create chaos. His funeral procession passed just a few yards from Zubaida's block of flats in Mecrorayan and was followed by a massive demonstration of thousands of party members through the streets of Kabul. The next day the government officials ordered the arrest of some of the PDPA.

A few days later, at midday on the *7th of Sour*, the second month of the Muslim Afghan calendar, which fell on 27 April 1978, Zubaida was hanging out her washing on the balcony of her flat in block 28 when the first bomb went off. It shook the whole city of Kabul. Zubaida rushed towards the big bookcase in their sitting room and picked up the holy Quran from the top shelf. It was covered with two or three pieces of material. She held it to her chest and started praying under her breath. She was shaking and anxious that something tragic might happen to her only son. 'Oh Allah please keep my Parwez safe wherever he is.'

Then the second bomb went off. 'Oh Allah, oh Allah please save my son,' she repeated, and opened a page of the Quran, to distract her from the dreadful reality. A third bomb went off and shook the whole of Kabul again, and smoke filled the blue sky. 'Oh my God, what has happened? In the name of God what has happened?' Zubaida could not concentrate on reading any more. She put the holy book back in its place and went out onto the balcony. Dark smoke filled the sky and the sound of explosions got louder and louder. Yes, it was the royal palace under attack, she thought. It was not very far from where she lived.

The city of Kabul collapsed. Schools sent children home, workers left their offices, shopkeepers closed their shops, and people emptied the streets and sat by their radios to hear what this madness was about. Things were serious, Zubaida thought. 'Oh God, please save Parwez.'

The bombing went on for three hours and was targeted around the palace. President Daoud, who was holding a meeting in the palace at the time, was killed with his entire family and bodyguards. The last remnants of Afghanistan's monarchy had ended. Daoud was from the royal family, the former King Mohammed Zahir Shah's first cousin. Back in July 1973 he had come to power by deposing his cousin and changed the regime from a constitutional monarchy to a republic.

Zubaida lived with her son Parwez on the third floor of a block of flats in an area built by the government with the help of the Soviet Union. It was built for middle class families and government staff. She looked from the window towards the palace and saw a cloud of smoke hanging over the whole city. Parwez had an important position in the army. He had just started working in that post and had already proved himself, making his mother very proud. He had a degree in political science from Kabul University and a Master's degree from the Soviet Union. Recently, Zubaida had realised that her son was not happy as he rarely spoke to her. Sometimes he came home late and did not touch his food. Occasionally he complained of headaches. She never dreamt that her son would be involved in any political activities. She had had enough problems with her late husband who had lost his life in Daoud's prison and she had never approved of his political activities.

Zubaida was in her late fifties, a language teacher at Zargona High School. She had grown up in a middle class family, was educated at college and university, and married a man of her own choice. Her late husband Easan, was an ambitious, honest man who had worked in a high position in the previous government, but he was secretly a supporter of the PDPA. He was attracted to the party from an early age and had joined when he was at university. When he married Zubaida he kept his political activities a secret, because Zubaida's father did not approve of a Communist system in an Islamic land and Easan found it easier to keep quiet about it. Occasionally, when Easan had a meeting with his party group, he made excuses to be out for a couple of hours.

The Daoud government arrested Easan for involvement in the hijacking of Adolph Dubs, the US ambassador. Dubs was kidnapped by a group of men in police uniforms. They took the ambassador to Kabul

Hotel and held him hostage, demanding in return the release of militant prisoners. Despite the embassy's intervention to stop the shooting, government troops fired on them, and Dubs and one of the kidnappers were killed while the rest escaped. The Communist Party blamed Daoud's government and Daoud blamed the Communist Party. Some people blamed the Islamic conservatives and by the end no one really knew who was involved. Zubaida's husband Easan was tortured and killed in prison. A few days later she received her husband's body. Zubaida never found out which group her husband had been involved in.

Zubaida kept praying, but Parwez did not come home that night. The next morning Kabul radio and TV announced that power was in the hands of the Revolutionary Council and that the regime had changed. The People's Democratic Party took control of the Ministry of Defence and the National Radio Station. Noor Muhammad Taraki became president of Afghanistan. Within a week, huge portraits of him were installed in every public space in Kabul. Sixty years old, he still was a handsome man. Babrak Karmal and Hafezullah Ameen became his deputy ministers.

Two days later three uniformed men knocked at Zubaida's door and informed her that Parwez had been killed. He had died a hero, they said, and had lost his life for the *inqulaab*, the revolution, for his people and his country. Zubaida collapsed on the floor. The men asked her neighbour to comfort her and left. Zubaida had no choice other than to face the reality that her son Parwez had been involved in underground activities and had supported the Communist Party like his father before him. They did not return Parwez's body. Apparently there was nothing left of him but they gave her a piece of his jacket with his fiancée's photo in the pocket. Parwez had been engaged to Fatana, a university student. Zubaida did not have any family in Kabul apart from her son. She had two brothers who had immigrated to Germany long before the *inqulaab*. She had a few distant cousins but had not been in contact with them because they had not approved of her husband's involvement in politics.

After her son's death the only thing that kept Zubaida going was the desire to find out how her son was killed and where his body was buried. For six months she went from office to office but found no trace of his death and which party he had been involved with. It was as though Parwez had vanished from the face of the earth, as if he had never existed.

One day she went to the Ministry of the Interior. A tall, smart officer with a dark moustache and thick lips approached her. He was dressed as if he was going to a wedding party.

'I want to see the minister.'

'Have you got an appointment?'

'No I haven't.'

'You cannot see him without an appointment. He is a very busy man.' said the officer. 'If it's urgent you can leave your message with me and I will pass it on,' he said.

Zubaida sat there patiently for a long time. The officer asked her to leave but Zubaida did not move. 'I just want to know where my son was killed,' she said. Gnawing the skin on her hands and biting her nails, she waited for an answer.

'Dear lady, your son is not the only person who was killed in the *inqulaab*. Many died and we cannot find out how and where they were killed. Be happy and proud that he is a martyr. He served his country,' the officer said.

When she insisted, the officer became agitated and raised his voice. 'Please do not disturb us. I told you, I do not know any more. Soon we will put the names of those who died on the wall outside the Home Office. You will find out how and where he was killed then.'

Zubaida left the office, broken-hearted. The next day she took her son's jacket, placed a small shovel and a long stick in her bag and caught the bus to Shohada-e Sualein, on the lower slopes of the big mountain where Sunni Muslims bury their loved ones. It took her hours to dig a hole in the hard ground and to bury her son's jacket with his fiancée's photo. She covered it with earth, stitched a green flag to one end of the stick and pushed it into the ground, murmuring to herself, 'My dear martyr Parwez. I hope your soul is in heaven, my martyr Parwez. I will come and see you every day.' She did not cry as her pain was so acute that it had dried up her whole body. Without tears, she continued lamenting to herself. She slowly got up and left the graveyard. No one was around.

Zubaida lost her job to a younger teacher for refusing to co-operate with the new regime and criticising them openly. Her neighbours supported the *Mujahideen* who at that time were considered 'freedom fighters' against the Communists. When they found out that Zubaida's son was a Communist supporter, they stopped socialising with her. Isolated, Zubaida contemplated committing suicide but could not go through with it, worried that she would go to hell according to Islamic faith. Gradually everyone forgot about Zubaida's son as they got caught up in the terrible political situation.

Soon after the new regime was installed, an exhibition was held in Kabul to demonstrate the wealth of the deposed President Daoud and how he had committed terrible crimes. As soon as the coalition government took power they started spreading their own ideology, which many ordinary people were not ready to accept. For them, the new regime were pushing a deeply religious and proudly independent country into Soviet-style modernity at gunpoint.

The political suppression spread, and anyone suspected of not supporting the regime was arrested. Many wealthy, upper and middle class and religious people were detained. It was well known that the prisons were already full and the only solution was to kill the most powerful and the influential prisoners. The victims were tied up and shot on the ground so as not to damage the walls. Then the bodies were dropped into a large hole and a tractor levelled the earth.

For Zubaida, life became hell. The only thing that kept her going was visiting her son's empty grave. She knew that the April coup was only the beginning of a longterm nightmare for the Afghan nation. Soon after the coup, a large opposition group went to Pakistan to gain support and weapons in order to fight the regime. Meanwhile, the new Communist government had its own internal conflicts. Within a short period of time, various leaders had been deposed, murdered, replaced and sent into exile. It was only after ten years of conflict that the Soviet Union finally withdrew, leaving Najibullah, the last Communist leader, to deal with the aftermath.

In 1989, the last of the soldiers returned to the Soviet Union, leaving behind a ruined land with thousands of mines planted all over the country. A million and a half Afghans had been killed, five million had escaped into exile and a large number of children had been orphaned. In 1992, when Najibullah was ousted, the country became a battlefield between different groups of *Mujahideen*. They fired rockets and missiles into Kabul killing an estimated fifty thousand people, destroying a beautiful country and levelling the land to dust.

Zubaida knew that each side was guilty of crimes. Kidnapping, rape, execution and murder became the rule. People had had enough of war, so when the *Taliban* came to power in 1996 many welcomed them with open arms. But the *Taliban* imposed the strictest interpretation of Sharia law ever seen in the history of Islam.

CHAPTER 11

Simeen closed the small gate behind her. She walked slowly, placing one foot ahead of the other. She felt as though she was dreaming. She walked along the dark road and did not notice the cold, the wind, the rain or anything else around her. The sharp wind blew away her black scarf and tore at her uncombed hair. All she could hear was her father's voice, 'I have no choice, I have no choice.' She looked around. No one was on the streets.

She walked faster and then began to run, not knowing where she was headed. Every few minutes she looked over her shoulder for fear of seeing her father running after her. She did not know who to turn to for help, where to go, nor who to tell about herself and her shameful tragedy. She was sure that her father had planned to kill her.

Finally she slowed down and began to walk aimlessly. She knew nobody in Kabul. The only person that she could rely on was the cook at Bibijan's house, but she could not go there because Bibijan had told her not to. Mid-morning she found herself in a deserted graveyard, hungry, tired and lonely. This was the only quiet place she could find to rest. She looked around and wished that she could find her mother's grave but it was impossible because most of the graves were unmarked. Even if the tombstones had had names on them, she could not read them. She sat down near a mound of earth and sobbed for a long time. She was exhausted, having not slept the previous night. After a while she fell asleep. She dreamed that her mother was weeping, then singing, then lamenting loudly while her father was trying to kill her with a kitchen knife. No, it was not her mother, it was her sister. Simeen gasped and woke up. She looked around and saw a woman bent over a grave, reciting a mournful song and weeping. When her lamenting concluded, she looked over. Simeen stood up to leave, but after a few steps she heard the woman calling her,'Wait a minute.'

Simeen turned her head and stared at a tall, grey-haired, woman, covered from head to toe in black. Simeen hesitated for a second, then returned to sit down at the exact place where she had slept.

The lady walked toward Simeen. 'Is this the grave of one of your relatives?' she asked.

'No,' Simeen said.

She sat next to her 'Why are you here then?' she asked.

Simeen did not answer. She just looked at the ground as though she was a disobedient student awaiting punishment for not doing her homework.

'What is your name?' the lady asked.

Simeen lifted her head for a second, 'I am Simeen,' she said and looked at the ground again.

'I am Zubaida,' the lady said with a gentle voice.

Simeen did not react but waited to be told what to do. Zubaida looked at Simeen sympathetically. She felt this girl's pain and gently touched her shoulder. Simeen started shaking and tears welled up in her eyes. The lady moved closer and tenderly wrapped her arms around her. Simeen hugged her back and started weeping loudly this time. They both hugged each other and wept for a long time. Simeen wept for her mother and the tragedy that she was facing and Zubaida for her martyred son.

After a long silence, Zubaida said, 'I feel that you are in some sort of trouble. If you tell me I may be able to help you.' Simeen did not answer. Zubaida did not push but gently said, 'Go home.'

Simeen did not move. And so Zubaida repeated, 'Go

home.' Simeen looked at her, 'I have no home. I do not know where to go.'

'Where is your husband?'

Simeen didn't respond. Zubaida thought that perhaps she had had a fight with her husband. 'Where are your mother and father? Do you have brothers or sisters?'

'My mother died a few months ago.'

'Oh I'm sorry. Is this why you're here? Is this your mother's grave?'

'No, I don't know where my mother's grave is. I wish I knew. My father said her grave was in Sakhi,' Simeen replied.

'Oh you've come to the wrong cemetery, girl. I know where Sakhi is. Would you like me to take you there?' Zubaida asked.

'No, thank you. I won't be able to find her anyway.

'Why not? You can read her name on the gravestone.'

'I cannot read,' Simeen said.

'I can read for you,' Zubaida insisted. 'What is your mother's name?'

'Gulchaira.'

Zubaida wanted to know more about Simeen so that she could help her. She stood up, adjusted her black head scarf and gestured toward her son's empty grave.

'That is my beautiful son sleeping there. He's a *shahid*, a martyr, he was killed during the *inqulaab*,' she said.

Simeen did not know what *inqulaab* meant. She knew that many people had been killed on *7th of Sour*, but she did not know why. She had been too wrapped up in her own misery and did not have the energy left to think about wider problems.

'Let's go,' Zubaida said and Simeen followed her like a lost lamb. They left the graveyard together. No one could have imagined the dreadful weight they shared in their hearts and minds.

'Would you like to come to my house and have a cup of tea?' Zubaida asked. Simeen prayed in her heart that this lady could help her. She did not say anything but kept walking.

When they reached Zubaida's home, Simeen was

tired and her dislocated shoulder was hurting. Zubaida made a poultice from egg yolk, flour and ginger, applied it to Simeen's shoulder, covered it with a warm bandage and gave her a painkiller.

Simeen stayed with Zubaida in her tiny flat in Mecrorayan, and after a week Zubaida knew everything about Simeen's short life. She began to think that Simeen would make a good companion, especially for visiting her son's grave. Meeting Simeen was perhaps a good opportunity for her to come to terms with her grief and accept the loss of her son. Zubaida kept thinking that finding Simeen in the graveyard near her son's grave was perhaps God's wish to help her. 'This was not an accident, it was a miracle. God had sent her a gift,' she thought.

A month or so later Zubaida suggested teaching Simeen some basic skills at home. 'I was a school teacher. Would you like me to teach you Dari?' She mentioned this casually, unsure what Simeen's reaction would be.

Simeen had never expected such generosity. 'Yes, I love the idea,' she replied excitedly.

It had always been her dream to learn to read and write but she had never had the slightest idea how this could happen. She had never touched a pen, book or paper before.

From then on Zubaida bombarded Simeen with books, pens and paper. Zubaida made a proper programme and timetable every day. This kept them both busy throughout. Despite her emotional uncertainty, Simeen tried hard to concentrate on her studies. She was so grateful to Zubaida and it was the only time that she did not think of her brothers and sister and her father.

After lessons, they went for long walks. Everyone knew everyone. The high rise block of flats was surrounded by trees and greenery and there was a shopping centre, a football ground and a tennis court where teenagers played in the late afternoon on summer days. Families walked around with their children and talked to their neighbours. The ice cream man parked nearby hoping to attract the children. This part of Kabul was different from the rest of city. For Simeen, this was far away from where her father lived and she felt safe, knowing that he could not find here. But Zubaida was cautious and tried to avoid people in case they asked about her new companion. She was equally concerned for Simeen's safety.

One day, after one of their walks, a neighbour approached Zubaida. 'I'm so glad you have company. Who is this young woman?' Zubaida was wondering how to introduce Simeen. She knew she could not say that Simeen was a relative as she had high cheek bones, a small nose, almond shaped eyes, and Asian features. Her dialect was also distinctive and gave her away. It was obvious that Simeen was a Hazara.

'She is my temporary maid,' she said, but immediately felt guilty and changed tack. 'She's living with me for the time being as her husband is a soldier fighting in Jalalabad and she doesn't have any family.'

'Poor woman. She's heavily pregnant,' said the neighbour.

Simeen did not mind being called a servant. It didn't bother her. She had worked as a servant and was grateful that Zubaida treated her like her own daughter. What was more important was that she was safe and living with a kind woman. After this encounter, Zubaida was reluctant to go out for walks.

Slowly Simeen managed to understand basic children's books and write simple sentences. Gradually her reading and writing improved and she began to read newspapers.

'What is *inqulaab*?' Simeen asked Zubaida.

'It is revolution,' she answered. 'When people are not happy with the government, they want to change the regime in a violent way. As a result many innocent people get killed. My Parwez was one of them,' she said. 'But it was not *inqulaab* as they claimed. It was a coup, organised by a small group of young and inexperienced men who created disaster. This coup destroyed my life and my happiness. It destroyed the dignity of ordinary citizens. The leaders claim that they are the guardians of law and order, according to their power and intellect, but they are blind to the misery that they have created for ordinary people. The society is now a battlefield between the Communists and the conservative Islamists, neighbours fighting neighbours, young people fighting old people.'

Simeen still did not understand most of the things that Zubaida said, but she was a good listener. 'What is a coup?' she asked.

'Oh it is difficult for you to understand. I will explain to you when your reading improves.'

'Why do some people not like the government, and what have they done?' Simeen asked.

Zubaida could have explained in detail, as she knew a lot about her country, but she knew it would be hard for Simeen to understand everything at once.

'The new government is trying to bring about change and improve the people's lifestyle at gun point,' Zubaida said simply. The hatred was clear in her voice. 'They are called the People's Democratic Party of Afghanistan. It was established long ago by university students in Kabul. I know because my husband was one of them. He died in prison.'

'What is a communist?' Simeen said.

'Oh you ask too many questions, my girl. Communists are people who do not believe in God, but my husband was a good Muslim and I don't think all the people who changed the regime are *kaffir*. I can understand why they did it. My husband was a good man. He wanted to bring about change, improve people's lives. But when the party gained power they wanted to change everything quickly. They killed people who disapproved of their regime and imprisoned many innocent people. I wish it had never happened. So many people suffered,' Zubaida said. 'Could you make me a cup of tea?' she continued, changing the subject.

Simeen went to the kitchen and Zubaida's thoughts drifted back to the past. She thought of Afghanistan when she had been at university. During the 1960s, Kabul University was the perfect location for all political debates. There, beside the pro-Soviet parties, were

Marxist, Maoist, different Islamist and nationalist parties, none of whom had any real connection with the real people of Afghanistan. In 1979 the Marxists managed to overthrow the present government. When they seized power they applied their authoritarian Stalinist ideology and quickly uprooted the religious groups.

She remembered April 1980 when the new government had announced the celebration of the first anniversary of their revolution. This had angered and mobilized people against the regime. In Kabul people protested. After that the government's treatment of civilians became much harsher. Every day, more young people were arrested and houses were searched for evidence of 'crimes against the government'. Many wealthy and religious people went to prison and a large group was killed again. The Communist party controlled radio and television and banned the free press and any opposition. Their first target were the religious leaders, many of whom were imprisoned or killed. The Communists demanded unconditional obedience.

Each area had its own party headquarters and those who had been given full authority to carry arms wore red armbands. Thousands of ordinary people were labelled 'Capitalists' and were threatened with death. Regular meetings involved denunciation and spying on one another's business became the norm. Parents were afraid of their children and could not talk about the regime in front of them because many young people were in the Communist youth clubs and had been indoctrinated. They were expected to spy on their family members and report them to the authorities.

Schoolchildren were divided into right and left. Each group bullied the other. Every class had to learn Communist literature and propaganda, overseen by the head teacher. The children did not need to worry about their exams as long as they were obedient and loyal to the party. All the teachers were expected to give a pep talk about the leader of Afghanistan for ten minutes before teaching. The students were taught to answer questions such as the leader's birthplace, his parents' names, his past achievements, when he joined the party and so on.

The government did not adapt their vision to acknowledge the reality and values of ordinary people. They did not believe that change should take place at grass roots level, and forced a quick modernisation programme. But this alienated people who were not willing to replace their Muslim ideology with an alien culture. The government's biggest mistake was that they underestimated the power of the proud people of Afghanistan.

The situation gradually deteriorated. The bridge of unity between the people and the government began to crumble. The more the government imposed their programmes, the angrier the people became. Zubaida knew Afghanistan was a poor country but previously it had been stable and peaceful. During this chaotic time, no one trusted anyone.

Many doctors, engineers, artists, writers, journalists and shopkeepers tried to escape. Many succeeded in getting out of the country but others, less resourceful, were arrested and imprisoned. Every family had relatives who were missing, either disappeared over the borders or in prison. Justice became arbitrary, cruelty was institutionalised and corruption spread through society.

Zubaida lost her job as a teacher after opposing the new regime. She had lost her son and her husband to politics. She remembered a time when she had been young and ambitious; one of her dreams was to study law but her mother had been against it.

'Why do you want to be a politician?' she had said to her. 'Politics is not for women. You cannot compete with men.'

'Mother! Times have changed. It is not the 18th century, it is the 1960s. We have the right to vote, we go to university and we work alongside men. Nothing is wrong with being a politician,' Zubaida argued. 'Women are much more capable nowadays. I'd like to study politics. It's a good subject and other friends are planning to study it.'

'Wait and see, my lovely daughter,' her mother said.

As a child, Zubaida had been impressed by the way

politicians lived, talked, dressed and convinced people what to do or not to do. She finished her schooling in 1968. After the argument with her mother she decided not to follow her dream and chose to study literature and history at Kabul University and became a teacher at Zargona High School. After losing her two men to politics, she was old enough to know that politicians were not clever people, they were no better than ordinary citizens. In fact some of them possessed less knowledge and wisdom. They just happened to be in the right place at the right time. Many of them abused their power and misled people to the point of no return with disastrous consequences.

In the evening, out of boredom, Zubaida and Simeen watched the only television channel broadcast by the government and full of propaganda. One night there was a documentary about the leader's childhood and how he had grown up in a nomadic family. His supporters had established a museum and exhibited the president's childhood clothes, his cradle, his parents' clothes and all their belongings.

Zubaida became frustrated. 'How can a nomadic family, who travel all their life, manage to keep all their belongings for sixty years? Those flatterers are trying to make a Prophet out of this man.,' she exclaimed and turned off the TV. A few months later this leader would be suffocated with a pillow by one of his rivals and the media covered it up by saying that he had died from an undiagnosed illness.

Gradually Zubaida reached the point when she felt unable to take any more. 'I can't live in that madness, there's nothing here left for me,' she thought. But where could they go? Where could she get help and direction? After many sleepless nights she decided to try and escape from the country that had created so much pain for her. She hated living in Kabul, the city she had once loved so much. The only thing that she was interested in was visiting the cemetery where she had buried her son's jacket.

Simeen was heavily pregnant and wouldn't be able to escape over the border, like so many others who   chose that route. They did not have passports so would not be able to go through normal borders or fly. This became a big dilemma for Zubaida.

That evening after turning off the TV, Simeen got up, went into the kitchen, washed the dishes and then went to her room. Zubaida read her book while Simeen looked at her bedroom ceiling for hours before she fell asleep. She missed her family and longed to hug her little sister Feroza and feel her body close to her.

Around midnight a wailing noise came from Simeen's room. Zubaida put down her book, knowing that Simeen was having another nightmare. Zubaida slowly opened Simeen's door and sat on her bed. She put one hand on her forehead and with the o t h e r touched her gently to wake her up. 'Get up my child. You are having a bad dream again.' Simeen woke up, still crying loudly.

'Did you have a bad dream?' Zubaida asked.

Simeen moved her head slightly and put the quilt over her face. Zubaida lay down next to her, held her tight and Simeen started crying silently.

'Would you like to see your mother's grave?' Zubaida asked.

'I don't know where her grave is,' Simeen said.

'Don't worry. We will find it,' Zubaida said. She knew where to find the Hazara and Shi'a cemetery. 'We can see if they have put her name on the stone. I am sure they have.'

Zubaida, born into a middle-class Sunni Muslim family, had no idea that most Hazaras did not put a name on their loved one's grave, believing that God created all human beings from earth and that they go back to earth when they die, or because they were poor and unable to afford a gravestone.

The next day Zubaida and Simeen took the bus to Sakhi and the shrine of Imam Ali.

The huge blue mosque was visible from miles away, located at the lower slopes of the mountain which separated the two parts of Kabul.

When they reached the graveyard, they noticed that there were no tombstones nor names on most of the graves. Some graves were old and overgrown with weeds, and others were new with plastic flowers on them.

They walked along the path but could not find Simeen's mother's grave. Simeen wept. Zubaida put her hand on her shoulder and stood silently next to her. The sky was heavy with clouds and the weather had turned cold.

Crying made Simeen feel better. Zubaida walked on and Simeen followed her. The first drops of rain touched the graves softly.

CHAPTER 12

Simeen woke up in the middle of the night. She felt uncomfortable with a pain in the lower part of her body. She moved position but it still hurt. She did not turn on the light, but tiptoed through the dark to the kitchen to have a glass of water. Zubaida was fast asleep.

Simeen's discomfort turned to a sharp pain in her stomach. She drank the water and tried not to panic but the pain was too much to bear. She knew what was happening and started to pray. She did not wake Zubaida up.

At four o'clock, when Zubaida went to the bathroom to wash for morning prayers she heard Simeen's wailing. She opened the door but could not see anything. She switched on the light but realised that there was a power cut and their block of flats was in complete darkness. She rushed to the kitchen, got the matches and lit a candle. Then she returned to the room to find Simeen face down on the floor soaked in sweat. Zubaida knew it was the time for the baby to come, but there was no way to get Simeen to the hospital as there was a curfew and she did not have access to a telephone. Even then, she would not have been able to call an ambulance as the whole town was in chaos.

Zubaida put her arm around her and squeezed her shoulders. 'Lie down on the bed,' she said.

'I'm frightened,' Simeen said, her voice soft and broken.

'You will be alright,' Zubaida said. The certainty in her own voice suprised her.

Simeen had a long , painful labour. Four hours later, she gave birth to a baby girl. It was an emotional time for Simeen and Zubaida. Simeen closed her eyes for hours and didn't want to see the baby so Zubaida took on the responsibility of mother.

After a few days, Zubaida asked Simeen about naming her daughter. Simeen did not answer. She buried her face in her arms and began to sob. Zubaida gently sat down next to her and put her arms around her small body and held her tight.

'What is done is done and cannot be undone, my girl. You had better face reality and I'm here to help you,' Zubaida said firmly. Simeen looked up into her kind brown eyes but couldn't shake the unbearable shame she felt.

Zubaida did not ask her again and named the child Sittara, meaning star. She wished the baby had been a boy and she could have named him after her Parwez.

Zubaida devoted herself to Sittara, washing her tiny body in the bathroom, changing her nappy, feeding her and hugging her. But Simeen kept her distance from the baby as much as she could although there were times that she couldn't avoid her. She had mixed feelings. She was sorry for herself and the baby. Every time she looked at Sittara's face she remembered that horrible night, the suffocating smell of alcohol on Jaweed's breath, and how helpless she had felt. She was reluctant to hold Sittara, although she recognised that it was not the baby's fault. But she also knew that this baby would never be welcome in Afghan society. There were many sleepless nights when Simeen wished they were both dead.

The worst thing was the breastfeeding. Every time the baby cried it was like torture, reminding her of her tragedy, of having a *harami* in her lap. The shame and anger were unbearable. She missed her sister, her brothers and even her father. After a few months, when Sittara began to smile at her mother, Simeen began to accept her fate, but she was still far from loving her.

A few months after the *inqulaab* the political atmosphere throughout the country was tense. People realized that the new regime was not going to bring stability. The new leaders were out of touch with the reality of their country and their people. They blindly followed their Stalinist ideology and tried to modernise a deeply proud nation by force, refusing to acknowledge that guns and tanks do not solve social, economic and political problems.

In every household there were secret talks but no one dared to speak publicly and express their real feelings about the government. Some people yearned for the return of the previous government while others blamed the previous government for the present chaos.The divide within society found its way into families.

One government project was literacy courses for adult men and women in rural parts of the country. They trained young teenagers from Kabul youth clubs to teach older and illiterate people in the villages. Those teenagers were given the authority to 'modernise' the older generation, the khans, the landlords and farmers. The trainees were not experienced and their arrogance angered the older generation. When they started adult education classes many men refused to sit next to women or be in the same classroom.

The most unrealistic project was Land Reform. The Communists tried to take land from the rich by force and give it to the farmers. Some farmers refused to take the land as they remained loyal to their landlords, but others took it, faced conflict with the landlord, and they often killed each other.

The rivalry and fight for power between the two coalition parties weakened government stability further. This deepened ordinary people's hatred of the pro-Soviet government. Eventually one party managed to get rid of the other. By then, people had had enough. Millions of desperate civilians left their homes and escaped over the mountains to Pakistan and Iran.

Not even in her darkest nightmares had Zubaida

imagined that she would ever witness such horrors. How could people be so evil to each other? Where was the humanity, where was the love and goodness? Was there no compassion left? Why had peace, harmony and trust evaporated from this country to be replaced by trauma, pain and hatred?

Throughout the following months, Zubaida and Simeen developed a mother and daughter relationship which both appreciated.

Simeen felt safe living with Zubaida and Zubaida was occupied with Sittara. The pair kept Zubaida's mind off her own tragedy. Every night after putting Sittara to bed, Simeen took her book to the kitchen and did her homework like a conscientious student. It was the only time that she was not thinking about her family. Soon Simeen managed to read and write fluently. Then she would go to her bedroom, lie next to her daughter and daydream about her childhood in Bamyan. Her earliest memories came to her mind like a film: playing in the green fields with other children, or sitting under a tree, or going with her father to the market every Monday where they would buy all sorts of things, from household goods to animals. Sometimes her father had carried Simeen on his back when she was tired. In those days her father had always been gentle and kind to her.

The fighting continued every day. After a year of living in fear, Zubaida decided to find a way to get out of the country. But she was not sure where to go and who to ask for help with passports. She could easily get to Pakistan or Iran on her own but to escape over the mountains with a young woman and a baby was too risky. Obtaining passports from the government also needed a large amount of money that Zubaida could barely afford. The only option she had was to find an official who would charge her less.

After two months she found the right person to provide them with passports. But Zubaida had no idea which country they should go to. After many sleepless nights she decided on India and started preparing for their journey without telling Simeen. Finally, their passports arrived. It was late afternoon when Zubaida came home with two passports and tried to break the news to Simeen.

'What shall we have for dinner?' she asked Simeen cheerfully.

'I have been waiting for you to tell me what to cook.'

'Some vegetable stew with nan bread would   be lovely,' Zubaida replied.

Simeen was surprised to see Zubaida, smiling. 'Why is she so happy today?' she thought.

'I hope it doesn't take long as I'm starving,' Zubaida said.

Simeen rushed to the kitchen to prepare the food. Zubaida was not sure how Simeen would react to her news. When dinner was finished Simeen cleared the table and went to the kitchen to wash the dishes.

'I have good news,' Zubaida said.

The first thing that came to Simeen's mind was her sister. 'Oh! You have news from Ferosa,' she said without even thinking. But quickly she laughed at her naïvety. Zubaida didn't know her sister. 'What could be the good news then?' she was wondering. 'What is it?' she asked. 'I have finally managed to get the passports.'

'What for? What passports?'

'To go abroad.'

Simeen's heart sank. 'You didn't tell me you had plans to go abroad.'

'I wanted to surprise you.'

The colour of Simeen's face changed. She sat on the nearest chair.

'Where are you going?

'To India.'

'Why?'

'You know I lost my husband, my son and my job. There is nothing left for me.'

Simeen was shocked. She did not say anything, but slowly got up and took the empty tea pot to the kitchen. Zubaida understood her anxiety and joined her. Simeen was crying quietly and tears were running down her cheeks.

Zubaida put her arms around Simeen's shoulders and hugged her. Simeen's body was rigid against her, as it had been in the beginning when they met at the graveyard. 'Why are you crying?'

Simeen did not answer, but simply sat, her fingers against her temples.

'I thought you would be happy,' Zubaida said.

Simeen put her head on the table and wept. Zubaida gently stroked her head. They both felt emotional and hugged each other, rooted to the spot for a long time without speaking to each other.

'What is going to happen to us if you go? Can you take Sittara with you?' Simeen asked, after a while. The hurt was clear in her eyes now.

Zubaida's heart sank 'I cannot take Sittara alone. I am not going without you both,' Zubaida said. 'Do you think I would leave you behind in this mess? We have come a long way together and we both are victims in our own way. I would never leave you in these circumstances.'

Simeen had never expected such generosity from her. After a long pause she said, 'Thank you. I thought you were going alone. I can't thank you enough. You are my angel.' Her heart filled with gratitude and tears ran down her cheeks again. But then she remembered her past. 'It means I will not see my family ever again, I mean my brothers and sister,' she said.

'You don't see them now and you don't know where they are. It will not make any difference to you. But don't lose hope. This is a small world, perhaps one day you will see them.'

Simeen lowered her head, looked at the floor and kept quiet. They did not talk about it any more that evening and for the rest of the following week.

Zubaida was worried that her meagre savings might not be enough. 'I have some valuable jewels, so if I need money I can sell them,' she thought.

On the night before they were due to leave Afghanistan, they were excited and anxious. They went to bed but couldn't sleep. Zubaida's mind travelled back to her past. Every single episode of her life was paraded in front of her eyes like a sad film. How her life had fallen to pieces. She also worried about how she was going to cope in a foreign land with Simeen and Sittara.

Simeen thought about her brothers and her sister. 'I will never see them again,' she thought. How would she be able to live in another country away from them?

Simeen sat on her bed, her back to the wall, her hands around her knees, her eyes glued to the baby a few centimetres away from her mother, fast asleep, knowing nothing of her anguish.

Zubaida remembered the happy occasion when her son Parwez was born in hospital and the whole family visited the lucky mother and the child. How happy her husband was that his first-born child was a boy. It was important to him. Parwez had had a very happy childhood, did well at school, college and university. His future had seemed bright. Now Parwez, handsome Parwez who had had so many dreams, was lying somewhere, and Zubaida did not know where he was buried.

At five in the morning, Zubaida went to the bathroom and washed for morning prayers. She returned to her bedroom, put the prayer mat on the floor, positioned herself toward *Kaaba* and prayed. This was the day that she was leaving her homeland for an unknown future and she had the responsibility of two other people. This felt like a heavy burden on her shoulders, but she had no choice. Their tragic destiny bound them together. She had to help them.

When Zubaida finished praying she gently folded the prayer mat and put it on the table. As she pushed aside the net curtain and looked from her top floor flat down to the ruined land, she felt a sharp pain in her heart. This place, this shared garden with neighbours, had been so beautiful in the past, full of colourful flowers and trees. Now it was all destroyed.

Zubaida was about to leave her country, for an unknown future. What would she do in another country with only a few savings and a young woman and baby who were not related to her?

She looked at everything around her. Her emotions ran high, she felt something inside her had died forever. With sad eyes she looked at the empty walls, the shelf full of books that had belonged to her beloved *shahid* son and her late husband. Their family photos smiled at her as if nothing had happened. She remembered the time when they went to Jalalabad for a short holiday and her husband had asked a stranger on the street to take their photos. She could see the tall trees behind them. They were all smiling. Happy days.

Zubaida felt like a bird without wings. She picked up the two precious photos and put them in her bag. She did not have much to take with her.

At seven o'clock the doorbell rang. Zubaida rushed to open it.

'Are you ready?' the taxi driver asked.

'Yes we are,' said Zubaida and ran into the kitchen to let Simeen know.

The taxi driver picked up the two small cases and walked down the corridor and down the stairs while Zubaida and Simeen followed him in silence.

After a long drive they reached Kabul airport. They passed through customs. An arrogant officer approached them, took their passports and looked closely at the photos. 'You're going to India?' he asked.

'Yes,' Zubaida said and prayed from the bottom of her heart that he wouldn't make any problems for them.

'Why are you going to India?'

'For health reasons.'

'Who is this woman with the baby? What is their reason to go?'

Zubaida could see that the man wanted to create problems for them. They had just twenty minutes left to catch their flight. Zubaida gently, without attracting attention, put some money in his hand. The officer's attitude softened immediately. 'OK now you can go' he said, and let them pass. They went through the barrier. Zubaida was all smiles for the first time. 'We have done it!' she said quietly.

Suddenly a massive explosion erupted and the whole building shook. The windows shattered, glass poured like heavy rain everywhere and smoke filled the huge reception area. There was panic, shouting and screaming. Outside they could see the two giant aeroplanes burning. Flames and smoke were rising high in the sky. Charred bodies lay on the ground. Zubaida felt a sharp pain in her upper body and saw blood pouring from her left arm. She looked around and saw Simeen lying on the floor, protecting her child and Sittara screaming under her mother's weight. The customs officer was lying unconscious under a shattered window, the money with which Zubaida had bribed him still in his hand. The sound of ambulances in the distance brought Zubaida back to reality. She shouted, 'Simeen where are you?' But Simeen had passed out.

The corridors and rooms in the Wazeer Akbar Khan Hospital were full of injured people, screaming in pain. Nurses and doctors were rushing around like mad animals. Zubaida had a broken arm, Simeen a minor injury and Sittara was unhurt. After plastering Zubaida's arm, the doctor discharged them and they took a taxi back to their empty flat. Kabul airport was closed for a long time.

The bloody war between the government and the *Mujahideen* continued. Kabul was like a graveyard in the evenings. The curfew started at 10pm. People rushed home for fear of being arrested by the police. It did not affect Zubaida as she hardly went out, even during the day.

Three months after the airport explosion, one evening around nine o'clock, Simeen put her daughter to bed and started studying. Zubaida turned on the TV to watch the usual government propaganda. Suddenly a huge explosion shook the area. The nearby block of flats was rocked by dynamite and shells and the sky brightened like a display of fireworks. The streets and houses were in flames, and windows were shattered. The TV programme stopped when the electricity was cut off and the whole area of Mecrorayan became dark. For at least half an hour it was quiet and then the sound of crying, shouting and wailing began to be heard. People did not know if they should stay at home or get out.

Zubaida and Simeen just sat and waited for what might happen next. They couldn't go to bed for fear of another explosion. After three or four hours Kabul seemed quiet again.

Zubaida did not have the energy to move, talk or sleep. She just sat on the floor unusually still. Simeen went to the kitchen, brought the dustpan and brush and cleared up the shattered glass. Then she went to the bathroom to wash for morning prayer. After she had prayed she cautiously moved the net curtain and looked outside. At first she could not see properly but once she focused her eyes, she saw several corpses were lying right outside their block of flats. The top floor of the opposite block of flats did not exist anymore. She screamed and Zubaida rushed to her. Simeen had lost her tongue and just pointed towards the dead bodies on the ground.

Zubaida ran downstairs without shoes and scarf, her hair messed up, her face white and her hands trembling. She did not know why as she couldn't do anything. She saw corpses lying all over the street, their intestines mixed with the rubble and broken concrete. She climbed back up the stairs. Just as she entered the flat there was a series of explosions. They seemed very close. The screams in the corridors grew louder. Zubaida and Simeen were shaking from head to toe as they stood in the middle of their tiny hall away from the windows. Zubaida went to her bedroom and withdrew her savings from under the mattress. She put the money with her son's photo in her scarf and secured it under her breast. Another blast filled the area. Zubaida held the baby in her arms and told Simeen to follow her along the corridor and down the stairs. They ran as fast as they could with other people who lived in the same block. They didn't look back until they were some distance away. The whole block had crumbled like a matchbox. Zubaida's flat did not exist anymore.

In the morning the whole town was soulless. People silently moved around as they picked up the dead bodies.

CHAPTER 13

It was six o'clock in the morning. Zubaida, found herself on the doorstep of a friend's house with Simeen's baby in her arms. Simeen stood behind her. It was cold but neither of them were wearing jumpers or shoes. Zubaida knocked on the door.

'Who is there?' said a sleepy voice.

'It is Zubaida.'

Her friend cautiously opened the door. It was not a big surprise to see Zubaida as it was wartime. Zubaida's friend, like many other people, was used to hearing the sound of missiles day and night. But she was surprised to see Zubaida accompanied by a baby and a young women. 'Surely they were not relatives,' she thought. 'Zubaida had no relatives.'

'Come in, come in,' she said and rushed to the kitchen to make some tea.

She brought them a big pot of green tea flavoured with cardamom. Zubaida explained how they had seen her block of flats collapse while they were only a short distance away. They both cried. After drinking the tea, Zubaida's friend asked her, 'Who are they?' She pointed towards Simeen and the child.

'Sorry, I forgot to introduce them,' said Zubaida. 'This is Simeen and her daughter Sittara,' she said 'They have no family, like me. Simeen's husband was a soldier, who was killed in Jalalabad province a couple of months ago. Simeen and her daughter have been living with me for the last couple of months. They are good company and helpful to me. I want to help them too.'

'God bless you, you have such a good heart. In this hard time people can't always help their own family let alone strangers!'

'Well, we are human beings and should help others who are desperate. That's why I am here. I need your help too,' said Zubaida.

Yes, of course,' said her friend.

Although it was early in the morning they had not slept all night and Zubaida's friend went to find some mattresses and blankets for them.

Zubaida looked around in surprise, as the room seemed very empty. Not long ago it had been well decorated with an Afghan carpet on the floor, white net curtains hanging in the windows, family pictures on the wall and books and other ornaments on the shelves. There were none of those furnishings anymore.

'Your room looks so different and empty,' Zubaida said.

'We sold some of our belongings,' her friend replied.

'Why? I thought your husband had a good job and you had a comfortable life,' Zubaida said.

Her friend hesitated for a few seconds and then said, 'If I tell you a secret can you keep it to yourself?'

'Of course I can. I'm your friend,' Zubaida replied.

'We plan to escape to Pakistan, but it is absolutely confidential. No one knows, not even our close relatives.'

'Why escape? Can't your husband get a passport? I thought he knew a lot of people in the government?' Zubaida said.

'No! It is not so easy. They are very strict now. '

'How are you going to get out, then?'

'My husband has arranged it with some traffickers who know the way to Pakistan over the mountains but they charge a large amount of money. This is the reason we had to sell everything,' she said.

'Can your husband help us too? We are desperate,' said Zubaida.

'I don't know. Let me talk to him. He may be able to help.'

'That would be great. I beg you. I don't have much savings.' Zubaida pulled up her blouse and showed her friend the small bundle of notes under her breasts.

'Do you want to take this young woman and child with you? Can you afford it?'

'Yes. I would not go without them.' Zubaida replied.

Within two weeks Zubaida, Simeen and Sittara joined the other family and two smugglers. They pretended to be going to a wedding party in Jalalabad, a town near the Pakistan border. From Kabul to Jalalabad the journey was not too risky and they did not meet any government officials, but the two-hour journey took them eight hours as the roads were so damaged.

In Jalalabad they had to wait for the right time to bribe the border police to let them cross. They demanded a large amount of money that they couldn't afford. So the group had no choice other than to go through the mountains.

They had to travel overnight, and during the day they slept in remote areas, hid in the forest, or paid a local person to let them into their house. The women covered themselves from head to toe even in the dark of the night. Sometimes they walked for hours on foot and sometimes they rode on a donkey. If they met any villagers the two smugglers had to pretend that they were Zubaida's and Simeen's husbands.

At last after fifteen hazardous days they reached Peshawar safely.

.

CHAPTER 14

After Karim Khan's death the division between his children over the unresolved inheritance became critical. It reached such impasse that they stopped talking to each other, while living in the same house. The political situation in Kabul had deteriorated farther and the city was almost empty.

Most of Karim Khan's children were able to bribe the government officials, obtain passports and leave for Europe or America. But Jaweed and his brother Rahmet stayed in Kabul. Their disagreements over their father's land and property caused their relationship to completely break down.

Rahmet refused to cooperate with the new regime, while Jaweed decided to support the government. Neither of them had a secure job, qualifications or work skills. Jaweed found a job in KHAD, the secret police, and was allowed a gun and a car with a driver. He became a devoted supporter of the Communist Party, and never missed any of their meetings or conferences. At every opportunity he talked about how wonderful the Communist system was and his position improved day by day. He flattered the people who had the highest positions and organised monthly political meetings in his house. He sent his children to the Communist youth clubs, which were important institutions for the regime.

They believed that children should know about their country's affairs from an early age and how to support the government.

Jaweed's older brother Rahmet continued to support President Daoud's regime. Rahmet lived with his family in the same house as Jaweed. Their mother Hanifa had developed a heart problem and was under doctor's supervision. She became depressed by her sons' arguments. Hanifa's illness reached the point where she couldn't move, couldn't do any work and the house, once full of servants, gradually emptied. She couldn't afford to have any more helpers and there was only one loyal servant left. The doctors could not help her any further. Nearing her last days she told her sons that she wanted to talk to them. The two men sat near her deathbed like two obedient children.

'You know I don't have much time left and I want to ask you to respect the only wish I have had since your father died. We were rich but it never made me happy. I had a painful life. Wealth does not bring happiness. I want you to be good brothers and not fight over issues that might bring hatred between you. Is this too much to ask?'

Jaweed held his mother's hand and kissed it. 'No mother, it isn't.' He touched his brother's shoulder and they hugged each other and tears ran down Hanifa's faded cheeks. 'We will not fight again,' Jaweed said.

She died on a hot summer's day. They held an extravagant funeral, borrowing money again. A small funeral would have brought shame to the family by suggesting that her sons did not care about their mother. A big funeral was therefore important, particularly if the dead person was elderly or the head of the family. For forty days, every Thursday night, they invited relatives to commemorate her life.

When Hanifa was alive the large family had dined together. After dinner they went to the sitting room to have their tea. This was the only time that the family spent together and talked to each other. Hanifa was always grateful for this and seeing everyone around the table. After her death, the cook continued to prepare the evening meal but unity was broken-down. The family ate separately and at different times. There was less and less conversation between them until they stopped talking to each other altogether. Hanifa's sons did not keep their promise to their mother. The fighting and the arguments continued but none of them moved out because the property remained undivided.

Rahmet was hoping to find a safe way to escape to Pakistan with his wife and children, but it was risky because his brother's children were in the Communist youth club and could have reported them to the authorities.

One evening he told his wife, 'I've found a smuggler to take us safely to Pakistan.' This was the easy part, Rahmet thought, knowing that Sakina wouldn't leave without him.

'Oh good! Tell me more about it. How did you find him?' said Sakina. 'Well it's not difficult but the problem is they charge a large amount of money.'

'He'll take you and the children first, then I'll follow you,' Rahmet said.

'We are not going without you.'

'I have to stay and convince my brother to sell the house and to ensure that I receive my share of the property. This could take a long time.'

'How are we going to live in Pakistan without any money? What if your brother does not agree to sell the house?' asked Sakina.

'I am going to borrow some money for you and the children and make sure there's enough until I reach you.'

'How are you going to live without money? You've lost your job.'

'I don't know. I'm sure God will provide for me. We cannot go in one journey anyway.'

'Why not?'

'Because the trafficker has to pretend that you and the children are his own family and that you are visiting their relatives. After you reach Pakistan he will come back to help me.'

Finally Rahmet managed to send his family to Pakistan. Within twenty-four hours, the secret police found out about their disappearance. Rahmet was arrested and without even going to a court of law they put him in jail. Two weeks later they informed his brother that he had died there. His family in Pakistan heard the news but couldn't go back for his funeral, knowing that their lives would be in danger. After a long struggle his wife and children were accepted as refugees in America. His wife Sakina blamed Jaweed for the arrest and death of her husband. Jaweed sold the shared house, the only property they had left in Kabul, as soon as he heard that his brother's family had reached America.

Jaweed was promoted to a higher position within the secret police and enjoyed his new position. He was allowed to carry a gun and arrest people. His son Abdullah and daughter Fatima enjoyed the Communist youth club.

However, the turbulent political situation soon overshadowed his life. The short-lived coalition between the *Khalq* and the *Parcham* Party, the two factions of the Communist Party broke down. Jaweed, who was from the weaker party, lost his job and many of his close friends went to prison. He himself could have been arrested at any time, so he decided to move quickly before it was too late. The only choice he had was to bribe a trafficker and escape to Pakistan with his family, but he knew that his reputation as a member of the Communist party would travel with him. And worst of all, having worked with the KHAD, the secret police, was unforgivable as far as the *Mujahideen* were concerned. Jaweed knew that he would not be welcome among the refugee community in Pakistan, especially among *Mujahideen* supporters, but he had no choice. If he stayed any longer he would end up in prison like his friends or get killed. He decided to confront the *Mujahideen* in Pakistan and try his luck. The best way to approach them was to repent and join them.

The second day after his arrival in Pakistan, after finding a place to live, he went to see the *Mujahideen* leader and to show his remorse, he admitted that he had made a mistake working for the Godless government. He said he was ready for his punishment and would pay any compensation. He asked for forgiveness and this was forthcoming in return for his savings. Jaweed voluntarily donated a large amount of money to show his support for the *Mujahideen* and joined their party. He grew a beard and attended public prayers in the mosque five times a day. He managed to secure his position by marrying his daughter Fatima to one of the *Mujahideen* leader's son, against her wishes.

'I am not going to give my daughter to that backward fanatical man, who knows nothing better than killing people,' his wife protested.

'He is not a killer, he is a brave freedom fighter, he's a *Mujahid*.'

'Look who is talking!' she said with sarcastic laugh. 'Were you not the one who supported the Communist regime wholeheartedly and even had a fight with your brother over it? You worked with the Soviet regime, you supported them and now you want to marry my only daughter, against her wishes to someone who is a stranger to her.'

'It is good for all of us,' he said.

'How about Fatima? Did you ask her how she feels about it?'

'She will have a rich husband. What else does she want?'

'I am not going to marry my daughter to him,' she said.

'Shut up woman. It is not your place to talk. I'm the father. When it comes to decisions it's up to me. You don't count.' He responded curtly.

After Fatima's marriage, Jaweed gained respect amongst many Afghan refugees. He found his place in the circle of the *Mujahideen* , but continued to look for a way to leave Pakistan. He did not really trust the *Mujahideen* and realised that he and his family would be in danger because of his previous politics and lifestyle in Kabul. He played a risky game with the *Mujahideen*. He did not drink, he wore the long white *shalwar khamiz*, and grew a long beard. But he hated all of this.

In Kabul, Jaweed had drunk alcohol and worn suits. He was nervous, in case the *Mujahideen* decided to go against him. So he contacted his wife's family in   Britain and asked for their help. Through his son in-law, Jaweed managed to obtain visas and passports and after two years of living in Pakistan, he arrived with his wife and son in Britain, relieved to leave the *Mujahideen* and to say goodbye to his bushy beard and baggy *shalwar khamiz*.

They were accepted as refugees and received income support and a flat. Within a year, when Jaweed had found his feet, he began to socialise with other Afghan refugees in Britain. In most gatherings he mixed alcohol with Coca cola and gave long speeches about Islam and how to be an honest Muslim.

CHAPTER 15

Share Ali woke up at five o'clock for his morning prayers. The room was dark and the children were fast asleep on the floor next to each other. He did not notice that Simeen was not there. He went to the yard, got the *aftawa*, filled it from the small water tank and went to the toilet. He then sat on the rock in the yard and washed his hands and face and got ready for his prayers. His mind was fully occupied with his tragedy. How would he be able to cope with this scandal and face his people? His dream of going back home to Bamyan was destroyed, as he had failed to look after his family honour. What would he say to his people?

He returned to his room, put the prayer mat on the floor and positioned himself towards *Kaaba*. He felt very emotional and covered his face with both hands as tears ran down his cheeks. 'Oh God, please help me!' He stood up on the prayer mat, both hands on his chest. He started with *'Bismilahi rahmani rahim '*, in the name of God who is merciful, and when his prayer finished he looked around and suddenly realised that his younger daughter was alone in bed. He picked up the quilt covering Ferosa to make sure that Simeen was not there. He called her but no answer came from the small corridor. He thought that perhaps Simeen had gone to the outside toilet. He waited for a few minutes and then walked into the yard but there was no sign of his daughter.

He sat on his prayer mat, deep in thought. He realised that Simeen might have been awake last night and heard his conversation with his friend and had run away. But where to?

Ferosa woke up alone. She looked around, and then went downstairs to the yard. Her father was sitting in the corner with his hands over his face, near the area where Simeen made tea every morning for them.

'Where is Simeen?' asked Ferosa.

Share Ali did not answer. He slowly lifted his head and looked at her, his eyes full of tears.

He tried to say something but his throat tightened and the words did not come out. His heart ached for Simeen and for himself. Ferosa could see that her father was upset. She went upstairs and lay in bed thinking that perhaps Simeen had died. She cried quietly under her blanket. Throughout the next few months Share Ali kept quiet about his daughter's disappearance.

'Where is Simeen these days? I don't see her around,' asked a neighbour one day.

'I sent her to my family in Bamyan,' Share Ali answered thinking to himself, 'What if she knew that Simeen had run away. What if she reported it to the police?' But no one suspected anything. People were wrapped up in their own problems and everyone was trying to flee the country.

A few weeks later, Share Ali had to face another tragedy. That evening, his son Moraad did not come home. He went out to look for him but could not find him. Share Ali did not sleep all night. Early the next morning he went to the butcher's shop where his son worked. He learned that Moraad, who was just sixteen-years-old, had been dragged to the war zone, despite not having any experience or training. He did not know where they had sent his son. He sat on the ground and felt as though his backbone had been broken.[iv]

Moraad had been captured by two recruitment officers on his way to the butcher's shop. They had stopped him near the shop.

'What is your name, boy?' asked one of the officers.

'Moraad Ali.'

'How old are you?'

'I'm fourteen,' he lied, knowing the government was desperate to recruit soldiers.

'Don't lie. You look seventeen to me.'

'I'm not lying.'

One of the officers stepped closer to him and studied his face closely to see if he had any hair growth on his face. Moraad had not bothered to shave. In a matter of seconds, before Moraad realised what was happening to him, the other officer pulled his baggy trousers up to his knee to reveal his legs.

'You have very hairy legs. You can't be fourteen.'

Moraad, paralysed with fear, stood firm and did not answer. The recruitment officers dragged the boy into the van and drove off.

'Please can I inform my father?' Moraad asked.

'You can tell him later. Now you have to come with us, we need you,' they laughed, happy with their recruitment. No one informed Moraad's father. They didn't even know where he lived.

Eventually, Share Ali found out that his son had been sent to fight in Faizabad, in the north east of the country. It was too late, they had already sent him to the war zone. Share Ali was devastated. Within days, a major operation started in Faizabad and after a long and bloody fight, the *Mujahideen* surrounded most of the Soviet-backed soldiers in a long gorge and killed them all. Share Ali was told that Moraad was among them. He was killed by a single bullet in the back of his head. He had fallen down like a tall tree, blood pumped from his wound and he tasted blood on his tongue for a few minutes before he died. A few metres away from him, fourteen other young soldiers were lying dead on the ground. Later the government soldiers found them with half their bodies missing. The area was covered in dead bodies and smelt of piss, shit and vomit which was overpowering in the silence of that deserted area. Moraad never understood why he was fighting and who the enemy was. A week later the authorities buried the dead bodies in   Faizabad and informed certain relatives. It was too expensive for them to deliver the bodies to their families. Share Ali's only remaining children were Rostam and Ferosa. Ferosa was traumatised after losing her mother, her sister, and her brother. She stopped talking to anyone for months. She never asked her father what had happened to Simeen or to Moraad, knowing that this would give him more pain.

Life became a living nightmare for Share Ali. He couldn't find work. After many long painful months and sleepless nights he decided to leave Kabul. He did not want to lose his other son, Rostam, who was then fifteen-years-old. Where could he go? He hated himself for not being able to provide food and protection for his family and he hated Kabul and the racism towards Hazaras. He had lost his wife to illness. He had lost his son to war. He had lost his honour and his daughter. He did not even know who had raped her and he was worried sick about his second son Rostam and little, motherless Ferosa.

He could not return to his village in Bamyan because he was still ashamed for not having protected his daughter's honour. Worst of all, Simeen had been engaged to her cousin when they were babies. Share Ali couldn't face his younger brother. He remembered their conversation when both their wives were pregnant. 'If we have a boy and a girl, they should be engaged.' This sort of arranged marriage was normal in rural parts of Afghanistan. Where could he go without any money? After a long struggle and many sleepless nights, Share Ali finally resolved to take Ferosa and Rostam to Pakistan.

He needed advice on what to do. His only friend was Moheb, the same man who had advised him to kill his daughter. The following day, Share Ali and Moheb were sitting patiently near a big roundabout waiting for work. It was where porters got together every morning in summer and winter, hoping and praying for someone to come and employ them. If people needed help building or moving house or any other heavy workload they could not do themselves, they knew where to come for help. When a car or a van approached the porters' area, it meant some of them were in luck. They all   rushed towards the van, pushing and shoving, in order to draw the attention of the driver. He would look at them carefully, trying to choose the strongest, those who would be capable of heavy work. The rest of the men would sit back in their places on the roundabout, waiting for the next car or van. When it was lunchtime they ate dry bread with walnuts or grapes, depending on the season, and drank water.

It was a rainy autumn day. Share Ali and Moheb were sitting side by side, their backs to the wall, waiting for a job to come by, but on wet days people did not do building work and there was no one around to ask them for work.

'I want to go to Pakistan,' Share Ali told him.

'What are you talking about?' asked Moheb.

'I've heard that one can find work in Pakistan.'

'How do you know that you can find work there? The drum sounds good from afar. Pakistan is a poor country and the people there treat Afghans, especially Shi'a Muslims, like dogs.' Moheb said.

'My life is worse than a dog here, anyway, and I'm fed up. I can't even feed my two children. Maybe God helped me by reducing my family members. He took my wife, son and daughter. I just need someone to tell me how to get there. I've heard there are thousands of camps set up for Afghan refugees who can get help from the Pakistan government,' Share Ali said.

'No, you got it all wrong,' Moheb said. 'I tell you, Pakistan is a poor country and cannot even provide food for its own people. How can they help Afghan refugees?'

'But so many Afghans go there every day. Where do they get help from? Who supports them?' Share Ali said.

'I don't know but I've heard that the United States and some Arab countries give aid to Pakistan's government to help the refugees. Their economy improves if the war in Afghanistan continues. Maybe you could get some help too. But I've also heard that they give weapons to the *Mujahideen* fighting Russia, rather than helping refugees,' Share Ali's friend said. 'Also you have to find a smuggler to take you there and that requires a lot of money.'

'Yes I know,' admitted Share Ali.

'These smugglers are not God-fearing people and they charge a lot of money,' Moheb continued. 'The smugglers are rich people. My wife works in the house of one of them and she says they even have a swimming pool at their house. It is *haraam* money.'

'Why do you say that? They are helping people and what is wrong with that?'

'Because they rip off disadvantaged and desperate people and charge them a large amount of money,' Moheb answered.

'If I can save my two children's lives, I'm willing to pay. Hopefully I'll find a job in Pakistan. Can you ask your wife if they will take us?'

Moheb made a clicking noise with his tongue. 'Don't be stupid, Share Ali! The smugglers' targets are the rich,' he said.

'You don't lose anything by asking, do you? Please ask your wife.'

'OK, I'll tell my wife to ask them but why don't you go to Iran. Most Hazaras and Shi'as go to Iran. You may find some work there?'

Share Ali shook his head and said, 'They are as bad as the Pakistanis. At least going to Pakistan is easier and cheaper. I have heard that the Iranians also treat Afghans very badly. They look down on us, swear at us and call us *pader sag*, your father is a dog.'

'Do you think the Pakistani people will treat you any better?'

'I don't know, but I'll try my luck there.'

Share Ali, with Moheb's help, found a way to Pakistan without having to pay a lot of money, but the journey was to be very difficult. One early morning, Share Ali, his son and daughter picked up their belongings and left the small rented room, which held so many bad memories.

The harsh roads that the smugglers chose were long and the weather was cold. But nothing mattered to Share Ali anymore. He was tired of life. His sleepless eyes were red like rotten fruit that the wind had dropped from a tree, his hair unwashed, his face sullen, his skinny body bent under his heavy, smelly coat. He was like a ghost walking with his two motherless children, carrying all the worries in the world. Why had all these tragedies happened to him? What had he done to deserve this? Where and when would this end? He had no answer to these questions. All he knew was that the shame, humiliation and disgrace had broken him to pieces.

The city of Kabul had destroyed his family beyond repair and he and his two children were alone on that bumpy road. Tired and hungry, they walked over the high mountains, hid in forests and slept rough. Sometimes they knocked at people's doors and asked for food. Sometimes the local people helped them, other times they slept in empty mosques. They begged for food and shelter throughout their journey and finally after fifteen days, they reached Pakistan, the land where Share Ali thought they would be safe and find work. There were millions of displaced Afghans in Peshawar who had escaped the war and had reached there through the mountains. Most of them had no documentation but Pakistan welcomed them with open arms. [v]

Arriving at a refugee camp in Peshawar with his two children, Share Ali found himself in a deserted sun-dried land bursting with refugees who had swelled the border city with tents and makeshift shacks spreading for miles and miles. The piece of land which had become a shanty town of canvas, corrugated iron and mud walls, was named the Afghan Colony. The refugees had no access to education or health services and crippling poverty drove many people to suicide.

Share Ali felt more powerless than he had ever felt in Kabul. There was no running water, no hospital and no medicine, but the cemeteries were filled with the graves of countless children who had died of disease or hunger, and a large number of women who had died during child birth.

Young children played outside the camps in polluted sand from morning to dusk. Flies buzzed around their heads and germs from the piles of rubbish infected their bodies. Their hair was unwashed and lice inhabited their tiny scalps like kings of the jungle. Their teeth were black and their feet were bare.

Jobless, tattered men and boys sat in the shade of their tents, their hands under their armpits, their eyes closed and sleepy. They suffered from the hot weather and drugs were rife. The smell of food wafted over from the town people's kitchens into the forgotten land of the camps. People could only dream about a dish of potato stew.

While the warlords terrorised the civilians, the gun-makers flourished and international traders accumulated wealth and built palaces for themselves. They drove in private cars with chauffeurs and bodyguards. America's first priority was to defeat the Soviet Union. Money poured in from the US and some Arab countries but international aid never reached the refugees who lived in filthy shanty towns. Conservative Islamists used the money to set up *madrassas*, religious schools, for refugee boys, while girls were forbidden to attend. *Madrassas* were the only hope for poor children to receive food and education.

Share Ali, was advised to send his son Rostam there, and he reluctantly agreed. Rostam attended the *madrassa*, while his sister Ferosa stayed in the tent with her father. Rostam could not read or write in his own language, Dari, but he learnt to read the Quran in Arabic, although he did not understand one word of it.

In the *madrassas* the teachers had no formal training and poor knowledge of the Quran. They beat the children for the smallest of mistakes. Rostam, fifteen years old, was soon able to read the holy book fluently and with passion. He had an angelic voice and could recite the Quran with his eyes closed. This made his father happy and despite their extreme poverty, he felt that he had made the right choice by coming to Pakistan. Whenever someone died, Rostam was invited to read the Quran.

After two years, Rostam had become a confident young man and a *hafiz*, master, who taught other children. When he turned seventeen, the mullah told his father that it was time for him to do his Islamic duty.

'He does his duty by teaching other children,' Share Ali said.

'No his duty is to join the army and fight for his country,' the *mullah* replied.

Share Ali felt a sharp pain in his heart. 'I lost one son to the war I don't want him to become a *shahid*, and he is the only son I have.' But Rostam decided to join the army training camp. After a few months of training they sent him back to Afghanistan.

After a few months, Share Ali learned that Rostam had been killed in a battle in the north of Kabul when a Soviet tank had crushed his young body. The *jihad* against the Soviets continued. Share Ali had no one to turn to except Ferosa who did not know how to comfort her father or herself.

Young *Mujahideen*, barely eighteen-years-old, walked around the poverty-stricken town of Peshawar, with long black beards, black turbans, black waistcoats and carrying Kalashnikovs on their shoulders. They enjoyed their status and felt respected.

In 1984 there were more than 9,000 *madrassas*. Children learned to hate women, Christians, Hindus, Jews and whoever did not believe in their faith. In a few years' time when the Soviets withdrew from Afghanistan, those barefooted, brain-washed children had become adults. The *Taliban* emerged in 1996 and established themselves with the help of the neo-*Wahabi*'s wealth. The *Taliban* grew out of the discontent of many of the younger generation of *Mujahideen* who felt that the older leadership had failed. They began to enforce strict Sharia law. The majority were students of the *madrassas* and chose the name *Taliban* (religious students) to distance themselves from the party politics of the *Mujahideen* and to signal that their movement aimed to cleanse the society of war and un-Islamic behaviour. Thousands of young male teenagers, who had spent their lives in refugee camps in Pakistan, joined the *Taliban*.

For days Share Ali did not sleep, did not eat and did not talk. He held one piece of Rostam's clothing against his mournful face and walked around his small tent in circles like a blindfolded horse. When he occasionally closed his eyes to sleep, the nightmare attacked him. 'Where was he? Was he awake or asleep?' He felt numb. He tried to escape, but his feet were stuck in one place. He saw around him dead bodies in battlefields. The smell was unbearable. He dreamed that he was stuck in a barn with unfamiliar animals. They were not sheep, they were not cows. They had the faces of humans but the bodies of animals with horns on their heads and they had cannons on their shoulders. He felt like a fly stuck inside a cobweb. He heard the sound of his broken ribs, woke and gasped for air. Sweat was running like a waterfall down his forehead, neck and back. He tried to lick his lips to moisten them, but felt a fresh taste of copper in his mouth like the smell of a gun.

Reality hit him hard like a punch in the stomach. He remembered everything, his wife, his sons, his daughter. He remembered his life in Bamyan, so sweet and full of joy. Poor but simple and free from fear, surrounded by family and friends. No conflict, no ill feelings, just a simple routine that became part of their lives. Their animals in the green fields, slowly chewing their hay. 'Why did I come to Kabul?' he kept asking himself. 'It would have been better if we had died of starvation together.' He remembered how his parents and grandparents had been born, lived and died in their homeland. They never travelled more than 30 miles from their birthplace. Images of the past kept coming back to him, although he tried to resist those thoughts. His brain was on fire.

What was done could not be undone. Share Ali succumbed to depression and withdrew into himself, cut himself off from human contact and never came out of his tent. Neighbours put food outside but he never touched it. The familiar odour of failure surrounded him. Slowly he lost touch with reality. He started seeing visions of his mother who had his wife's hair or his father who shouted at him. He began seeing different people in his head.

During the day, Ferosa played outside the tent with other children, and the women from the neighbourhood gave her food. When dark she entered the tent and slept near her father who did not look at her and did not know whether she was there or not. Through the summer, Share Ali's condition went from bad to worse and he stopped eating and drinking. He died in his sleep on a cold winter's night while his daughter lay asleep in the same bed. When Ferosa woke in the morning to find her dead father, she did not scream or shout. She just slowly moved her hand from his cold body and went out to inform the nearest neighbour. She knew this would happen, had been waiting for the last member of her family to disappear.

The Afghan refugee families collected a small amount of money and bought a few metres of white cotton. They washed Share Ali's body and wrapped him in the cloth, dug a deep hole in the ground and buried him. Someone volunteered to read a few lines from the Quran over his grave. After the funeral, Ferosa stopped talking again. She did not speak to anyone, she did not cry, she did not play. People tried to be kind to her but she covered her face with her hands and lay on the floor like a hand-made rag doll. Her brain was preoccupied with her mother, father, brothers and sister. They had all gone. The hurt and emptiness showed in her small body and downcast grey eyes.

Ferosa had nowhere to go and no family to take responsibility for her. She stayed with a kind neighbour, Nisar Khan and his family, who were hardly able to feed themselves. Nisar's wife put her arms around Feroza's cold body and held her for a long time, feeling her unsteady breath against her face. Her pain soaked through the woman's shirt, skin and bones to be absorbed into her heart. 'God, it was too much for a child,' she thought. After a couple of weeks Nisar said to his wife.

'What do we do with this child?'

'We do not do anything, she can stay here with us,' said his wife.

'Well we cannot afford to feed her. We have to give her to a rich family,' said her husband.

'Over my dead body,' replied his wife.

'She is not our responsibility. We should inform the *Mujahideen*'s office. They get money from everywhere and should look after the orphan children. After all they are responsible for this bloody war.'

His wife clicked her tongue and laughed sarcastically. 'How naive you are, Nisar. Do you really think they can look after a child? You know what? They will marry her to a man who is the same age as her grandfather.'

'But we cannot afford to feed her; we already have five mouths to feed.'

'One more mouth does not make much difference,' she responded.

It was the last conversation they had over Ferosa. She became part of the family and stayed with them. The war reached its height in Afghanistan. The teenage children from the camps, who had studied in the *madrassas*, were sent back to Afghanistan to fight the infidel Communists. Nisar Khan's family had sleepless nights over their sons who attended the *madrassa*. They were powerless against the *Mujahideen*, who could easily send their sons to the front.

'We should find a way to save our sons,' Nisar Khan's wife said.

'I can't see any way out,' replied her husband.

'Maybe we should go to Iran.'

'Where would we get the money from? We barely manage to have a decent meal.'

'I can sell my engagement and wedding rings, and I have some small pieces of jewellery.'

'It's not enough. The smugglers want a lot of money,' he argued.

'If we can manage to go back to Kabul, we can borrow some money from my brother,' said his wife. 'The money from my jewellery should be enough to take us back to Kabul.'

Nisar Khan agreed to take his wife's jewellery to the centre of Peshawar. He sold her rings for half the price they were worth. A week later they returned to Kabul in the hope of going on to Iran through the mountains. They had five children including Ferosa. In Kabul the situation had deteriorated. The war against the Soviets had reached its height. Like a non-stop train at night it hammered civilians' sleep and stole their comfort and laughter. Eventually the family found their way to Iran with the help of some relatives. In Iran they found life even more difficult than in Peshawar. The majority of Afghan refugees were Shi'a Muslims while they were Sunni and spoke Pashto. But they continued to treat Ferosa as part of the family, and even after the fall of the Communist regime, did not return to Afghanistan.

CHAPTER 16

It took Zubaida a week to find her way around Peshawar. She and Simeen did not know anyone who could help them. After a long search Zubaida rented a small room in a crowded area near the refugee camps, on the third floor of a block of flats. The room was unfurnished, but it did not bother Zubaida too much. After a few nights sleeping on the carpetless floor, they managed to buy two pillows, a blanket and one thin mattress. What bothered Zubaida most was dealing with the world outside their tiny room.

The male domination in Peshawar was much worse than in Kabul, even during war time. They were not supposed to go out for a walk, without a *mahram* or a male blood relative to chaperone and protect them. She was shocked to see women walking around with their heads down and their faces hidden. She found it difficult to live like this, but it was too late and she could not go back to Kabul. At least she had some money and they did not have to live in the camps. She had no choice but to accept their new environment. Zubaida was not worried about herself but felt responsible for Simeen and Sittara. They had given her the will to continue her life.

Zubaida was brought up during a period in Afghanistan known as the 'Golden Time or the Spring of Hope'. Women could walk freely without covering their heads. They had the right to vote, to work, to go to university and to get involved in every aspect of life. She remembered that in the 1940s a minority of women went to college. In the 1950s women worked in government alongside men and, by 1959, some women were engaged actively in the socio-economic and socio-political life of the country. Her interpretation of Islam was that women should not be stopped from moving forward. In 1960, Afghanistan had female doctors, teachers, professors, radio presenters, journalists, office workers and businesswomen.

Zubaida had experienced this process of change and was a product of the 1960s modernisation. Zubaida's heart heaved with the weight of sadness as she remembered how the conservative Islamists had changed the lifestyle of modern Afghan women, like herself, making them powerless. She was heartbroken that all those Afghan women, who had worked hard for decades to bring equality and make Afghanistan a modern Islamic society were washed out like ink from the pages of history. Zubaida believed deeply that it was not Islam that was keeping women from moving forward, but certain men. The Soviet invasion, the US war against them and the civil war took away any hope of sustaining the 'Golden Time' in Afghanistan.

She cried to see barefoot Afghan refugee children in the camps playing in the dirt, with messy hair, unwashed faces and hungry stomachs, with no home, no mother and no father. The Afghanistan which had been called the Paris of Asia had stopped breathing. The *Mujahideen* were not just fighting the Soviets, they butchered each other and ordinary people.

In Pakistan, Zubaida's activities were focussed on teaching Simeen and looking after Sittara. Sittara had a sweet way and a gentle smile and quickly became the centre of Zubaida's life as her son Parwez had once been. She started talking. Occasionally Zubaida wrote some poems and read them to Simeen but her level of Dari was not good enough to understand poetry. All Simeen knew was that Zubaida's poems were sad. Writing them calmed Zubaida down and helped her to relax.

In Peshawar, Simeen realised that the war had left its mark on every family in the camps but she didn't know that her sister Ferosa was among those refugees just a mile away from her, living with strangers. She didn't know that her brothers Moraad and Rostam had been killed in the war. She didn't know that her father was also dead.

Simeen, Sittara and Zubaida lived in Peshawar for nearly two years. One day, they heard a knock on the door. Simeen rushed to see who it was.

'Don't open the door. It's not safe and we are not expecting anyone,' Zubaida said.

Simeen stopped. A few minutes later, Zubaida cautiously opened the door and found an envelope on the floor. She picked it up and opened it. The page contained just one small sentence: 'We know who you are.' This was a death threat and Zubaida knew that it was just a matter of time before they would be a target of one of those young *Mujahid*. She guessed that somehow the warlords had found out that her husband and her son had been supporters of the Communist regime. Her face lost its colour, her body started shaking, and she sat on the floor, with the note in her hand. Zubaida knew that this sort of threat was very serious. She knew all about revenge killings and the murdering and kidnapping, which happened every day in Peshawar.

Early the next morning they left their tiny room and disappeared into the fog. Zubaida had decided that they had no choice but to move to Islamabad where there was less chance of the *Mujahideen* finding them. They found another tiny cheap room to rent there. Day and night Zubaida was filled with fear and thoughts of how to get out of this miserable, dark, hot room.

Eventually she found a way, through another Afghan family who were about to leave for America. Zubaida met the mother by chance while shopping for food. Sharing each other's misery, they began talking and became friends. Zubaida told her that she desperately needed help to get out of Pakistan as their life was in danger.

'Where do you want to go?' asked her friend.

'Anywhere in the world. I just want to get out of Pakistan,' said Zubaida.

'Have you applied to the American Embassy?'

'Yes, but I was refused.'

'What about Germany?'

'I was refused.'

'How about other countries in Europe?'

'I have lost hope. I don't know anyone else who can help me.'

'You do not need to know people there. Just fill in the application forms.'

Zubaida had no luck. At last, in desperation she asked her friend again, 'I have tried all the embassies and been refused. Do you or your husband know anyone who could help me?'

'There are smugglers around but they are ripping people off. They want their money in dollars, not in Afghanis, and it's a large amount. Can you afford it?'

'I have some savings and some jewellery. At least I have to try.'

A few days later her friend came to visit her. 'My husband has found a man who might be able to help you. Would you like to meet him?'

'Oh yes please. Where and when can I meet him?'

'I think it would be better if you come to my house.'

The night before the meeting Zubaida was nervous and sleepless. 'What if he cannot help? What if he asks for a large amount of money that I cannot afford to pay? What if we are caught?' Her troubled mind was on fire. When she was in this state all she could do was pray. It was the only thing that made her relax.

The next morning she went to meet the smuggler. The man was in his forties, strongly built, dark-skinned and had a sullen face. After the introductions, without wasting his time, he began to talk business.

'Where do you want to go, *hamshera*, sister?

'Do I have a choice?'

'Yes, but it depends on your finances. Europe is cheaper than America. But wherever you go I get half of my money now and the rest when you reach your destination.'

'I'd like to go to Europe, probably Britain. How much do you charge?'

'20,000 dollars for each person.'

'I do not have that much.'

'Well it's up to you. I don't charge a lot. People generally pay more. It's a risky business.'

After a tiring process of negotiation the smuggler said, 'Dear lady I'll do you a favour because you don't have a husband or male relatives. I'll charge you 17,000 dollars for three of you and that is final. But bear in mind that it will not be an easy journey, especially when you have a small child with you. I have to take you through many different countries before reaching Britain. Sometimes you'll have to walk through the night, sometimes you'll have to sleep in unknown places on your own, sometimes travel with groups. You'll have to cross the sea in a small boat. In each country you may be with a different smuggler as I can't be with you all the time.'

'I'm willing to take the risk,' Zubaida said, thinking of their miserable life in Pakistan.

'From this moment on you have to be prepared to go at all times. It could be in a week from now or in six months,' the smuggler said, leaving Zubaida in a state of panic.

Early one Monday morning, Zubaida and Simeen collected their few belongings, including some simple clothes for Sittara, and left Pakistan for an uncertain future with a man they hardly knew. Zubaida felt very emotional as she travelled further away from her beloved Afghanistan. Her roots were there, where she had grown up, where she belonged. But she was happy to be leaving Pakistan, where she and Simeen had suffered greatly from the heat, where poor Afghan refugees begged on the streets, where the rich people, warlords, businessmen, smugglers, drug dealers, swaggered around in snow-white shalwar and khamiz, and the best Kashmiri shawls on their shoulders.

The long journey was as dangerous as the smuggler had warned. At one point they travelled in an old lorry which was boarded into two sections. The women and children sat in the upper part. The men and the boys squashed down below. The journey started at two o'clock in the morning when the roads were empty and the possibility of being confronted by the authorities was less. They were not allowed to get out for hours, even to relieve themselves or to get fresh air, for fear of getting caught by the police. Some of the children's urine leaked through the wooden boards onto the heads of the men and the boys underneath. They had no choice other than to laugh about it and not take it too seriously.

In July 1985, Zubaida, Simeen and Sittara safely reached London. By this time Zubaida's savings had been spent on the smugglers' fees, but she was happy to be safe. She did not know how many men had been involved in smuggling such a large group into the UK, or who they had bribed.

The council placed them in a small flat in south London. After living in one room in Pakistan, this tiny flat seemed like a palace to them but the displacement had left scars on Simeen and Zubaida and, unable to speak English, they felt isolated.

Simeen applied to enrol in adult education courses to learn English. She was excited but nervous. Everything had happened so fast in her young life, she found it hard to adjust. It was not easy for her to join in a mixed class sitting side by side with men, but she had no choice.

When her English improved she applied to go to college. The classroom was full of students from all over the world: Asia, Africa and Europe. The only Afghans were Simeen and Akbar. Simeen felt odd among all those strangers.

Zubaida stayed at home to look after Sittara. After a while, she joined the local playgroup. Zubaida's heart was full of gratitude for the help they had received in the UK, unlike their experiences in Pakistan. She recalled travelling with her husband on an official visit to one of the Arab countries in the Middle East, where the Muslim immigrants and refugees lived in appalling conditions and were not allowed to travel from one part of the country to another without police permission. They were treated like second-class citizens and the race and class discrimination was so strong she found it disturbing. She was grateful that they had been treated with compassion in the UK. But the loss of her homeland left an emptiness, like a big hole, in Zubaida's heart and she couldn't fill it with anything.

Zubaida was mostly housebound. She had no friends, no family and no country. She hated the fact that she was invisible to people on the roads, in the park or in the shopping centre. She hated the weather, she hated the damp, cold, the rain and the need for extra layers of clothing. Most of all she hated not being able to communicate with people in English. Sometimes she wanted to scream and let them know how her beautiful country had been completely destroyed, but she couldn't.

Her only activities during the weeks and months that followed, apart from looking after Sittara, were walking around the block, and waiting for Simeen to return from college. There were no Afghan families nearby and they had no contact with the Afghan community in London.

Zubaida tried hard not to think about her past, but sometimes her emotions drove her nearly mad. During one of her walks, a kind English woman approached her and started a friendly chat. She smiled at Zubaida who smiled back.

'Lovely weather, isn't it?' the English woman said.

Zubaida nodded her head in agreement. When she found out that Zubaida's English was poor, she offered to teach her at home which Zubaida accepted gratefully. However, she knew that she wouldn't be a good learner at this stage in her life because her brain was occupied with so many tragedies. She accepted Laura's offer because she was desperate for a friend.

After a few sessions Laura started to bombard her with leaflets from her church, to help improve her English. This continued for a few months. Zubaida didn't want to lose her English friend, but she felt deeply humiliated at being pushed to convert to a new belief.

'Why do people force or bribe others to believe what they believe? Isn't being an honest human being not enough for any religion?' Zubaida thought. The last straw for her was when Laura bought her a Bible translated into Dari. Zubaida refused to accept it and the friendship stopped. She was lonely again. Life became more difficult without a friend.

One Thursday morning, Simeen picked up a letter which had come through the letter-box, and gave it to Zubaida.

'What is it?'

'I don't know,' she said.

'Open it,' Zubaida said nervously.

Simeen opened the brown envelope. 'It's from the Home Office,' she said. Both of them were alarmed. Simeen read it through quickly but she did not understand it fully as she was so nervous. Then she started reading it again slowly while Zubaida stood beside her patiently, watching her reactions.

'What is it? Tell me,' said Zubaida, impatiently.

'It's good news. We're accepted,' she said. 'They are granting us Leave to Remain.'

They were accepted as refugees, but the letter said that they could travel anywhere except Afghanistan. Zubaida understood the reasons but this was extremely upsetting for her. Afghanistan had so many connections for her, how could she not go there again? How could she forget about that beautiful land that she missed so much?

Zubaida placed the letter on the dining table, went to her bedroom and closed the door gently behind her. Simeen did not understand why Zubaida was so upset. Simeen's feelings for Afghanistan were not as strong. In fact she had many bad memories – the inequality, racism, the social system and all the pain she had been through. She had no desire to go back. But Zubaida's connection with Afghanistan was deep.

Zubaida relived her past every day. The future was so uncertain. She was lost between two worlds, one in which she no longer belonged and the other where she couldn't belong. Her memories paraded themselves one after another through her heart and mind. She remembered her flat, the colour of the walls in the kitchen and the sitting room, the book case and the top shelf with her son's picture smiling down at her and the plants on the windowsill. Every single thing about that flat was precious and fresh in her tired mind.

She remembered that in the1960s, as a young woman at university, the future had seemed so bright and hopeful. It was the best time of her life, the golden age of change. King Zahir Shah tried to bring freedom and democracy to the country, and people appreciated life. Zubaida never dreamt that her beautiful homeland would erupt as a flashpoint between the Communists and the conservative Islamists and that every town and village would be transformed into graveyards. Hundreds of thousands of healthy young men had died without any memorial service.

Zubaida knew that nothing would fill her empty heart. She remembered everything, especially when she closed her eyes. She saw the dead bodies on the floor of Kabul airport and heard the people's screams. Her only refuge was her notebook. She would make herself a cup of tea, go to her bedroom and close the door. In the familiarity of that small room, her mind would race through her life. Sadness overwhelmed her. She looked at the only photo on the bedside table, those three happy faces. Zubaida with her son and husband. She picked up the frame, touched it and put it back in its place. The room was still, the only sound she heard was from the clock in the small corridor.

She got out of her bed wiped her tears, opened the tiny drawer, opened her notebook and wrote what she felt at that particular time deep in her empty heart.

Like a dry leaf from an old tree
From a faraway land
On a stormy day
I ended up in a strange land.
The storm has died down
But the old tree has fallen.
Its unity has broken to pieces
Its past has vanished
As if it never existed.
The well of my eyes has dried up
There are no more tears
There is nothing in me

INNOCENT DECEPTION

And then slowly the pain of nothingness
Invades my whole body and finds its comforting bed
There forever and ever.

CHAPTER 17

During the last term of college Akbar dared to ask Simeen out for a cup of tea. It was something that Simeen had never expected. She was thrilled but felt it was wrong to accept his invitation. 'Thank you for inviting me but I can't. I have another engagement. Sorry,' she replied.

Akbar did not ask her again for a long time but, seeing her every day in class, he gradually fell deeply in love with Simeen and decided to write to her and try to express his feelings. He wanted to know more about her, but this was exactly what worried Simeen the most. 'What if he's not serious? What would be his reaction if he found out about Sittara? Would he still be interested in me?' she thought. Akbar kept writing and asking to meet. Through the following months they occasionally talked, but always in a group. These were casual chats, but they found they had many things in common. They were both refugees, from the same background and ethnicity. They had their share of misery back home and both had lost their families. Simeen did not tell Akbar about her tragic past, her daughter and her family but Akbar told her everything about his life, how he had lived with an English foster family, that his uncle was waiting for him to send money home, that from time to time the smuggler approached him and demanded money and that he still had nightmares.

Simeen started to like Akbar, but she was reserved and shy. This was the first time that Simeen had had a friendship with a man. She kept it a secret from Zubaida, and felt guilty. She did not know how Zubaida would react if she told her, and she did not know if Akbar was serious about her. But most of all she did not have the guts to tell anyone about her child, let alone Akbar.

Then Akbar dared to invite her out again. 'I would like to talk to you. Is it possible to go to the college canteen?'

Simeen was nervous but agreed as the canteen was a public place. 'What do you want to talk about?' she said, feeling her face redden. 'If it's not urgent can we talk about it next week please?'

'Yes sure,' Akbar said.

Finally, Simeen decided to tell Zubaida. One evening after dinner she tried to be brave. 'I would like to talk to you about something,' she said.

Zubaida was alarmed. 'Yes what is it?'

'I keep receiving letters from a class mate.'

Zubaida felt uncomfortable and her face clearly showed her feelings. She imagined what the letters were about. But she asked, 'Is he an Afghan?'

'Yes he is an Afghan.' Deep down Zubaida was relieved.

'What does he want?'

Simeen didn't answer but went to her room, took all the letters that she had received from Akbar and handed them to Zubaida.

Zubaida leafed through the letters and then asked 'If he is an Afghan why has he written in English?'

'He can't read and write in Dari. I believe, like me, he did not go to school in Afghanistan.'

'Are these love letters?' she asked

Simeen blushed and did not answer. Zubaida looked at the letters again and put them on the table. 'I'm concerned about you and Sittara,' Zubaida said.

'Yes I know. That is why I want to know what you think about him.'

'I cannot judge because I do not know what he has

written to you but you have to be very careful about your life – most men are not trustworthy. They play with women's feelings and then break their hearts. A respectable Afghan man would ask his family to approach your family, not write these letters,' Zubaida said.

Simeen did not tell her that Akbar had no family. She did not want to give any further details to make Zubaida even more anxious about her friendship.

'If he's serious about you, why doesn't he approach your family? You know it's the right way. I would love to see you settled, but you have to be careful. We're not in Afghanistan. This is a good, free country where you can live on your own as well as with a man who may create problems for you in the future. Does he know about your daughter?'

'No, he does not know anything about me because I do not talk to him. This is why he has written to me.'

Zubaida was relieved. 'If he is serious about you, tell him that I want to see him and his family. Tell him about your daughter, tell him you were married before and that your husband was killed in the war. Don't ever tell him about Sittara's real father and what happened to you in Afghanistan. It's not good for your daughter. This secret has to be kept forever.'

Simeen was aware of the issues. In Afghanistan no one would want to marry a used woman with an illegitimate child.

The following day, when class had finished for lunch and the students were rushing toward the canteen, Akbar approached Simeen.

'Can I talk to you please?'

'Sure,' said Simeen.

'Can we go somewhere else, somewhere quieter please?'

'I prefer the canteen' she said but felt guilty, thinking she had betrayed Zubaida's trust.

'Would you like something to eat or drink?'

'A glass of water would be lovely,' Simeen said nervously.

Akbar bought their drinks and found a quiet place outside where they sat on a wooden bench. It would have been a perfect day for two adults to talk about their future if Simeen hadn't felt so guilty. The sound of music from the canteen and the crowd of students talking loudly made her nervous.

'Could we meet some time? I'm serious about you and want to know about you. It would be good to know each other better. What do you think?' Akbar asked.

Simeen took a few seconds to think. 'I'm not an English girl and I do not like dating. I come from a different background. And you do not know about my past,' Simeen said quietly, her eyes on the floor.

'That's the reason I want to get to know you better.'

'What if I'm not what you expect me to be?'

'What do you mean?'

'What if I've been married before?' Simeen said.

'Are you teasing me?'

'No I'm not.'

'You're too young to have been married before. How old are you?'

'I am twenty-one-years-old. I was married before and have a six-year-old daughter.' Akbar never expected to hear this. He did not talk for a few minutes. Simeen was in a state of panic, but she felt relieved to have told him about her daughter. It was the hardest part.

'Have you divorced him or do you live with him now?'

'No I don't live with him,' she said, hearing the voice of Zubaida in her conscience. 'Don't ever say the truth, this secret must be kept for ever.'

'Where is your husband now?'

'He was killed in the war.'

'Do you live on your own?'

'I live with my mother and my daughter,' she said

'How about the rest of your family? Where are they? Do you have brothers and sisters?' Akbar asked.

'I have a sister and two brothers, we lost them in the war. We don't know where they are.' Simeen wept.

We are both in the same boat, Akbar thought. For a while Akbar couldn't find the right words. Then he said, 'I lost my family too. At least you have your mother with you.' Akbar looked at the ground as he remembered the time when he lost his entire family in one day. Then

moving to his uncle's home, the harsh journey to Pakistan, the begging for food, the miserable life that the refugees led in the Pakistan refugee camps, the brutality of the warlords and the savageness of the *Taliban*.
Simeen's heart started beating fast. Akbar looked into her eyes.

'I can't hide my feelings for you and I don't care if you were married before. Thank you for telling me the truth. I love you. Your daughter will be like my own child,' Akbar said. Simeen felt even more guilty knowing that she had kept her secret.

'I love you and we have the chance to leave our pasts behind and live in peace in this country,' Akbar said.

Simeen did not look at him, she did not say a word.

'Don't you have any questions for me?' Akbar asked.

'No,' Simeen said, not looking at him.

'I feel obliged to tell you about my position,' Akbar continued. 'I live with my foster family, they are amazing people, they changed my miserable life to a happy one and I'm ever grateful to them. But hopefully one day we'll live together and have our own family, if that's OK with you?' Akbar said.

Simeen did not reply. She found the proposal odd. Everything was happening so fast.

'I know in Afghanistan this kind of meeting happens between parents but I do not have any one in this country. I would very much like to meet your mother if she wants to meet me,' Akbar continued.

'I don't know — let me think,' Simeen replied.

They both finished college with good grades. Akbar continued to study for a law degree. Simeen started working as an administrator for the local council. They married on 17th March 1990. The *nikkah* took place in a local mosque, and the *Imam* recited verses from the Quran.

Simeen was twenty-two and Akbar twenty-one-years-old. The wedding ceremony was small and simple with Zubaida on Simeen's side and Akbar's foster family on his. After the ceremony they all went to have dinner nearby at a presentable restaurant and Akbar's foster family happily paid for the food. It was the only time that Simeen felt relaxed and bloomed like the daffodils.

The couple had decided to live with Zubaida, who was a great support. They shared a three bedroom flat in south London. Simeen never imagined living without Zubaida as she owed her life to her. Zubaida continued to write poetry. The only other thing that made her happy was helping Simeen.

Two years later in May 1992, Jamila, light-skinned small and beautiful, was born and at last Simeen felt at peace with herself. The deep scars that she carried in her heart were slowly healing. Akbar loved his new family. He liked and respected Zubaida, while Sittara loved Akbar and happily accepted him as her father.

Zubaida used to get up to pray every morning at 5am and then would return to her bedroom to sleep or read a book. She didn't want to disturb the young family as they were all rushing to get to work or school. One morning, in December 1993, Simeen made Zubaida's tea as usual and took it to her room. She gently knocked on the door but did not get any response. 'Your tea is ready,' she said, as she walked in and put it on the bedside table. But Zubaida did not reply. Simeen thought that she must be in a deep sleep and then she noticed that Zubaida's eyes were wide open. Immediately Simeen knew something was wrong. Zubaida's breathing was ragged and her face colour had changed. She tried hard to speak but no words came out, just an unfamiliar bird sound. Zubaida shut her eyes and the tears ran down her cheeks. Simeen shouted to Akbar who was getting ready for work. He dropped his tooth brush in the bathroom sink and rushed toward Zubaida's room.

'What's happening?' he asked.

'I don't know,' Simeen said, shaking badly. By the time the ambulance came Zubaida had gone into a coma. In hospital they put her on a life support machine. Four days later she died. Simeen felt as though she had lost her mother for the second time.

CHAPTER 18

In the early morning the postman knocked at Number 23. Simeen was in the kitchen making breakfast. She put her tea on the table, opened the door, received the parcel and signed for it. It was for Sittara. Simeen put the package on the dining table and went back into the kitchen to make breakfast. After a few minutes she remembered the telephone conversation of a few days ago and that Sittara was waiting for a book. She rushed back to the room but it was too late. Sittara had picked up the parcel and opened it.

'Oh Mum, look, the Afghan man has sent me this book,' she said cheerfully.

The colour drained from Simeen's face but Sittara was excited about the book and did not notice. Simeen looked at the title, *Afghanistan During The Course of History*. It was translated into English.

'It doesn't look like an easy read. I would have thought it wouldn't interest you as Afghanistan's history is so complicated,' was all Simeen managed to say. She was boiling with rage at herself. 'Why did we go to that bloody *Nawroz* party,' she thought

'I will try. Can you help me, I mean, explain the parts of it that I don't understand?'

'I don't know anything about Afghanistan's history. I didn't go to school,' Simeen replied coldly.

'Why not? Isn't education compulsory in Afghanistan?'

'No it isn't,' Simeen replied and went into the kitchen to avoid having to talk about her past. Sittara found it strange that every time she tried to find out about her mother's life, she wouldn't tell her anything.

Simeen was hoping and praying that the relationship between Sittara and Abdullah would not go any further than the exchanging of books. She tried, unsuccessfully, to keep her mind busy but deep down she knew that this was the beginning of her tragedy.

That evening Sittara showed the book to Akbar. 'Look what I received today!' she said excitedly.

'What a big book! Where did you get it?'

'That Afghan man kindly sent it by post,' she said

'Oh yes. I remember.' He put his tea on the table, picked up the book and leafed through the pages. 'It seems quite a complex book,' he said.

'I'd really love to read it. Can you help me?' Sittara asked.

'I don't know much about Afghanistan. I didn't go to school.'

'Oh really, Mum said the same. Why not?'

'Because the war stopped everything and I left Afghanistan when I was very young.'

'I'd really like to thank him. Would it be OK to send a card or phone him?' she asked her father, looking at the address on the back of the envelope.

Akbar knew that Simeen was not happy about the book. 'Well, a simple phone call can do no harm, I suppose, but you must know that some young men can't be trusted,' he said mildly.

'Oh I know that, but he seemed such a nice man,' she replied.

Simeen did not want to react to their conversation, which might make matters worse, but deep down she was upset. She was quiet for a while and then couldn't help getting involved.

'Akbar, why don't you call him and thank him from Sittara? It is not good for a young Afghan woman to speak to a man,' she said.

'I don't mind thanking him, but he sent the book to

Sittara. If I call him it means that we don't trust our daughter,' Akbar replied. Sittara picked up the phone and dialled Abdullah's number.

Simeen was in turmoil. 'What would happen if Akbar discovers that Sittara is illegitimate? What if Abdullah and Sittara fall in love? How can I protect my daughter and myself from this scandal? Do I have the guts to tell her that Abdullah is her half-brother? What if Akbar leaves me? My life would be over. Our life would be over'. She repeated all those questions again and again and couldn't find the right button in her brain to switch them off.

She remembered Akbar always telling the children to be truthful. 'Honesty is the best thing in life,' he emphasised. He will hate me for my disloyalty, she thought. 'Oh God, please help me.'

Simeen began to lose weight. She had lost her appetite and interest in anything and grew depressed. She withdrew to her bedroom but couldn't sleep. She jumped at the slightest sound. Somehow, deep down, Simeen knew a big tragedy was unfolding, a big earthquake, a big flood but she did not know how to protect her family from these disasters.

After a few weeks, Akbar noticed that his wife was not well. 'Is anything wrong? You seem so quiet lately,' he said.

'I'm just a bit tired, too much work at the office.'

'Maybe you should see your GP. You've lost weight. Or maybe we both need a week's holiday together somewhere?'

'You mean without the children?'

'Yes without or with the children. It doesn't matter.'

'It's not half term yet.'

'We can go without them.'

'Who will look after them then?'

'They can look after themselves, the flat is quite safe and Sittara is eighteen. Soon she'll be going to university.'

'It's not urgent. In two weeks' time it will be half term. Then we'll go together.'

Simeen became more withdrawn. There was no conversation when Akbar came home. They had their dinner together and Simeen would go to her bedroom.

Akbar was concerned at Simeen's deepening depression. 'Just tell me what is wrong with you? Did I do something to upset you? Did I not do something you wanted me to do? I'm desperate to help you but I don't know if you don't talk to me.' Simeen felt even more guilty. She walked towards her husband and gently put her arms around him. 'No, you are the perfect husband.' For a second or two she wanted him to know everything about her past but she was too scared. She changed her mind.

'Tell me what's wrong, I may be able to help you.'

'I'm thinking about my brother and sister, I miss them so much and they are in my mind lately. I don't know where they are,' she said.

Akbar put his arm around his wife and gently kissed her face. 'Don't lose hope. When the war stops we'll go to Afghanistan and search for them,' Akbar said.

'I don't think they're still alive.'

'But you don't know if they are dead either, so there's some hope.'

Simeen stopped working and most of the time she stayed in her bedroom, slept or listened to sad music that made her more depressed. Akbar took on the responsibility of cooking and cleaning.

'Simeen! Why don't you see your GP? I know that something is wrong with you,' Akbar remonstrated with her.

'Nothing is wrong with me. I am just upset about Sittara leaving for university.' Simeen said. 'Don't worry. She's quite capable of looking after herself.'

In September Sittara left for university. She had enrolled to study journalism at Luton. She had a passion for media and wanted to go to Afghanistan one day to report on the situation there. The book that Abdullah had sent her had proved very useful. Afghan history was complicated, but interesting. Over the months she was busy and forgot to send the book back to Abdullah. She enjoyed university. She was happy that she had more freedom than at home and her social life was busy. In the summer holidays she moved back to be with her family – staying at university was expensive. Having been away from home for a whole year, she found it hard to be under her mother's control again. She also knew that her mother had developed some sort of depression and was frustrated not to be able to help her. One evening, after dinner, the phone rang. Sittara picked up the phone.

'Hello!'

'*Salaam*, can I speak to Sittara please?'

'It's me.'

Abdullah paused for a few seconds. 'This is Abdullah. I hope you remember me. I sent you a book a while ago,' he said.

Sittara felt guilty for not having returned the book. 'Yes of course I remember you,' she said. 'I'm so sorry for not sending your book back. It took me a while to finish it and I've been busy at university, I'm so sorry.'

'No problem. It's not important. When did you start university?' Abdullah asked

'Last September,' Sittara said.

'Which university are you at?'

'Luton.'

'Oh, I have a friend there,' Abdullah said. 'He studies social economics.'

'Oh really? Is he an Afghan?

'No, he's from Iran.'

'Did you manage to read the book?' Abdullah asked.

'Yes and it was very informative. I really enjoyed it but it's a sad book. Now I know much more about our history. The fighting, killing and rivalry,' she said. 'I suppose all countries have a similar history. Perhaps it is human nature not to live in harmony and peace. Anyway I have your address. I will post it to you first thing in the morning,' Sittara concluded.

'Don't worry! It's not urgent. I'm planning to come to Luton to visit my Iranian friend. It would be a good excuse to see you too, if it's OK with you.' He hoped she would say yes. 'When does your term start? '

'We return in the first week of September. Good. You'll save me postage,' Sittara said, laughing.

They arranged to meet in Luton. She put the phone down, and realised that her mother had just entered the room and heard the last bit of her conversation.

'Who was that?' Simeen asked.

'A friend of mine, a girl. We're meeting when university starts again,' she lied, reading her mother's thoughts. Lately, she had noticed that her mother was overly concerned about her and sometimes asked strange questions about who she was meeting or where she was going.

In September, Sittara and Abdullah met in the university cafeteria. Sittara wore a pair of jeans, a sleeveless T shirt and white trainers but Abdullah came in a smart suit. He looked handsome. He was nervous, but Sittara felt quite relaxed.

'*Salaam*,' said Abdullah and extended his hand toward Sittara.

'*Salaam*. How are you?'

'I'm fine thank you.' Abdullah spoke Dari fluently while Sittara only spoke broken Dari which sounded sweet and foreign.

While they sat in the cafeteria, drinking coffee, Sittara opened her bag and took the book out. 'Thank you so much for lending me this. I am happy to have learnt so much about Afghanistan. Sorry it's taken me so long to give it back.'

'Oh, it's not a problem, I've read it anyway but it's good to have it back on my bookshelf. It was a good excuse to see you again,' he said.

Sittara felt slightly embarrassed and did not reply. She was impressed by his general knowledge of Afghanistan's politics and history. She wanted to know more about her homeland. 'I hope I remember correctly, you are at SOAS, but I forget what you are studying?' Sittara asked.

'It's a four year law course. Hopefully I'll be a lawyer one day.'

'Wow good for you! We need our own lawyers in Britain,' she said. 'My father is a lawyer.'

'Really?'

'Yes.'

'What field does he work in?'

'He works with a law firm, dealing with immigration, mostly with unaccompanied minor children coming from war-torn countries. Sometimes he gets very emotional as so many cases remind him of his own experiences when he came to the UK as a child without parents,' she said.

'Oh really? I didn't know that,' Abdullah said.

'Sometimes when he comes home he is very upset and he doesn't talk about his work. I suppose he bottles up his emotions,' said Sittara.

'I am surprised that you grew up here and are still so keen to know about a country you'll probably never visit,' Abdullah said.

'I don't know. We all need to think that we belong somewhere. Perhaps it is human nature. When I look at pictures of Afghanistan on the internet, the landscape seems so beautiful, a natural beauty. It is such a shame that the war forced people to leave. I'll always feel that I belong to that poor nation. I wish I could do something to help those desperate people, especially the women and children,' Sittara said. 'Sometime I think how wonderful the world would be if we were all one big country, just one big nation, one big religion and all of us belonged to the world, with no war, no politics, no greed, just peace and harmony.'

'Don't forget if we were one nation and one religion the world would be such a boring place. With no wars and no disagreements what sort of a world would that be?' Abdullah said and laughed loudly. 'War is the core of life.'

'I hope you're not serious. Sometimes I don't understand men. They always have a hunger for war. Once they get hold of weapons they never let go. It's is like an addiction, an intoxication. The world would be a better place without men,' she said. They both laughed.

'You could be right,' Abdullah agreed.

'The world is getting more corrupt every day. It's like a big jungle and the lion always eats the deer,' she continued. 'I've started reading more books about Afghanistan's recent history, but they are all written by foreign journalists or politicians.'

'Yes, and they don't really understand the Afghan culture, language, traditions or life style. It's hard to write about people you don't know well. Even if they go for a short visit it's not enough to write about an ancient country and its history,' said Abdullah.

'I wish I could read more books in Dari to know what

other Afghan historians have written, but unfortunately I can't,' Sittara said.

'Mind you, sometimes even those books written by Afghans can't be trusted as the historians are never completely objective,' Abdullah said.

When they had finished their coffee, Sittara looked at her watch. 'I must be going, my class starts right now. Thank you again for collecting the book. It's much appreciated.'

'Can I have your email please?' Abdullah asked.

'Yes, sure,' she tore a page from her notebook, wrote down her e-mail address and handed it to him.

'I hope to see you some time soon,' Abdullah said.

'That would be lovely.' Sittara couldn't help blushing. She held out her hand and said goodbye.

Sittara could not concentrate on the lecture. She was thinking about Abdullah with a feeling that she had never experienced before. He was extremely respectful, polite, pleasant and funny, she thought. She knew how her parents felt about her future. They had always emphasised, especially her mother, that she should marry an Afghan man.

'Do not bring disgrace onto the family,' Sittara's mother said to her when she left for university. Sittara knew what she meant. She knew that her father was more liberal than her mother. Simeen would die of shame if Sittara married anyone from a different ethnicity. Sittara knew it was inevitable that one day she would marry an Afghan man. It would be so good if she was able to marry someone of her own choice. And who better than Abdullah, she thought. Meeting Abdullah gave her hope. She liked him, but did not know anything about his family.

At university, Sittara had the freedom to get in touch with Abdullah if she wanted to. But she did not make the first move. She was waiting for Abdullah to contact her. After a few weeks he emailed her and they kept in touch in that way. Abdullah bombarded Sittara with journals, magazines, newsletters and history books about Afghanistan. He always looked for an excuse to be in touch with her. He talked about anything but never mentioned his family and how they managed to come   to

Britain.

Slowly, over the months, they built up a friendship, emailing, phoning each other and occasionally meeting at her university campus. It was the only place they felt comfortable and their conversations were always around Afghanistan, Sittara's favourite subject. They never talked about their personal feelings or their families. After months of seeing each other, one day Abdullah asked her out properly.

Sittara did not tell her mother about her friendship with Abdullah, knowing how she would react. Sittara was also wondering why Abdullah never mentioned his family, what they were like or what they thought of their friendship. Sittara had the impression that his family did not know or were not happy about their relationship. Abdullah wanted to finish university. His family were newcomers to the UK and were not completely settled yet, so it was hard for Abdullah to break the news about Sittara to his parents.

In the final year of university, after much thought, Abdullah decided to speak to his father one evening after dinner while his mother was in the kitchen.

'Father I want to talk to you about something,'

'Yes, what is it? I hope nothing bad or serious has happened,' Jaweed replied.

'Not bad but serious,' said Abdullah. 'Can we go out and talk?'

Jaweed was alarmed and thought Abdullah was in some sort of trouble. He quickly picked up his coat and they left the flat and walked side by side in silence for a while.

'I hope you're not involved with drugs or the police.'

'Do I look like a criminal or an addict to you, father?'

'Just joking, my son. You are much better than I was at your age, I'm proud of you. Tell me what is bothering you.'

'Well, I'm seeing a girl.'

'You had me worried sick. I thought you were in some sort of trouble. That's good news. Who is this lucky girl? I hope she is not one of those English tarts?'

'What is wrong with English girls?' Abdullah asked.

'They are good for fun, and I don't forbid you to have

that, but when you marry them, you are their servant and you have to wash and cook and clean for them.'

'No, she is from Afghanistan, but she was very young when she came to this country. She is really British,' said Abdullah.

'As long as she doesn't make you clean the house that's fine by me.' They both laughed.

'Where did you meet her?'

'Do you remember a few years ago when we went to the Bukhara Banquet Hall to celebrate *Nawroz*?'

Jaweed interrupted his son. 'Oh yes, yes I remember. I hope it's not that Hazara girl we sat with at the table with her family. That chatterbox who talked non-stop about politics.'

Abdullah felt a sharp pain in his heart. 'She's a nice, educated young woman, Dad.'

'Oh, it is that girl then?'

Abdullah did not look up and continued walking, sensing that his father was not happy. After a long pause, Jaweed put on his authoritarian voice and said, 'Listen son, I read a poem long ago in a book. It stuck in my memory because it's true and made sense to me. I want to repeat it to you.'

Abdullah was confused and did not know why his father wanted to read a poem at this particular moment when he should be happy at his good news, but he waited patiently for him to repeat the poem knowing that it would not be a positive one.

Kaboter ba kaboter baz ba baz
konad hamjins ba hamjins parwas.

Abdullah understood the message of the poem clearly, but boiling with rage he asked 'What does it mean?'

'It means that the phoenix flies with the phoenix and the pigeon flies with the pigeon. Have you ever seen a phoenix fly with a pigeon? It means that if you are a phoenix, marry a phoenix not a pigeon. You have to find someone from your own race and class. She is Hazara, from a very low class and not equal to us.'

'Ethnicity, race and class do not matter, father. We

181

are all from the human race. She is highly educated,' said Abdullah.

Jaweed grew irritated. 'You read a few books and you think you know all about race and ethnicity. There are different races and some are not good.'

Abdullah did not say anything, but waited for a further lecture from his father.

'Those mouse-eater Hazaras were our cleaners, water carriers and porters for a hundred years. We came from a very prestigious and respected family and people know us, even in the UK. If you marry her, you're making a big mistake and you're going to be sorry. You are too young to understand now. If you marry a Hazara, that will bring shame to the family and damage our honour,' his father concluded.

Abdullah remembered that his grandfather had come to Afghanistan with nothing but the clothes that he was wearing, and that he was not from a prestigious family. He worked hard and became wealthy. He was not from a higher or lower ethnicity. Abdullah had a lot to say to his father about family honour and respect, but just said one sentence.

'What honour are we talking about father?' He saw rage in his father's eyes. Jaweed understood exactly what his son meant.

Abdullah was old enough to remember what his father used to be like, using every female servant to satisfy his lust, and the pain that his mother went through. How she had kept quiet for the sake of their family honour. Oh yes, he remembered every detail of that summer morning when his mother found his father with his pants down in the servant's room again. He remembered the fight between them.

'I can't tolerate this scandal anymore,' she had shouted. She had packed her belongings to leave her husband. The whole family gathered in the garden to see what was happening. Yes, Jaweed had disgraced himself again and it had affected the teenage Abdullah. It was hardly the story of a respected family, Abdullah thought, and deep down he felt ashamed of his father with his artificial Arab pride. He also thought about the time that they were in Pakistan and his father joined the *Hazib-*

Islami Party, one of the *Mujahideen*'s most conservative parties. He contributed a large part of his savings, which was not just his money. It was the money from selling the inherited house in Kabul, half of which belonged to his brother who had been killed by the Communists. Abdullah knew his father was supposed to give half to his brother's family, but he didn't.

'Don't talk to me in that tone, my son. I am your father.'

Abdullah decided not to speak about his feelings anymore, but he was not going to give up without a fight. They both walked back to the house in silence. Jaweed went to the sitting room and turned on the TV. Abdullah went to his room and closed the door quietly behind him.

'What is the matter? You both seem upset?' Hosna asked her husband, when she came into the sitting room.

'Ask your son,' Jaweed answered.

'I am asking you what is wrong?'

Jaweed did not answer. After a few seconds he stood up, closed the door, and sat down at the dining table. He took off his shoes and socks and pushed them under the table.

'What's the matter?' his wife asked again.

'He wants to marry someone.'

'That's good news. What's wrong? It's the right time, isn't it? asked his wife. 'We should be happy for him.'

Jaweed put on his self-righteous expression. 'Do you know who he is going to marry?'

'No, tell me!'

'He wants to marry a Hazara girl.'

Hosna was silent for a few seconds and then said, 'If my son is happy, I am happy.'

'How can you say that? What will people think?'

'I do not care what people say or think, he is our son and I want him to be happy.'

'You are talking rubbish, *zan*, just shut up!' he said.

'No I'm not talking rubbish.'

'Of course you're talking rubbish. You always do.'

'You broke our daughter's heart, marrying her to a gunman in Pakistan to save your position. Now you are trying to break our son's heart,' Hosna dared to argue.

'I told you to shut your mouth. Just shut up!'

Irritated, Hosna got up and went to the kitchen to wash the dishes knowing if she said one more word there would a big fight and as always Jaweed would be the winner. 'Will I never be able to stand my ground?' she thought.

Abdullah tried to avoid his father but remained polite. He had never been close to his father anyway and he had always felt sorry for his mother for having to put up with such a man. He knew his father was a hypocrite and that when he was angry with his wife or his son he shouted and screamed at them and had even been violent.

In June Abdullah was studying hard for his final exams. He hardly went out. He did not have time even to see Sittara. In September he received the date of his graduation and his parents were invited to celebrate the happy occasion. Jaweed refused.

'It's his big day. We have to go and celebrate with him,' Hosna said.

'I'm not going to celebrate that spoiled son of yours.'

'He is your son as well. Don't ruin his day,' she said.

'Don't preach at me and get out of my sight.'

Hosna watched as beads of sweat appeared on her husband's upper lip and he moved towards her with clenched fists, but Hosna did not move. 'I told you to get out of the room.' Before Hosna could say anything, he slapped her hard in the face. 'I told you to get out of the room,' he repeated.

Hosna did not move and shouted back 'You nasty selfish man!' He slapped her again. Abdullah heard them and rushed in. He gripped his father's hand in mid-air before he could hit his mother again and pushed him away. It was the first time ever that Abdullah had dared to stand up to his father and take his mother's side.

'If you ever touch my mother again, don't blame me for whatever happens to you, father,' he said.

'Well, well, look who's talking. You dirty little mouse, now you've found your tongue. Are you challenging me?'

'Yes I am. You've abused my mother all her life. I was a witness, but you can't hit her, not anymore.'

'She is my wife, and I'll do what I like to her.'

'No father, this is not Afghanistan. It is a different country. If she complains you could end up in prison,'

Abdullah said.

Jaweed had never seen his son so angry.

'Get out of my house,' Jaweed said.

'Father, you forget that it's not your house. It is a council flat the *kaffir* government, as you always call them, gave to us because they pitied us, because we are refugees.' He stared his father straight in the eyes for the first time.

'Ungrateful, stupid son. I came to this country to save you. I was a respectable person amongst the *Mujahideen* in Pakistan. Is this the way you pay me back?'

'No father! You bought the respect you had in Pakistan by giving my sister in marriage to a warlord, to a gun man. You came here for your own interest and spend your time drinking alcohol,' Jaweed retorted. 'You are not my son anymore.'

'I am very happy to be disowned.' Abdullah replied outraged.

This was the last conversation they had. After that even the smallest communication stopped between father and son, and this broke Hosna's heart. Abdullah always stayed in his room and Jaweed stopped beating his wife. On graduation day, Abdullah went with his mother to receive his law degree. After a few months he moved out, rented a small flat with two of his classmates from university and found a temporary job.

His mother went to pieces as she watched her son gather his belongings. Throughout the winter she became more and more depressed as she had no one to talk to. Hosna was not allowed to go to English classes as Jaweed thought it was too late for her to learn. She had no Afghan friends. Apart from cooking and cleaning the small council flat, all she did was to go for long walks to clear her head and get away from her abusive husband. Jaweed never recovered from his son's insult. No one had ever stood up to him in his entire life.

On 11th September 2001, Hosna informed her husband that she was going for a walk.

'Make me a cup of tea before you go,' Jaweed said.

Hosna made the tea and left it on the table.

The weather was warm and Hosna enjoyed walking and window shopping. She walked slowly towards the town centre as usual. She suddenly noticed that a group of people had gathered outside a TV shop window and were watching in horror as New York's twin towers collapsed. People were shouting and screaming and trying to escape from the burning buildings. At first she thought it was an action film. 'Why are people watching it outside the shop window?' she thought. Then she realised it couldn't be a film. Something was seriously wrong. It didn't occur to her that it was related to her country. After a long walk she went home and found her husband glued to the TV in shock.

'What is wrong?' she asked. 'I saw these scenes in town. Something very serious has happened today.'

'It's in America. Some group attacked the Twin Towers.'

They both sat and watched in horror.

A few days later the British media went mad about Afghanistan. The tragedy affected many Afghan families who faced racism and aggression. The powerful western media influenced people's perceptions. President Bush appeared on every channel promising his nation would retaliate against the *Taliban* and Osama Bin Laden.

In October 2001, the USA and UK led the bombing campaign against Afghanistan. Jaweed never missed the news. American and British forces began an aerial bombardment, targeting *Taliban* and al-Qaida forces in Kabul, Kandahar, Konduz, Herat and Jalalabad. In November 2001, the US bombers carpet-bombed Mazar-e-Sharif. The bombs fell on villages and residential areas, which were already damaged from the long years of civil war. An estimated 400 civilians were killed in the first week of bombing also. The number of dead reached an estimated 4,000 in the following months, many more houses were destroyed, animals were killed and 2.2 million people were internally displaced. Bombs were dropped on fleeing refugees, the majority of them women and children. Ambulances carrying injured refugees were also attacked. UN mine-cleaning officials noted that 14,000 unexploded cluster bombs killed and maimed between forty and 100 people a week.

The bombing campaign broke down the already fragile infrastructure of aid distribution which had existed under the *Taliban*. UN and international relief agencies warned of the catastrophic consequences of continued bombing as hundreds of thousands were on the brink of starvation. In response, George W. Bush stated that at the same time as they were targeting the *Taliban* and al-Qaida, food and medical supplies would be dropped to the starving people of Afghanistan. The purpose of the bombing campaign was to oust al-Qaida members and their leader Osama Bin Laden and to punish the *Taliban* government for supporting al-Qaida. By mid-November, the *Taliban* and al-Qaida had regrouped their forces in the mountains of Tora Bora near Pakistan's border. The US air strike on Tora Bora led to the defeat of *Taliban* and al-Qaida forces. However, Osama Bin Laden and other important al-Qaida figures, escaped to the tribal border areas between Afghanistan and Pakistan. They soon regained their strength and began launching cross-border raids on NATO forces. The *Taliban* also used the rural regions of the four southern provinces of Kandahar, Zabul, Helmand and Uruzgan, to launch attacks.

Hamid Karzai was installed by the West and many Afghan families who had fled abroad returned home. Some were homesick, some aimed to rebuild their country, some just wanted to grab job opportunities, and others returned to make money. Afghans and non-Afghans rushed to establish their businesses. Thousands of foreign aid workers went to Afghanistan and they all needed some where to live. The price of land and properties rocketed. The Afghan currency lost its value and was replaced by dollars. Some women removed their *burqa* and found jobs. For many, hopes were shattered and the country lapsed back into corruption.

In 2004, Jaweed decided to return to Afghanistan.

'I'm going home,' he told his wife.

'Why, what for?'

'Now that America is there and pouring money into rebuilding Afghanistan, there are job opportunities. I am going to find work and live in my own country. What is wrong with that?'

'I thought you hated those imperialist Americans.'

'Who told you that?'

'Well I thought you supported the Communist regime.'

'Times have changed and so have I. It's a good opportunity.'

'Don't you feel a little bit guilty about supporting America now?'

He looked at his wife in surprise, as if he was seeing her for the first time. 'Don't preach at me! Grow up, woman! Don't be so sentimental! Life is not about fantasy and loyalty. America is pouring money into Afghanistan and I would be stupid if I refused it.'

'Good for you! But I 'm not going,' she said.

'I am not asking you.'

Jaweed went back to Afghanistan, but didn't look for a job. He felt too old to participate in the rebuilding of Afghanistan, but he was not too old to make money. In a country where everything was possible he forged documentation, bribed corrupt officials, and reclaimed his father's properties that he had sold when he left. Jaweed knew that the price of property had gone sky high, and owning property made him a rich man. He left his wife in the UK and Hosna was happy to be away from him.

CHAPTER 19

When the phone rang Simeen was in the kitchen preparing dinner. She dried her hands on her apron and rushed toward the phone. It was Sittara on the line.

Sittara had finished university with a good degree in journalism, and had moved back to her parents' flat. She found a small voluntary job at a local newspaper to improve her skills and to be out of her mother's way.

'*Balie*, yes?' Simeen said.

'*Salaam*, Mum,' Sittara said. 'I would like to speak to you about something.'

'Is something wrong?' Simeen immediately felt anxious. 'Are you OK?' she asked.

'Yes I am fine, but I want to tell you something before I talk to anyone else because you are my mum and I love you,' she said. 'There is a boy very keen to meet you.'

Simeen was alarmed. 'What for? What does he want? Who is he? I hope he's not British?' 'No Mum, he is not British.'

Simeen kept quiet for a few seconds.

'I thought university was a place for studying, not finding a husband,' Simeen said sarcastically. What's his name? Is he Afghan?'

Sittara's anger doubled. 'Mum you are the closest person in my life. You've always encouraged me to tell you the truth, whatever happens. I haven't done anything wrong. Why are you making such a big fuss?'

Simeen knew her daughter was being reasonable but she felt that a big disaster was unfolding. She couldn't bear to think that she could lose everything, especially her beloved Akbar who was so kind and gentle, and her children. 'Akbar will never love me if he finds out, about my past,' she thought.

Sittara paused for a few seconds, 'He wants to see you for ...' She could not finish her sentence.

'It must be very urgent if you couldn't wait to come home and tell me. So who is this young man?' said Simeen. She fell silent as though crushed under the weight of what her daughter was going to say next. She felt agitated.

Sittara was hurt by her mother's response. 'Why does she always act so strangely?' Sittara thought. Sittara had grown up in Britain with a different approach to her mother. They were not in touch with the Afghan community and her family did not know other Afghan families. Sittara often behaved like a British woman, which her mother found difficult to accept, but she always tried to be honest with her family.

Sittara knew that Akbar was more understanding than her mother but she wanted to tell her about the man she loved, before talking to her father. She felt upset and decided to end the subject.

'Forget it Mum, there is no one,' she said, putting the phone down.

Breathing hard, Simeen put the phone down and went back to the kitchen. She repeated to herself, 'I hope it is not him. Oh God please help me, oh God please help me!' Simeen couldn't sleep that night or the following nights. She couldn't talk and couldn't eat. Who should she talk to? She had no close friends. There were bags under her eyes and she looked as though all the blood had been drained from her body. She was torn deep inside. The great pain of lying to Akbar consumed her and she lost more weight.

One late afternoon Akbar came home from work with a huge parcel in his hands. 'What's that?' asked his youngest daughter, Jamila, excitedly.

'It is not for you this time,' Akbar said. 'It's a present for your mum,' Akbar said.

Simeen was in her bedroom. She heard Akbar talking to Jamila but couldn't hear what they were saying. She slowly got out of bed, put her dressing gown over her shoulders and went into the sitting room, her face pale and her hair untidy.

'Look Mum, you've got the biggest present!'

Simeen smiled. 'What is the occasion?' she said.

'No occasion,' Akbar replied. 'It's for you. Go ahead and open it.' Simeen was consumed with guilt. She smiled at him and carefully opened the present. It was a small TV with a digital box for their bedroom. In recent times, Simeen had barely left her bedroom.

'Just for you to watch TV in the comfort of the bedroom,' he said.

Simeen tried to hide her tears. 'Thank you! You shouldn't have spent that much money on me. We have a TV in the sitting room,' Simeen said.

'You deserve more than that. One day when I get rich, I'll buy you the biggest diamond ring in the world.'

'Why a ring?' Simeen asked.

'Because I love you and because when we got engaged I was not able to buy you a proper engagement ring,' he said.

Simeen's guilt punched her stomach but she still felt that she had to guard her dreadful secret. 'I love my engagement ring, even if it's a cheap one.'

Akbar remained worried about his wife's depression. Buying a present was the only thing he could think of to try and help her. He took the TV out of the box and put it on a small table. 'Look, you can see hundreds of channels now, even from Afghanistan and Iran,' he said. Simeen embraced her husband.

'I thought it would make you happy. Why are you crying?' he asked.

'Because, I'm very happy. Thank you,' she replied and kissed him.

Akbar set up the TV, and searched the channels until he found a programme in Dari that they both watched. Simeen loved it. During the day, Simeen watched TV absent-mindedly, occasionally she watched sad drama films.

A few weeks later Simeen discovered an interesting programm called *Chashim Bara* - Waiting For You. It was about displacement in Afghanistan and how hundreds of thousands of families had been separated from each other and were scattered throughout the world without knowing where the rest of their relations and friends were. The programme tried to reunite families. It was on the Ariana channel, broadcast from America. The TV presenter, a young woman, read 'Raziq Samady from Canada, desperately looking for his brother, Asmat Samady, who was lost during the war in 1989. If anyone knows of his whereabouts please call this number.' The number came up on the screen.

Simeen watched with much interest and wishing that she could find her brothers and sister. 'God knows if they are alive or dead, I wish I could find one of them,' she said under her breath but Akbar heard what she said.

'There's no harm in trying,' Akbar said, and he picked up a pen and quickly noted down the number.

'I don't know,' Simeen said, uncertain as always.

The TV presenter read a few more names and requests and the programme finished. Simeen's mind travelled hundreds of thousands of miles back to Afghanistan, to her childhood in Bamyan, to living in Kabul in that tiny room where her mother had died, where her father had nearly committed the crime of killing her, where her sister Ferosa slept near her at night. She wondered whether they were alive or dead. The death of her mother, the separation from her brothers and sister, the war and the trauma of rape had had an enormous impact on Simeen's life and personality. She had become a sensitive and emotional woman who had never recovered from these tragedies. Even making a small decision was hard for her. She was exhausted keeping so much emotion inside her that sometimes she felt as though she was going to explode, but there was no one she could talk to.

Simeen went into the kitchen, made tea and poured some for herself and for her husband. Eventually, Akbar said, 'What has happened to you? We used to talk for hours and never got bored with each other. You are so withdrawn. If we don't discuss our problems how can we help each other? Please tell me what is bothering you.'

'If I only knew myself' said Simeen. 'There seems to be a part of my mind that does not want to acknowledge that I have any problems.'

'So you don't understand what is bothering you. Is this what you are saying?'

'Yes.'

'We are not living in a remote village in Afghanistan, Simeen. Here there is a lot of help for people who are not feeling good about themselves. I think you should see your GP.'

'Yes I should.'

'Would you like me to go with you?'

'No, thank you, I will make an appointment tomorrow.'

'Do you want me to call this number?' Akbar suggested. There is a small chance that you might find one of your family members. You never know.'

Simeen panicked. 'What if something nasty comes out of it and Akbar finds out about my past?' she thought to herself.

'No, I don't think there is any chance that my family will have a TV. They are poor people.' She tried to change the subject, but Akbar was determined to help his wife. He knew that Simeen was depressed and that if she could find her family it might help her.

'Look Simeen! You know I love you and it's hard for me not knowing what is bothering you, and what goes on in your mind. You have been depressed for a while and I am trying hard to help you. You don't talk to me, but maybe you need some professional help? What do you think?'

Simeen wept but was not able to open up to her husband. No words could express her pain, which had accompanied her all those years, which had penetrated her heart and her soul. How could she tell him that her daughter Sittara was the product of a rape? How could she say that she had not been married before and that she had lied to him? How could she tell him that Jaweed is Sittara's father? How could she tell him that Abdullah, Sittara's sweetheart, is her half-brother. There were so many lies and deceptions. Would he forgive me? Would Sittara forgive me? Knowing that Akbar would be hurt, how could she tell him that their life was built on a lie? Akbar was so honest, so truthful and kind. He had told Simeen everything that had happened in his life and expected the same from his wife. Would Akbar be able to forgive her? To believe that she had been raped? How could she tell her beautiful daughter that her father was the nasty man they had met in the Bukhara Banquet Hall a few years ago?

'Yes, I think I should get some help,' Simeen said. 'I'll make an appointment to see my GP tomorrow.'

'Good,' said Akbar.

Simeen made the appointment the next day knowing that the doctor wouldn't be able to help her. She went to keep Akbar happy. This was the only thing she could do for her beloved husband.

Two weeks later Simeen was sitting on a low chair in the basement of a mental health room waiting for the counsellor. The room was small, airless and dark. It had a tiny window, level with the street above. Simeen couldn't see anything outside but could hear the sound of cars passing. The old flowery carpet smelt of food and sweat which made Simeen more depressed. The sunshine that came through the small window brightened the room and Simeen saw particles of dust dancing through the air. There was just one table and two uncomfortable chairs in the bare room. She sat and waited. A young, well-dressed trainee counsellor entered the room. She was business-like. And Simeen couldn't find any sympathy or compassion in her over-decorated eyes.

'I am Barbara West. What can I do for you?' she said and indicated for Simeen to sit down.

'I'm Simeen. I think my GP sent you a referral letter.'

'Oh yes, I believe you are not feeling good about yourself and I am ready to hear your problems. You have forty-five minutes.'

Simeen found it odd, to try and open up to a complete

stranger. She looked at the flowery carpet in silence and the tick-tock of the clock on the wall seemed extra loud. Simeen wept, her tears running like a fast river over rocks. The young counsellor looked at her and said nothing. Simeen finally said that she was not ready to talk.

'OK perhaps next time,' she replied.

In the course of eight sessions, over four months, Simeen was not able to say anything to the counsellor. Her relationship with Sittara did not improve, and her panic attacks continued.

Simeen was waiting for a storm, a disaster to come, and she did not know how to safeguard against it. Four months of counselling did not help her. She was not able to tell the truth about herself so she dropped it.

One day, Simeen was alone in the house watching her favourite programme, *Chashim Bara*. She heard the presenter mention a name, Ferosa from Iran, looking for her sister. Seconds later she was shocked when the presenter mentioned her name. How could this be possible? How could she find her sister by phone? What was she doing in Iran? There were hundreds of questions in her mind. What if she is not my sister and there is another Simeen and Ferosa? She quickly wrote down the number on the TV screen, her heart beating fast. With trembling hands she dialled the number and heard a man's voice. Simeen put the phone down. No she couldn't do it. But after a few minutes she tried again.

'Hello,' a very thin voice answered. Simeen didn't recognise the voice. Her throat tightened with emotion, she tried to speak but nothing came out. The pressure was too great. She put the phone down again. Her brain was on fire, her emotions high. For the third time she picked up the phone, praying under her breath, 'Please God help me! Oh God please help me!'

'Can I speak to Ferosa?' she said.

'Speaking. This is Ferosa,' Simeen's heart was beating faster and faster. She could not manage to talk for a few seconds and then said, 'I got this number from Ariana TV.'

Before she had finished her sentence the woman on

the line shouted excitedly, 'Oh my God, oh my God! Did you find her? Her name is Simeen. She is older than me, I lost her long ago, do you know her?' She spoke non- stop and Simeen couldn't hear anymore. She collapsed on a chair and passed out, dropping the phone on the floor. The voice from the other end said, 'Hello, hello, hello,' and then the line went dead. Simeen slowly came round but did not have the courage to dial the number again. She waited for Akbar to come home.

Their reunion by telephone was something that they had never dreamt was possible. Now Simeen found out about her family. That both her brothers had also been killed in the war, that her father had died of starvation in the refugee camp, and that a kind family had adopted Ferosa and taken her with them to Iran. Ferosa had married a good man and had two children. All this did not help Simeen but troubled her greatly. The only thing that she was grateful for was having found her sister. But Simeen could not tell her about the rape, about Sittara and about the problems she was facing at that moment.

It troubled her even more to realise that she found it hard to speak to her sister about anything. After twenty years of separation, Simeen realised sadly that they had drifted apart and that she was totally cut off from her family. Ferosa had turned deeply religious, while Simeen had lost her faith. After she lost Zubaida she had stopped her daily prayers. Simeen felt that she had also somehow lost her daughter. Sittara kept herself at a distance from her mother, and Simeen found it impossible to talk to her.

One night Akbar picked up the phone to hear a man's voice, 'Can I speak to Mr Ali please?'

'Speaking,' said Akbar.

'I am Abdullah Karimi. We met at the Bukhara Hall a few years ago, I hope you remember me. I would like to speak to you about something that is very important to me. Could I come and meet you, please?'

'Yes, sure. Can you tell me what it's about?'

'It's very personal, I cannot tell you over the phone. I won't take much of your precious time. Just let me talk to you, please.'

Akbar immediately guessed that it was about Sittara.

What else could it be? He knew he had sent a book to her a while ago. But what puzzled him was that the young man had contacted him directly. According to Afghan custom, his family should have been in touch. Akbar was open-minded. He did not mind meeting the young man, but he didn't know how to bring up the subject with his wife. He wanted to tell her about this meeting but was not sure if it was definitely about Sittara. Abdullah had not mentioned her. Perhaps it was about something else.

They arranged to meet the next day in a cafeteria near Akbar's office during his lunch break. Normally Abdullah was very confident but that day he was nervous and did not know how to approach Akbar. He shook hands with him and looked at the ground.

'Nice to meet you again. How can I help?' asked Akbar.

'I would like to speak to you about Sittara.'

'Yes, what about Sittara?'

Abdullah paused for a second or two but couldn't find the words that he had practised last night in front of mirror. 'I would like your permission to marry Sittara,' he said and immediately felt stupid.

'Have you spoken to my daughter? Have you got to know her?'

Abdullah did not know how to answer these questions. If he said yes Sittara could be in trouble. If he said no then how he could expect to marry a girl that he did not know. He looked at the floor. 'I love your daughter, sir, and would like to spend the rest of my life with her,' he said quietly.

'Can I ask you a question? Why did you come to meet me? As far as I know this is your parents' responsibility. Is there a problem?'

'I must be honest sir. My father and I have some difficulty speaking to each other, and I am not living with my parents.'

'What about your mother?'

'Unfortunately my mother cannot drink a glass of water without my father's permission.'

'When we met your father in Bukhara Banquet he seemed a very understanding and knowledgeable man to me.' Abdullah kept quiet. Akbar didn't push him.

'Let me talk to my wife and my daughter and get back to you. I don't know what problem you have with your family but it's not wise to build a new life without your family's blessing. They should be involved with their son.'

They parted, but Abdullah felt annoyed with himself that he had not had the confidence to speak the truth about his father's feelings towards the Hazaras. He felt that he had given the impression that he was not respectful towards his father and this made him angry with himself. How could he tell Akbar that his father was racist? How could he tell anyone that his father had many faces and different personalities? How could he tell anyone there were so many family secrets that he felt ashamed to even think about them.

They parted, and Abdullah went home with the feeling that his meeting with Akbar had not been fruitful. He felt frustrated and cross with his father. Yet there was some hope in his mind. He would call his mother and try to convince her to meet Sittara's family.

Akbar tried to find a way to talk to his wife. Knowing that Simeen was suffering from depression, he thought that perhaps it was not a good time, but it was Sittara's life and Simeen should be happy to see her married to a respectable, well-educated Afghan man. Abdullah seemed a good, responsible person, although he did not know the real reasons why the young man was unhappy with his family.

As a solicitor Akbar knew that there were various problems that refugees and immigrants faced in the west, due to the clash of cultures. He knew that Afghan families were strict with their daughters' social lives outside their own community, but that sons were mostly free to socialise with whoever they wished. It didn't matter how mature the young women were, they were not allowed to go out late at night while young men were out most of the time. Young men were not expected to do any house work, while women were expected to do it all. Akbar knew that children found it hard to live under their parents' pressure to retain their culture while parents found it hard to adjust to the western environment where their children were brought up.

Akbar knew that many Afghans found it hard to integrate in their host country. The more they pressured their children, the more they faced arguing with them. He had experienced young people rebelling against the older generation by leaving home and channels of communications breaking down. Akbar imagined there must have been similar disagreements between Abdullah and his father.

'I would like to talk to you about something important,' Akbar said to Simeen.

'OK', said Simeen, resigned.

'It's about our daughter Sittara.'

'What has she done?'

'Nothing. Nothing at all. We must be proud of her. I think it is the right time for her to get married,' he said.

'What are you talking about?'

'A decent Afghan man came to see me today and he is very serious about Sittara.'

'Why didn't he send his family first? What is his name?'

'His name is Abdullah. Do you remember we met his family at that New Year party? I think he has some problems with his family, but he seems to be a decent young man.'

Simeen heard nothing else, the colour of her face changed and she rushed towards the bathroom.

'Are you all right?' Akbar called after her.

'Yes! Yes, I'll be back,' she said. She closed the bathroom door behind her. Akbar heard Simeen vomiting. She did not come out for a while, and when she finally emerged she had no energy to talk to him. Akbar made her a cup of tea and decided to leave the subject for another time.

'Before I go, can I do anything for you?' Akbar asked.

'No, thank you. I will be OK.'

Within a week Simeen's health had deteriorated and when Akber took her to her GP they found out that she had had a mild heart attack. When she came out of hospital Akbar brought up the subject again.

'What is bothering you? Every time I talk about Sittara's future you react strangely. I don't understand. Is there something I should know?'

'She is too young to get married,' Simeen said.

'You married her father when you were fifteen. Sittara is twenty now and I think they are in love. What is wrong with that? We were in love, remember? Let the young man come to see us. He seems very nice.

Simeen didn't answer. She just sat there like a mute, defeated animal, her left hand under her chin, her mind on fire.

'What is bothering you Simeen? I'm your husband, the closest person in your life. I've never kept a secret from you and have always been honest with you.'

'That is the problem,' Simeen said, without thinking, and regretted it immediately.

'What do you mean? Is my honesty bothering you?'

After a long pause Simeen said, 'There is a lot on my mind. Just give me one or two more days. I do want to talk to you,' she said.

'OK, thank you.' Akbar was puzzled. He gently got up and sat next to his wife, kissed her face and held her hand.

'I know you are depressed, but whatever it is on your mind you have to trust me. You have my full support, but we have to talk about it.'

'Yes I know we have to talk, but give me a few more days.'

'OK,' said Akbar.

They didn't talk about it further. Akbar watched his wife's mood and waited for her to open up about Sittara. But she didn't. Akbar knew that Sittara and Simeen's relationship had deteriorated and the atmosphere in their home was uncomfortable. He wanted to make peace between them, but didn't know how.

One evening, after dinner Akbar made a cup of tea for himself and Simeen and attempted to talk to her again. He put the tea on the table, 'Can we talk?'

'What about?' asked Simeen.

'About Sittara.'

Raising her head, she glanced around the room.   Her

gaze lingered on the family photograph. The picture was a happy one. They all were smiling.

'It is a bit late and you are working tomorrow. Why don't we talk about it at the weekend when you will have more time? I have things I need to say,' Simeen said.

'Yes that's a good idea,' Akbar said. He didn't want to upset his wife, knowing her condition.

On Friday morning, Simeen woke up late. No one was at home. She reluctantly dragged herself out of bed and went to the kitchen. She made a cup of tea and sat at the kitchen table, deeply troubled. She made no attempt to wipe away the tears that ran freely down her cheeks. She couldn't find a way out. She was petrified at the thought of what she was about to do. The flat was so quiet, so still. She went to her bedroom and opened her bedside table, removed her notebook, tore out a few pages, got her pen, sat down again and started writing. After a few lines, she put the pen down and turned her head to look out of the window. Through her veil of tears she could barely see the small patch of greenery outside. The tightness in her chest made it difficult for her to write anymore. She sat very still for a few moments and waited for her heartbeat to return to normal. She put on her coat and went for a long walk. This helped her. She returned calmer, she found the pen and the paper waiting for her on the table. She started writing again. When she finished she did not read it over. She put it in an envelope, sealed it and left it under Akbar's pillow. Then she left the house.

Akbar came home at six in the evening. Simeen was not at home. This was unusual.

'Where is your mother?' he asked the girls.

'I don't know,' Sittara said.

Akbar went into their bedroom, changed out of his office suit, and started watching the television. At 7 o'clock, he started to panic. He called Simeen's mobile, but it rang in their bedroom. Akbar put on his coat and went out. He looked around the block and local shops. But there was no trace of his wife. At 10 o'clock he called the police and they began to search the area. Akbar and the girls couldn't sleep all night. The next day the police found Simeen's body in a lake far away from their flat. Akbar was the immediate suspect. The police returned to search the house and found Simeen's letter under Akbar's pillow.

It read:

Dear Akbar.

I hope you'll forgive me for what I am going to write and what I am about to do. Remember a few days back when I said my problem is your honesty. You were shocked. But it is true. Your honesty and trust pains me. I admired you when you told me everything that had happened in your life. How truthful you were. Whatever you said I knew, deep down in my heart, that it was true. When we married and over the years, I realised that nothing would make you more upset than dishonesty. The more I loved your honesty, the more it pained me. You know why? Because my life with you was based on a big lie from the start. Living together for fourteen years, I never doubted your honesty, commitment and love towards me and the children.

The fear of losing you killed me almost every day. Through my life with you, I tried hard to be a mature, sensible woman, the way you always wanted me to be. But inside is a vulnerable, terrified child who never managed to get over her fear. Inside me, is a little girl who always looked for security, identity and belonging. Fear of life, fear of losing you and my children. I don't know who I am anymore. I get up in the morning with fear and I go to bed in the evening with fear. Fear is the price I pay for love. What if after fourteen years you find out that I am not the person you believed me to be? What would you do? When I met you I thought my wounds would finally heal. How wrong I was.

You remember the time I met you, when you told me everything about your past, how gentle and truthful you were. You told me that nothing made you more upset than dishonesty? This was killing me because from the start I had to lie to you to keep you for myself. I know now that it was stupid, but I didn't know any better. Now that everything is out of my hands, I have to tell you the truth about Simeen. Only two things are true about me, first my name. Yes I am Simeen. And the second is that I love you dearly. The rest, what can I say to make your pain less? The rest is a lie. I told you that Zubaida was my mother. She was not. I'm not even related to her. I told you that I married Sittara's father. This is not true. I told you lies because I was scared of losing you. I was raped by that nasty man we saw in the Bukhara Banquet Hall a few years back. I was working in his house as a maid and he raped me. That man left his dirty mark on my life and I was never able to wash it out. Sittara is the product of that rape and the man who wants to marry Sittara is her half-brother. I escaped from my father's house when I found out that he planned to kill me. Zubaida was a godsend, the kindest lady who saved my life and helped me. She allowed me to live with her and she supported me. My life has been a disaster, one thing after another. The only good thing that happened to me was that I fell in love with you and we had a few good years together but the lie that I told you at the beginning of our marriage has been killing me all these years. I can't even ask you to forgive me. You may, but I don't forgive myself. I know you don't deserve this but I'm tired of life. Please tell Sittara that Abdullah is her half-brother. Tell her to forgive me if she can. I know you still love me but I don't feel that I deserve you. Tell Jamila to forgive me. I hope you will all forgive me.

    Simeen

ABOUT THE AUTHOR

Shabibi Shah Nala has a degree in journalism from Kabul University and worked as a teacher for 12 years in Afghanistan. She led a comfortable life in Afghanistan as a college teacher married to a political journalist and a mother of three children. Then her life was torn apart by violent political events.

Her husband Zafar was imprisoned by the then Communist regime. Shabibi managed to secure his release and Zafar escaped across the mountains to neighbouring Pakistan. Two weeks later Shabibi followed him with her three young children. The journey was terrifying but they finally arrived in Peshawar on the Pakistani border where Zafar was waiting. A year and a half later, in 1984, they arrived in England as refugees.

Shabibi was faced with bringing up her three children, and caring for her sick husband in a completely new culture with not a word of the language. When her husband passed away in 1993, she succeeded in learning fluent English and wrote her autobiography, *Where do I Belong?*

She now works as a foster parent for young unaccompanied minors and has successfully fostered three boys from Afghanistan. She is actively involved in helping refugees. She is a published poet in her first language Dari.

Innocent Deception is her first novel.

GLOSSARY

Aftawa: can used for washing hands and feet
Azan: call to prayer
Burqa: enveloping outer garment worn by women in some Islamic traditions to cover their bodies when in public
Chalam: water pipe
Chador: scarf
Chapan: robe
Charpiee: bed
Danbora: one of Afghanistan's oldest and most traditional musical instruments
Eid: religious holiday
Espand: the plant rue
Hamshera: sister
Haraam: unlawful
Harami: bastard
Inqulaab: revolution
Kaaba: the direction that Muslims turn to for prayer
Kaffir: infidel
Khan: clan leader
Mahram: male relative
Manto: pastry filled with mince and onions,
Moallem, teacher
Nawroz: the Afghan New Year's Day
Nikkah: marriage ceremony
Noqul: sugar-coated almonds
Oshaak: pastry filled with leeks served with mince
Shalwar khamiz: trousers and tunic
Shahid: martyr
Taweez: talisman
Tabla: drums
Zan: woman

ENDNOTES

i

The long black robe has been imposed on Afghan women since the 1990s and was never worn in Afghanistan before. The black robe and veil came with the arrival of the *Taliban* and the influence of *Wahabi* Arabs on Afghan culture. The wearing of the veil had originated long before in Persia amongst royal families to distinguish themselves from the common masses.

The history of the blue *burqa* in Afghanistan (a tent- like garment which covers the whole body with a small window-like piece of embroidery in front of the eyes) does not go back any further than 200 years. It was invented by the Afghan royal family to distinguish their women from other women in the country and was a symbol of status and privilege. Wearing such luxurious clothing required money, which poor village women could not afford. Also the *burqa* was simply not practical for women working in the fields alongside men. Even today, in rural parts of Afghanistan, women walk freely without *burqa*.

Slowly the *burqa* moved from the royal families to the wider community and became fashionable among the upper class and rich families in the city. In 1920 the liberal young king Amanullah Khan abolished the *burqa* from the cities. However, it spread widely among village women and today has become part of their culture. The *burqa* has no religious meaning or base in the Quran. Islam required women to dress modestly like any other religion, in fact the headscarf was worn by Christian and Jewish women before Islam but the Prophet Muhammed did not impose it on women. Male dominance and female subordination can be traced back to pre- Islamic civilisation in Afghanistan and that region as a whole.

Even after the introduction of the *burqa* Afghan women could choose its colour but during the *Taliban's* time it became light blue and no one knows the reason and it remains a mystery to this day. Now with the growth of conservative Islam in the 1990s women are hidden behind the veil not just in Afghanistan and other Muslim countries but even in the west.

ii

This was the time while the United States and the Soviet Union used Afghanistan for their own political game. The warlords were supported by USA against the Soviet Union. In the classrooms hundreds of hungry children sat side by side in rows, the holy book on their laps, reading it in passionate and loud voices, moving their heads to and fro, not understanding a word. Apparently the meaning of what they read in Arabic was not the point. The purpose of reading the Quran was to be saved from the hell fire of the judgement day. The children were terrified by the sermons of these self-righteous *mullahs*. Everything was about sin. If a child was naughty he was sinful. If a child made a mistake in reading the holy book or laughed in the class he was in big trouble. The *mullah* had every right to beat these children severely in return for giving them food and shelter. When the children were older the *madrassas* demanded absolute obedience to practise *jihad*, 'the holy war' against Jews, Hindus, Christians, the West, democracy, even against moderate Muslims.

For many Muslims *jihad* is defined as a sincere effort to live according to the highest teaching of the Muslim faith. It is an inner spiritual struggle to fulfil the religious knowledge of divine law to command what is right for you. However, in the context of the *madrassas* the meaning of the term was reduced to the holy war. During the Russian invasion these children became adults, fully brainwashed and ready to do what ever was asked of them. After the fall of the Soviet Union and the civil war they emerged from the *madrassas* and became the *Taliban,* a group who shook the modern world with fear. They organised themselves and became bigger and stronger with the support of conservative Muslims and other brain-washed men from other countries. The Inter-Services Intelligence (ISI) of Pakistan backed them financially to recruit thousands more men and give them weapons to fight the other warlords. No one realised the deep psychological impact of the *madrassa*. No one dreamt that in a few years time that starving and naïve children would be able to cause total global chaos.

iii

The traffickers built palaces for themselves in their own countries and living quietly in the UK, enjoying double lives without a conscience. They knew those children despite separation from their families were under a lot of pressure. They knew once the teenagers reached their destination the traffickers' investment was secured. But it did not matter if the boys missed their families or if they went mad with emotions or if they became involved with drugs and alcohol as long as they made their profit out of desperate children.

iv

At the beginning of the invasion Russian soldiers were not directly involved in the war against the resistance, and the government soon became desperately short of fighters, so Afghan young people were targeted to join the army, especially university students and older school boys. Many families escaped

the country to avoid being recruited into the army.
Some succeeded but others failed and soon the shops,
parks, cinemas and restaurants were empty of young
men.

v

Afghan refugees in Peshawar divided into many
different groups – rich and poor, Shi'a and Sunni,
politically motivated and ordinary people. The well-off
rented houses, the poor lived in the refugee camps. The
rich built up a business or managed to go on to America
or Europe, while the poor begged on the streets.
Politicians established parties in exile, fighting the
Soviets and sometimes among themselves. There were
many individuals who believed in democratic values,
were not allied with any of the parties, and fought
bravely to free their country from the grip of the Soviets.

Back in 1977, General Zia ul Haq had turned Pakistan
into a conservative Islamic state and imposed Sharia
law. One of his aims was to have Afghan conservative
Islamists on his side in order to secure the western
border with Afghanistan. Refugees arrived in their
thousands and it felt as though Peshawar had become an
Afghan colony. Pakistan was financially supported by
billions of dollars from the United States and rich Arab
countries in the region, through the Inter-Services
Intelligence (ISI), to help the Afghan refugees and to
defeat the Soviet Union. The ISI provided guns and
money to train Afghan fighters, but this also created
warlords.

One of the warlords who benefited the most from the
Pakistani ISI was Gulbaddin Hekmatyar, a conservative
Islamist who had a criminal record for killing a young
poet named Saidal Sikander and was known for throwing

acid at women's faces at university. General Zia welcomed him with open arms and he quickly established himself as a warlord in Pakistan.

15975280R00129

Printed in Great Britain
by Amazon